SANTINO

THE CAMBOY NETWORK

BOOK 4

LINDEN BELL

Cover Designer: Cate Ashwood

Proofreader: Helen Smith

Content Warning: explicit sexual content, alcohol consumption (casual drinking during party), major depressive disorder, suicidal thoughts, mental health crises, self-condemnation, ableist language, panic attacks, low self-worth, major fatigue/low energy, loss of appetite/weight loss, erectile dysfunction.

SANTINO

SANTINO

He's the one I reach for in the middle of the night.

SANTINO

My life is going nowhere fast, so why not go out to New York for a few weeks and try my hand at something new? I crash with this guy, Hayden, who is gorgeous, sweet, and smart.

But there's something dark lurking beneath the surface, threatening to pull him under. I can't just stand by and do nothing--I have to help him. And in the process, I might end up helping myself too.

HAYDEN

I love my life. My job. My friends. Everything's great... until my mind betrays me. I'm sad and angry all the time, and I don't know why. There's a cloud hanging over my head, an ache in my chest, and a voice in my head that scares me.

I'm becoming someone I don't recognize, and Santino is the only one who notices that something's wrong. He's the only one who can keep the darkness at bay.

Santino is a hurt/comfort, forced proximity, sunshine/sunshiny-er MM romance between a golden retriever camboy struggling with depression and an empathic newbie looking for meaning in life. Expect lots of cuddling, late night chats, gentle showers, food as a love language, reading aloud to each other, blanket burritos, found family, and a very slow burn. It is the fourth and last book in The Camboy Network series, but can be read as a stand-alone.

CONTENTS

CHAPTER
ONE

HAYDEN

It's a beautiful summer day in New York City and I'm miserable.

Okay, maybe not miserable, but I'm definitely not happy.

The sun is shining, the temperature is a warm seventy-five. The sidewalks are filled with locals and tourists, all wearing bright smiles. The outdoor patios are packed with diners enjoying a late weekend brunch.

I should feel alive and cheerful. I should be buzzing with energy. But I'm not—I'm just… bleh.

I can feel the sun on my face, but I'm not basking in it. I can feel the light breeze stirring the air, but it doesn't feel refreshing. I can hear the chatter and laughter of the other pedestrians on the sidewalk, but I'm not swept up in the liveliness all around me.

My brain's registering everything, but that's about it. It's not making me happy like it normally does. I'm not the cheerful, upbeat person I used to be. I haven't been for a while.

Rhys, my best friend, hangs off my arm as we stroll down the sidewalk together. "Angel thinks it's too expensive, but I'm like, if we're going all the way to Disney World, we might as well stay at a Disney hotel, right?"

"Mmhmm, yeah, makes sense to me." I try to inject as much enthusiasm into my voice as I can and hope that Rhys doesn't notice how flat it is.

"I'm going to get him one of those hats with the Mickey Mouse ears. OMG, he's going to be so adorable," Rhys gushes.

"Yeah, I'm sure he will." I force a chuckle and it sounds, well, forced.

Rhys glances up at me, brows drawn together in concern. "Are you okay?"

"Yeah, of course I'm okay." I paste a smile on my face that tugs uncomfortably on my cheeks. "Why wouldn't I be okay?"

Rhys studies me for several moments, long enough that I'm afraid my smile is going to slip. But then he jostles me gently. "I'm just worried about you."

"Worried?" I make a sound that's halfway between a scoff and a laugh, but to my own ears it sounds strangled. "There's nothing to worry about."

Rhys sighs dramatically. "You keep saying that…"

"Because it's true." The lie slips off my tongue and a little part of me dies inside.

Because it's *not* true. There *is* something to worry about. I'm just not sure what.

A year ago, I would've been ecstatic and bouncing with excitement on a day like today. The weather is beautiful.

I'm going to brunch with my best friends—Rhys, Sebastian, and Noel. I have a job I love and I live in the best city in the world.

But in the past year, things have gotten… weird. Off. I don't really know how to explain it. I'm not usually someone who gets bothered by things. I'm an easy-going, optimistic guy. I like seeing the positives in every situation. I like celebrating all the good things in life.

But things have been getting to me. At first, it was the big things. Like when our monthly brunch date with the four of us got pushed back a week because Rhys had to spend the weekend with Angel's family.

I mean, in the grand scheme of things, it's not a big deal. We've had to reschedule brunches before. But then it got pushed back again because Sebastian's boyfriend, Christian, planned a surprise getaway for them. Then again because Noel's fiancé wanted to go to Burning Man. Then all of a sudden, an entire month had gone by and we never managed to squeeze it in.

Honestly, Old Hayden wouldn't have even noticed we missed a month. Old Hayden would've been happy that his friends were doing such cool things. But it got to me for some reason. It really bothered me.

Then it became smaller and smaller things. Like I'd make enough dinner for me and Rhys, like I always do, even if he's not home to eat it with me. But then he messages to say he's having dinner with Angel instead. Or like I'd ask Sebastian if he wants to come over to play League of Legends and he's busy working out with Christian. Or like I'd send a message to the group chat and no one responds for a couple hours.

It's all perfectly normal. But it bothers me.

"I don't like that you're in the apartment all by your-self," Rhys says and I get this strange pang in my chest.

That's something that just started recently. It's almost like an ache, right underneath my sternum. It's not a physical pain. At least, I don't think anything's physically wrong with me. But I have to, like, breathe through it as if it were a muscle cramp.

"I don't think I'd ever want to live on my own. It must be so lonely coming home to an empty apartment."

"No! It's not lonely. I mean, I miss having you there, obviously. But I'm good." The ache in my chest grows with each lie.

Rhys debated for months before deciding to move out of the apartment we've shared for half a decade and in with his boyfriend. He wanted to move sooner, but he kept putting it off because he was concerned about me. I knew if I'd asked him to stay, he totally would've. But that would've been a dick move on my part. He and Angel went through a lot to be together and they deserve to be happy without having to worry about me.

"Are you sure?" Rhys casts me a skeptical look. He knows me better than anyone else in the world, so I make sure to smile with my eyes too.

"Of course! Besides, I won't be alone for long. Bellamy's friend is moving in soon."

Noel's fiancé, Bellamy, used to live in San Francisco and the guy who's moving in with me was his roommate, I think. I'm not too clear on that whole situation, to be honest. All I know is Noel and Bellamy are getting married. Sebastian convinced them to film the entire planning process and make a documentary out of it. And this guy is coming to play Bellamy's friend-slash-best man in the film… I think.

Sebastian's always got these genius ideas that he ropes the rest of us into. I remember thinking this one was really cool when he first explained it to us, but the details are kind of murky now.

Rhys lights up. "Oh yeah! What's his name again?"

"Uh…" See, that's one of the murky details I can't quite conjure up. I kind of see the name in my mind, kind of feel the way it sounds on my tongue, but not entirely. Like his name is a ghost who disappears if I focus on it too hard. Same with when exactly he's getting here or how long he's staying.

Rhys gives me a funny look. I'm usually pretty good with random details, but the harder I try to remember, the more I lose the shape of it.

"No worries. We'll ask Sebastian at brunch." He picks up the pace, dragging me along the sidewalk.

Half a block later, Rhys directs us toward a restaurant and I hold the door open for him to go in first. Sebastian and Noel are already seated at a table, sipping Bellinis, and Rhys and I slip into the two empty chairs.

Sebastian doesn't bother saying hello and launches right into business. People who don't know him think he's a little intense, but he's the mastermind who turned a ragtag group of camboys into The Camboy Network, one of the leading adult entertainment studios in the industry. "Are you ready for Santino?" he fires off at me.

Who? What? I stare blankly at him while my brain scrambles to catch up.

"Bellamy's friend? He's staying with you?" Noel

prompts. He cocks an eyebrow at me like I've forgotten my own name.

That's when it clicks. "Oh! Santino! Yeah, totally ready." I swallow down the nervous laughter that would definitely give me away.

"Good," Sebastian says, not missing a beat as he turns to Noel. "His flight lands at three-twenty on Thursday afternoon. You and Bellamy are going to pick him up from JFK."

Noel huffs an annoyed sigh as if he's being asked to personally drive the guy from San Francisco. Noel's annoyed a lot. It's a part of his bad-boy persona that his rabid fans love so much. "Yeah, I guess."

"No guessing. You are," Sebastian corrects.

"I still don't get why he can't just take a cab or whatever," Noel grumbles.

"I still don't get why he can't stay with you and Bellamy," Sebastian shoots back, pinning Noel with a pointed look. "He's Bellamy's friend. It would make more sense for the doc."

Noel pouts and slouches down in his chair. "We like having our privacy."

"More like you're jealous of him and you want to keep Bellamy to yourself," Rhys jumps in with a smirk.

"Fuck you. What would I have to be jealous about?" Noel's pout deepens.

"Oh, I don't know. Maybe because he's known Bellamy longer than you have? He used to live with Bellamy? Or maybe you're just a jealous bitch who doesn't like to share," Rhys says, his voice taunting.

Noel's pout turns devilish. "Oh, I like to share just fine." There's more than enough innuendo in his voice for us to know exactly what he's talking about—and it's not food.

"Anyway," Sebastian cuts in, bringing us back on track. "Santino's flight lands at three-twenty. I'd give him at least thirty minutes to disembark and get through the airport. Pickup is no later than four o'clock. They should be at your place around five-ish, Hayden. You'll be at home to meet them?" Sebastian phrases the last sentence like a question, but we all know it's an order.

Seeing my friends around the table like this, just being themselves and bantering, it deepens the ache in my chest… which makes no sense at all. I should be thrilled right now. I should be ecstatic. I've missed spending time with the guys, so I should be soaking it all in and savoring it. Yet all I can think about is how rare these opportunities are and dread the moment we all go our separate ways again.

But I put on a brave face, a smiling one. "I'll be there!" My voice cracks on the last word when I try to force a little too much cheerfulness into it.

Sebastian gives me a puzzled look before continuing. "Good. I'll double-check with Christian, but I'm pretty sure he finishes work at six. We can all have dinner together to welcome Santino to the city, then head to The Bronzed Rail. You'll be performing?" he asks Rhys.

"I've actually got a new pole dance routine I'll be doing," Rhys answers. "Angel's already planning on being at the club, so he can meet Santino too. It's perfect!"

Sebastian nods like that was a part of his plan all along. "Excellent. It's all set then. We'll have a pre-production meeting on Friday afternoon at Noel and Bellamy's. Shooting starts on Monday. Questions?"

The waiter comes over to take our order and after he leaves, the conversation turns to who everyone thinks will be nominated for the Grabbys. Noel and Bellamy won the industry award for best flip-fuck last year and Noel's convinced they'll win it again this time. Rhys thinks Angel will for sure be nominated for best male newcomer. And Sebastian is keeping his fingers crossed for best director.

My name doesn't come up, which is fine. Really. It is. I've done some good videos this past year, but nothing earth-shattering or record-breaking. I've never been nominated for the Grabbys and I'd be surprised if I ever will. I'm not that kind of performer... you know, flashy, charismatic, memorable.

Don't get me wrong. I'm hot and hung, two basic requirements to be a gay porn star. But there are dozens of guys who are hotter and more hung than I am—three of whom are right around the table with me. I'm more than happy to see my friends up on stage while I cheer them on from below. I like being the supportive friend who celebrates when they succeed.

So why is the ache in my chest growing? Why does it feel like it's cracking my chest open? Why does it feel like it might swallow me whole?

**CHAPTER
TWO**

SANTINO

My stomach swoops and I can't tell whether it's just the change in altitude from the plane descending toward JFK or if I'm nauseous because I'm nervous. Both. Both. It's probably both.

I've never really liked planes—they're thin metal tubes catapulting through the air, just waiting to fall out of the sky. But I've also never done anything like this before—take off to the other side of the country all by myself, without telling my family, to work with a porn studio.

When Bellamy called me up months ago with this idea, I thought he was joking. Me? Go to New York? Work for The Camboy Network? Did he mix me up with someone else?

But nope, apparently he's getting married and the whole thing is getting filmed and turned into a movie and he wants me to be his best man. *Me,* plain old Santino Baldoni from a small city in the middle of California, who hasn't done anything worthwhile in my twenty-five years on the planet. Like, what? We're not even that good friends.

I mean, we lived together for a few years in San Francisco, and we get along well and everything, but we're definitely not best friends or anything like that. Hell, he was fucking Noel on the DL for *months* before I found out on social media. The dude didn't even tell me himself.

But like, whatever. If Bellamy wants to fly me out to New York for a few weeks, all expenses covered, be in a movie, and get paid, then, hell yeah, I'll pretend to be his best friend. I'll be the best fucking friend he's ever had.

But it's more than that.

I managed to move out of my parents' house and into San Francisco after high school. I was going to do big things, make a life for myself, be somebody. But all I managed to do was odd jobs like being a porter at a hotel, selling ferry tickets at Fisherman's Wharf, and delivering other people's food orders on the side. Some life I've been living.

My mom's been bugging me for ages to move back home and join my dad's pool maintenance company. It's the last thing I want to do, but it's becoming harder and harder to say no. What excuse do I have? "No, Mom, I can't because I'm making the big bucks washing dishes at some random restaurant. Yay…"

So yeah, when Bellamy offered me this chance, I jumped at it. And maybe there's some teeny tiny part of me that's hoping something will happen in the few weeks I have here—something that will get my life back on track.

To be honest, though, I'm terrified. It's silly, I know. A fully grown man scared of being on the other side of the country from his family. But I've never been this far away from home before. Completely on my own. Without my parents or my older sisters just a phone call away.

I know. I know. I'm desperate to get out of the shadow of my family, and yet I'm afraid of being so far away from them. It doesn't make sense. But it's normal to be scared of something you've never done before, right? It's normal to be nervous when it feels like my entire life rides on the success of this trip.

And like, the crazy thing is that I kind of want to call my Mom about it? Like, I want her to tell me it's okay, I should go have a good time, everything will turn out fine. But I know she won't say that. She'll flip out and demand I come home. She might even lock me in my room. I know, it's extreme, but my mom's been through some shit and she's not good at dealing with people leaving.

Besides, how would I even explain what I'm doing? "Oh, hey, Mom, I'm working with this porn studio, but don't worry, I'm not in a porno. It's a documentary about two porn stars who are getting married? How do I know porn stars? Oh, you know, I used to live with one of them." Yeah, not happening.

The plane lands with a jolt and my stomach lodges itself in my throat. I grip the armrests and hold my breath, willing my organs to settle back in place instead of projectile vomiting out of my mouth. When the seatbelt sign blinks off, I let everyone else elbow each other off the plane first. I need a minute to make sure I won't be sick.

Except the nausea doesn't fade when it's my turn to shuffle down the narrow aisle toward the exit. Actually, it gets worse as I follow the flow of passengers through the airport. By the time I collect my suitcase and make it out to the pickup zone, I feel like I'm up in the air again and the plane is about to plummet to earth.

The heat doesn't help. The second the sliding doors open and I step outside, I'm hit with a wall of humidity. It's so much hotter here than it is back in San Francisco.

I'm in the middle of taking my hoodie off when a shiny black Range Rover comes barreling around the corner. I jump backward just as it screeches to a halt right in front of me. "What the fu—?"

The passenger door flies open and Bellamy jumps out. "Yo! Dude!" He rushes over and pulls me into a full-body hug.

It takes my brain a second to react and tell my body I'm not being attacked, then I relax into the embrace. It's nice, actually. Grounding. I don't feel like I'm being tossed around a tin can at thirty thousand feet anymore.

"Man, I'm so stoked you're here! How was your flight?" Bellamy grabs my suitcase and stores it in the trunk.

"Bro, I fucking hate flying. I thought I was going to die."

Bellamy laughs and the sound takes me by surprise. I've heard him laugh before, of course. We laughed all the time back in San Francisco. But I've never heard him laugh like this. Like he's high on something, but also like, totally sober at the same time. Like he's really, genuinely happy.

He slams the trunk shut, then clasps a hand on my shoulder. "I'm so glad you're here. You're going to love New York. Trust me."

I want to trust him. I really want to love it here. I'm not sure what I'll do if I don't.

The backseat of the giant SUV is as big as a fucking

living room. The seats feel like a full-sized leather couch and there's so much leg room, I can't touch the front seats with my feet.

"Hey, Noel! Thanks for picking me up!"

From the driver's seat, Bellamy's fiancé throws a bored look at me through the rearview mirror. "Yeah, sure."

Oookay. Honestly, Noel's a weird guy and I never really got what Bellamy saw in him. I mean, yeah, he's got that whole bad boy vibe going for him, but every time I've tried to actually talk to him, he's been kind of a jerk. Who wants to spend the rest of their life with that? But whatever, not my problem.

The second Bellamy's door closes, Noel floors it. The car catapults forward and I'm thrown back in my seat. Jesus Christ. Maybe I should be more worried about this drive than I was about the plane.

"Hey, so, we're taking you to Hayden's place right now. You'll stay with him while you're here. He's a great guy, super sweet, amazing cook, happy all the damn time. It'd almost be annoying if he wasn't so nice."

"*Almost* annoying?" Noel chimes in a second before he slams on the brakes.

I practically get clotheslined by my damn seatbelt.

Bellamy's arm flies out to give Noel a back-handed smack on the arm. It doesn't look very hard, but Noel flinches and rubs the spot with a pout. "Ow."

"Don't be an asshole, babe," Bellamy says like he's asking Noel to pass the salt. "And this isn't Grand Theft Auto. Tone it the fuck down."

In the rearview mirror, I see Noel's lips twitch like he's trying not to be smug, but surprisingly, his driving actually does calm down a little.

Bellamy turns toward me again. "So, after we drop you off, you can chill out for a bit. Then we're all going out for dinner and you can meet Sebastian and the rest of the gang. Sound good?"

"Totally." It sounds great, actually. I love meeting new people, learning about who they are, and what they're all about. But this is a little more high-stakes than just going out to dinner with a bunch of new friends. I'll be working with these people. I want to make a good impression. I want them to like me. If they like me, maybe they'll want me to work with them again. Maybe they'll let me join their group.

Thirty minutes later, Noel turns down a narrow street and parallel parks in a spot that should've been too small for the massive car. But he squeezes the damn thing in without a scratch.

I climb down from the car and when my feet hit the sidewalk, I take a deep breath of the thick, hot air. It smells different here—richer, warmer. Maybe it's the humidity, or maybe it's just my imagination playing tricks on me. Walk-up buildings line both sides of the street with trees pushing up through the sidewalk concrete every few yards. The wind rustles through the full green foliage and piles of black trash bags sit next to the curb.

I'm in New York now. This could be the start of the rest of my life.

Bellamy pushes the buzzer on the intercom and a couple seconds later, the door unlocks for us. I follow him up the stairs to the fourth floor, dragging my suitcase behind me. Noel takes up the rear, but he doesn't offer to help me with my bags.

On the fourth-floor landing, Bellamy knocks on a door and we stand there awkwardly, waiting for it to open.

Except it doesn't.

Bellamy and Noel share a look that I don't understand and Noel raises his hand to knock again. It's another minute or two before the door flies open.

Okay, confession time. I might've looked up Hayden Summers when Bellamy first told me I'd be staying with him. Can't blame a guy for being curious, right? And like, I might've gotten a little obsessed and watched every video I could get my hands on and stalked him on social media. I mean, just a little. Because the dude is really hot. Tall, built, strawberry blond hair that's a hint more strawberry than blond. And eyes so green they look like actual emeralds.

But all of that? None of it compares to the real Hayden Summers standing in front of me. Like, not even a little bit.

I'm a very respectable five-eleven-and-a-half, but I have to tilt my head back to see his face. His wavy hair falls over his forehead like he's tried to quickly comb it with his fingers, but didn't succeed. His lashes are a shade lighter than his hair, so it looks like he's got feathers lining his eyes. And those eyes. Holy shit. I swear, they fucking glow.

I'm stunned as Bellamy introduces us in the hallway. This is actually him. Hayden Summers. In the flesh. Looking like a Greek god. That really hot one. I mean, I think they're all supposed to be really hot, but the hottest of them all. That's him—Hayden Summers.

They expect me to live with this guy? Share a bathroom with him? Sleep in the room next to his? Shit. I'm going to be walking around with a permanent hard-on for the next few weeks.

"Hey! Welcome!" His voice is so deep, I feel it more than hear it. He holds out his hand and when I take it, his fingers swallow mine up whole. His smile is so bright, it feels like the sun is breaking through the ceiling and shining directly down on me.

I make a strangled sound that's supposed to be a hello.

He leads us down a long hallway that opens up into a living area. It's not huge, but it's got all the essentials—big couch, big coffee table, big TV—with enough room for five or six guys without feeling claustrophobic. Two large windows look out on to the street and in one of them is an air conditioning unit pumping cool air into the apartment. Thank fucking god.

Hayden crosses the living room, talking as he goes. "This is the living room, obviously," he says with a laugh that sounds a little on edge. He pushes his fingers through his hair and tugs on the hem of his t-shirt with the other. Then he hikes up the gray sweatpants that are hanging low on his hips.

"Kitchen's through here. Help yourself to anything in the cupboards or the fridge. I like to cook, so let me know if there's anything you want to eat and I can make it for you. Oh, and if you have any allergies or anything."

He doesn't seem to know what to do with his hands. They slip into the pockets of his sweatpants. Then he pulls them out and clasps them together. He folds his arms across his chest, then unfolds them again to gesture to an open door. "That room there is yours. I just changed the sheets and the towels on the bed are fresh. The bathroom's right next to it. Feel free to use the shampoo and soap.

Most of it is left over from Rhys, so it's all pretty good stuff."

He spins around a bit, gaze darting everywhere, like he's trying to make sure he isn't forgetting anything. "Um, I think that's it? It's pretty basic. Sorry."

Okay, so the guy looks like a Greek god, but he's actually pretty adorable. Real golden retriever vibes. Like he has more excitable energy than he knows what to do with and wants to be everyone's best friend.

It makes him way less intimidating and I manage to stop fanboying enough to speak. "Oh man, don't be sorry. This is amazing. Thanks for letting me stay here."

The smile he flashes me practically melts my insides. "No worries at all. Seriously. I'm not really used to living alone, so you're like, doing me a favor. And um, sorry, I didn't get a chance to clean up before you got here. It's not usually this messy."

I don't know what he's talking about because the place is basically immaculate. There's one empty glass on the coffee table, a few Amazon boxes broken down and leaning against the wall, and a couple piles of books sitting around the room. "Seriously? You should see my place. It's never this clean."

"It's true." Bellamy backs me up. "We always had empty takeout containers and greasy pizza boxes everywhere."

The horrified look on Hayden's face is so fucking cute. "But you'll get mice and cockroaches if you don't throw that stuff out right away."

Bellamy and I share a pained look. "We might've had a mouse or two," I admit. "But I promise I won't leave anything out while I'm here, I swear," I add quickly when Hayden's expression of horror grows worse.

He nods and murmurs a quiet, "thanks," but I don't think he's convinced.

Great. Way to make a good first impression. Now the Greek god thinks I'm a disgusting slob he'll have to put up with for the foreseeable future. I'll be lucky if he doesn't kick me out the second Bellamy and Noel leave.

"If you're all done talking about cleaning—" Noel shudders visibly. "Can we get out of here now?"

Ugh, what is wrong with the guy? Does he really have to be such an asshole *all* the time? Bellamy smacks him again with an indulgent shake of his head, but Hayden doesn't seem fazed at all by Noel's attitude.

"Thanks for picking Santino up from the airport!" he says instead. Which like, he doesn't have to thank Noel on my behalf, especially not Noel of all people.

But he's being so polite, so now I guess I have to be nice to Noel too. "Yeah, thanks so much."

Noel's only acknowledgement is a half-hearted raise of a hand before he turns for the door.

Bellamy's a little slower to follow. "You guys good to meet us at the restaurant later?"

Hayden nods eagerly. "Yeah, we're good. I've got it covered. Leave it to me."

"Awesome. Thanks, bro. See you later."

Hayden sees them out and when he returns, it's just the two of us standing in the living room. I don't usually have a problem talking to strangers, but I must be fanboying again because I can't think of a single thing to say. Hayden rakes his fingers through his hair. He doesn't seem to know what to say either.

"Do you want something to drink—"

"I guess I'll go get settled—"

We end up talking over each other, then dissolving into nervous giggles. When our gazes meet again, the vision of him takes my breath away. Goddamn, this man is gorgeous. And now I'm living with him. I don't know if I'm the luckiest bastard alive or if I'm fucked. Both. Both. It's probably both.

CHAPTER
THREE

HAYDEN

So... yeah... I kind of forgot Santino was coming today. Sebastian even texted me yesterday to remind me, but I don't know what happened. I thought I had more time? Like an extra day or something? I didn't realize today was the day until the intercom for my building's front door buzzed.

I hit the button to unlock the door, then raced to put clean sheets on Rhys's old bed. That was the fastest I've ever put on sheets in my entire life.

I'm not usually a forgetful person and I wasn't lying when I said I was looking forward to living with someone again. The apartment is too big and empty just by myself. Most of the time, I end up holed up in my room so I'm not constantly reminded I'm all alone.

It's not like I was super busy with other stuff either. I did a couple social media promo things, tried to read some of the library books I need to return soon, and lay around in bed a lot. I think I went for a run at some point. But other than that, I've mostly been doing nothing.

And I still forgot. Forgot to put clean sheets on the bed. Forgot to do the dishes. Forgot to take out the recycling. Forgot to shower. I don't think there's much food in the fridge and I almost went to answer the door wearing nothing but my boxers.

I'm such a mess. Rambling on about allergies and shampoo? Then I basically accuse Santino of being gross when he makes the comment about take-out containers and greasy pizza boxes. Way to make a guy feel welcome, dude.

"Do you want something to drink—"

"I guess I'll go get settled—"

Laughing, I meet his gaze and for the first time since he walked into the apartment, I take a really good look at Santino.

He's not as tall as me, but he's still pretty tall with a slim build. Dark hair, dark eyes, deep olive complexion. He's the definition of tall, dark, and handsome, but not the edgy, mysterious kind. He looks playful, mischievous, fun.

"You go first," I say after a moment of us staring into each other's eyes.

"I'll take some of that water." He gives me a lopsided smile.

"Uh... water. Yes! I also have, um..." I rush to the kitchen and pull open the fridge to see what other options I have. I usually keep it stocked with at least some LaCroix, but there's only the half-empty Brita filter. Oops. "Sorry, I just have water."

"Water's great. Just something cold would be awesome. It's a fucking sauna out there."

I chuckle as I pour out a cool glass and hand it over.

Santino brings it to his lips and downs the whole thing in one go. His throat works as he swallows, his Adam's apple bobbing up and down. I catch myself staring at him, mesmerized by the length of his neck as he tilts his head back. I drag my gaze away. Watching him drink is weirdly intimate and I don't want to be the creepy new roommate who doesn't understand boundaries.

I can still see him out of the corner of my eye, though. He finishes the glass with a sigh of satisfaction and presses the back of his hand against his mouth to wipe away the few drops of water that escaped.

"Thanks." He holds out the empty glass and our fingers brush when I take it from him. He notices, I think, since his lips quirk into that lopsided smile again, a knowing look in his eye. "I'm going to go unpack a bit."

"Oh yeah! Sure! Let me know if you need anything. I'll be…" I wave my hands around. "You know, here."

His smile widens. "I know where to find you."

I jump into the shower and change while Santino unpacks, then start tidying up the apartment. I'm drying the dishes when Santino comes back out. He picks up a book sitting on top of the pile by the couch.

"Are these all yours?" he asks, flipping through the book in his hands. "You do a lot of reading?"

"Uh… they're not mine. I borrow them from the library." I busy myself with putting the dishes away, trying to avoid his second question.

I *used to* do a lot of reading. I haven't actually been able to finish a book in… a while.

"What's this one about?" Santino holds up a paperback with a cube floating in midair on the cover.

I wrack my brain, trying to remember. That's one of the books I tried to read yesterday, but I couldn't get into it. I don't know why. I was really excited about it when I saw it at the library. But when I cracked it open, the words lay flat and boring on the page.

That almost never happens. Not until recently, at least. I love reading. It's my guilty pleasure. I'll read anything. Non-fiction books about random topics: deep sea creatures, the Mongol Empire, how ceramics are made, the human digestive system. Biographies, memoirs, and self-help books. Horror, science fiction, fantasy, even romance. There's just something so cool about words on a page coming alive as I read them.

But I can't for the life of me remember what this book is about. The only thing I can think of is science because that's what the cover looks like and that's what the author is famous for. "It's about the history of physics, I think. I haven't read it yet."

Santino carries the book with him into the kitchen, reading the back. I catch a whiff of warm cinnamon when he leans on the counter beside me. "Other dimensions. Parallel universes. Shit. I don't think I know half the words in this paragraph."

He holds it up for me to see, but I'm not looking at the book. I'm caught by his big brown eyes ringed by thick lashes. There are tiny golden specks in his irises that make them sparkle. I wonder if anyone's ever tried to count the specks before. I bet there are at least a couple dozen in each eye.

"Um… yeah… uh…" Suddenly, my mouth is dry.

Santino's eyes drop to my lips when I try to wet them. His own lips part in a silent inhale. The air around us feels too warm, even though I've had the air conditioning running all day. We sway toward each other, almost like we're opposite ends of two magnets being drawn toward each other.

I'm stopped by the book hitting my chest. Embarrassment rushes at me, hard and fast. What am I doing? Santino was holding up the book so I could read the back and all of a sudden, I'm trying to… what? Kiss him?

Why would he want to kiss you? He just met you. Don't be a creep.

"Sorry," I sputter, spinning away. I grab the last glass that needs drying and nearly drop it in my haste.

"No, I'm sorry," Santino replies, taking a step back. "I shouldn't be randomly touching your stuff. I'll go put this back." He moves stiffly, shoulders raised, like he's nervous and uncomfortable.

"No!" It comes out a little too loud in my eagerness to put him at ease.

Santino stops in his tracks and gives me a deer-caught-in-headlights look.

"You can touch my stuff." I hear the way that sounds a second too late. I wince and Santino's lips twitch with a suppressed laugh. The tension between us vanishes as quickly as it appeared.

"I mean, you can read any of the books," I clarify.

Santino shrugs, flipping the book back and forth between his hands. "I don't really read, but…" He scans the room and the random piles of books I haven't tidied yet. "Who knows? Maybe I'll give it a try while I'm here."

He smiles at me and there's something about his expression that makes me pause. It's goofy and unserious. Lighthearted and carefree. It feels so familiar and yet so far out of my reach. Like it's a place I used to go to all the time, but I haven't been back in so long, I've forgotten what it's like.

The moment passes as Santino returns the book to its pile. I hurriedly give the kitchen counter one last wipedown, then get ready to leave for dinner.

The restaurant Sebastian made reservations at isn't far from The Bronzed Rail. On our subway ride into Manhattan, I try to tell Santino about each stop and the things he can find there if he wants to explore the city. He soaks it all up like every word out of my mouth is the most fascinating thing he's ever heard. I can't tell if he's for real or not. Noel would've told me to shut up already by the second stop. Rhys would've patted me on the arm and subtly tried to change the subject. Sebastian would've half-listened while checking his emails on his phone.

But Santino listens with his whole body. He angles himself toward me, gaze unwavering and attentive. He doesn't just respond with the normal "I'm listening" sounds at the right times, he asks questions—lots of them.

Do I prefer walking the bridge from the Manhattan side or the Brooklyn side? Do I have a favorite restaurant for spring rolls? Do I think it's worth going to see the Statue of Liberty? What do I think is the most underrated neighborhood in the city?

It's a little strange, honestly. The questions don't feel like casual small-talk type questions. He keeps phrasing them like he wants to hear my opinions and my preferences. Like he's not interested in getting to know the city, but rather, he's interested in getting to know me. I've never had someone pay that kind of attention to me before. Like they really want to know what I think. Like what I say matters to them.

It's not just you. You're not special. He probably does that with everyone.

At dinner, Santino sits in the middle of the long table while I grab the empty seat at the end. Rhys tells story after story about all the funny and cringey and hilarious-after-the-fact stuff that's happened during video shoots. Bellamy cuts in to explain things Rhys glosses over or to correct him when he exaggerates a little too much. Then Sebastian goes on about how we started The Camboy Network and some of our more recent projects.

No matter who's talking, no matter what they're talking about, Santino looks right at them as if they're the only person in the entire room. He's quick to laugh and generous with his smiles. He seems to find everything "hella cool."

By the time dinner's over, it feels like Santino's been a part of the friend group since forever. He's already got some inside jokes going and whenever he says something funny, the whole table erupts in laughter. Even Christian and Angel, the two quieter guys in the group, are chiming in on the conversation, and Noel doesn't look as annoyed as he usually does.

I push my chair back. No one looks up when I leave the table. I'm just going to the restroom, no big deal. When I get back, everyone's still talking and laughing and having a great time. I slip back into my seat and no one looks in my direction.

They didn't even notice you were gone. They probably wouldn't notice if you didn't come back.

A pang hits me in the middle of my chest, hard like a

sledgehammer. It's sudden and out of nowhere, leaving me struggling to draw in air.

The distance between me and the rest of the table feels like it's growing, like I'm drifting away, even though nothing's actually moving. All my friends are over there, having so much fun. And I'm over here, all by myself.

I don't want to be alone on this side of the divide. But I don't know how to get back over there. I can't close the distance.

A dark, looming feeling teases around the edges of my mind and memories start to surface. Not any specific ones. Just fuzzy impressions of times when I felt like my friends were moving in one direction and I was moving in another. They feed into the growing darkness.

I don't know what this is or why it's happening. But it's getting bigger and stronger and I'm scared it's going to eat me alive.

CHAPTER
FOUR

SANTINO

Bellamy's friends are fucking dope. They're all so cool and dinner is so damn fun. They treat me like I'm one of the guys, giving me shit and cracking jokes at my expense. I've only known them for a handful of hours, but it kind of feels like we've been friends forever.

Hayden grabbed the seat at the far end of the table when we first arrived—too far for me to say anything directly to him without shouting, too far to even make eye contact naturally. But even then, I keep glancing over at him every few minutes. I can't keep my eyes off him.

He's hot, we've established that. But he's really damn cute too. He gets flustered kind of easily, which for some reason, I find adorable.

And that moment in the kitchen? Fuuuck. I don't know what that was about, but for a few seconds there, I swear to god he was going to kiss me. If only I hadn't been holding the damn book between us. When he turned away so abruptly, I thought I'd screwed up, for sure. But then that line about touching his stuff. Oh my god. Ded.

Seriously, though. I'm not sure I've got a good read on the guy. He seemed, I don't know, nervous? In the apartment? But totally cool and super knowledgeable about everything on the train ride here. And now, he's really quiet around his friends.

I mean, I get it. Rhys is especially hard to compete with. The petite guy has long blue hair and a full face of makeup, while wearing a crop top and mini-skirt. He looks like he's used to being the center of attention.

Not that that's a bad thing or anything. A couple of the other guys are kind of like that too. Bellamy's always been this magnet for attention whenever he walks into a room. And Sebastian has this real "I'm in charge" vibe going on.

Near the end of dinner, Hayden gets up from the table and I see him head toward the restroom. When he comes back, he's even quieter than before. He keeps his chair pushed back from the table, arms wrapped around his middle. His head is bowed, he won't look at anyone, and that gorgeous smile he has is nowhere in sight.

He looks like he's not feeling well. Or maybe he's upset about something. He seemed fine on the train. Maybe something happened earlier? Or who knows, maybe this is his normal. Maybe he's always quiet in large groups. What the hell do I know? I met the guy a few hours ago.

By the time we're finished dinner, Hayden looks fucking miserable. Like someone kicked his puppy. I kind of want to say something. Maybe ask if he's okay or if he wants to go home. But I'm the new guy. I don't want to poke my nose into other people's business and none of the other guys seem to think anything is wrong. So, I keep my mouth shut.

At The Bronzed Rail, we're welcomed inside like VIPs, which apparently we are—or they are. The Camboy Network has some sort of agreement where they help promote the club on social media in exchange for VIP access and a reserved table. Rhys and his boyfriend Angel disappear backstage so Rhys can get ready for his pole dance performance and the rest of us are ushered to our table.

Hayden's a full step behind us, almost like he doesn't want people to think he's with us. When we sit down, he takes the seat that's on the very edge of the group. He looks like this is the last place in the world he wants to be. Like he's forcing himself to stay.

The house lights dim and a spotlight illuminates the stage. The curtains pull back and a tall drag queen struts out. "Are you ready to get railed?!" she calls out and the packed nightclub erupts. "Welcome to The Bronzed Rail! I'm Anna Conda and I'll be your host for the evening!"

The first couple performers are drag queens lip syncing to classics like Britney and Mariah. They're good, dancing wildly across the stage, doing the splits and cartwheels and other crazy stuff. Then it's Rhys's turn and the second his name is announced, every single person in the club is on their feet.

Remember when I said Rhys looked like he was used to being the center of attention? Yeah, that totally tracks. He's glowing as he comes out on stage wearing black fishnet stockings and matching gloves that extend all the way up his arms and attach across his upper back. His knee-high platform stilettos are the same electric blue as his hair. He's a small dude and when he gets his hands on that pole at the front of the stage, he looks like he's floating through the air.

There are a couple of taller guys standing in front of me, so I have to crane my head side to side to be able to see Rhys. Then out of nowhere, a pair of strong hands wrap around both my arms and gently move me to the left where I have a better view.

I glance behind me to find Hayden only inches away. He gives me a sheepish smile that's way too fucking endearing, then ducks his head. I'm torn. I want to watch the rest of Rhys's performance, but I also want to see Hayden's smile again. What's up with him? Is he upset? Is he cool being here? I wish I could hit pause on time and take a minute to figure him out.

He's standing really close behind me. So close I can feel the heat of his body and if I "accidentally" sway backward, my back brushes up against his front. He doesn't shift away when I do that, but he doesn't lean in toward me either.

Which like, doesn't mean anything, obviously. But that moment in the kitchen keeps replaying in my mind. Was he going to kiss me? Did I just imagine it?

Or maybe I'm just a horny fanboy who's reading way too much into every single thing because I more than a little obsessed. Yes. Yeah. That's it. I need to chill the fuck out.

When Rhys finishes his dance, I maybe, kind of, accidentally pull my chair away from the table so I can sit next to Hayden. "Dude, that was dope!"

Hayden flashes me a quick smile, then drops his gaze

to the floor. "Yeah, Rhys is really good. He practices all the time and takes dance classes two or three times a week. Not just pole dancing, but like ballet and other stuff too."

"Did you see what he was wearing on his feet?" Rhys's boots had a six-inch platform under the sole and heels that looked like stakes. "How does he walk around in those things?"

Hayden chuckles softly, gaze still trained on the floor. "I used to be his crutch when he was practicing in our apartment. He twisted his ankle once and had to take two weeks off from dance classes. He was so pissed."

He sounds so proud of Rhys and the fondness in his voice is unmistakable. But there's also a hint of something else in there. I don't know what it is… maybe like, nostalgia or something? "It must've been fun living with your best friend."

Hayden's smile falters. "Yeah, it was."

A wave of sadness pulses out of him and I shift in my seat when it hits me. Listen, I just met the guy, right? I don't know who he really is or what he's got going on in his life. But if anyone asked me, I would've said this dude's dealing with some heavy shit.

I've seen something like it before. It reminds me of when my grandmother passed away and my mom kind of fell off the deep end. I got the same feeling of sadness from her, so thick it made the air around her difficult to breathe. She got better eventually, but there was about a year when it felt like I lost both a grandmother and a mother.

I hope that's not what Hayden's going through. Because that would suck big time.

I put my hand on his knee and give it a reassuring squeeze. "I bet you miss him, huh?"

Hayden's eyes flick to me, looking like a deer caught in headlights. Stunned, eyes wide, like I've somehow uncovered a deep, dark secret. But come on. That's not such a big leap, is it? I mean, they're best friends who lived together, who enjoyed living together. Then one of them leaves and the other is left behind in their shared apartment. That has to be hard.

Hayden sucks his bottom lip in between his teeth and chews on it for a couple moments. Watching him, I get the urge to tug the poor lip free and soothe it with my thumb.

But then Hayden's gaze drops again and he lowers his head like he's ashamed of something. "How did you know?"

He sounds so small and fragile that my heart sinks. Fuuuck. This feels exactly like it did with my mom. That's definitely not a good sign.

I give him a light bump with my shoulder. "I'd miss my best friend if he moved out on me."

For a second, nothing happens. Then Hayden lifts his gaze from the floor and it collides with mine. All the air is expelled from my lungs and I forget how to breathe. I can't see the green of his eyes in the dark club, but even then, it feels like I'm looking into his soul. There's hurt there, and sadness. Confusion and loss.

It's so much like Mom that I feel like I'm back there again. Helping her through the depression. Coaxing her back to life. I wouldn't wish that on my worst enemy. I certainly wouldn't wish it on someone like Hayden.

"Incoming!" Bellamy shouts as he barges past us with a tray of fresh drinks he deposits on the table. Craft beer, whiskey, margaritas. He waves everyone over and hands out the drinks.

I pass a margarita to Hayden and he throws me a smile of thanks before melting toward the back of the group. I follow him, suddenly afraid that he'll disappear if I lose sight of him.

Bellamy throws an arm around Noel's shoulder and holds up his glass with the other. "I just want to say thank you to all you guys for welcoming me into the fold. I know I was 'the enemy' for a long time—"

"No, you weren't!" Rhys interrupts. "We all liked you just fine. It was only Noel who had a stick up his ass."

Noel gives him the middle finger while laughter ripples through the group. Hayden tries to laugh too, but it feels awkward and stilted.

"Well, now I've replaced the stick with something better." Bellamy reaches down and gropes himself.

Noel rolls his eyes, crossing his arms over his chest in a pout. But his lips still tilt up at the corners like he can't quite fight back his grin. "Anyway…"

"Anyway…" Bellamy continues. "Noel and I are both really excited about this documentary. It means a lot that you're all helping out with it. This is our family in New York and we're super grateful to have you in our lives. Here's to The Camboy Network!"

Beside me, I feel Hayden shift and I look over just in time to see him slip away. He takes up a spot against the wall a few feet down and stares into his margarita like the bright pink liquid holds the answers to all of life's secrets.

I glance around at the group. None of them seems to notice Hayden's not with us anymore. And if they have, they don't seem worried. I'm not sure what to do.

With Mom, sometimes she needed us to pull her out of her loneliness and back into life. But sometimes she just needed to be alone and recuperate. I don't know Hayden well enough to know what he needs. Hell, I'm not even certain he needs anything from me or if he needs anything at all.

I shouldn't be jumping to conclusions about what's bothering him. Just because he's sad doesn't mean he's depressed. Just because I think he's sad doesn't mean he's actually sad.

His friends know him better than I do. They're all so tight with one another. They would know if something was seriously wrong, right? They would've done something about it, right?

Hayden slides down the wall an inch, like his legs aren't quite strong enough to hold him up. He must feel me staring at him because he lifts his head and our eyes lock across the distance.

Maybe I'm imagining it, but I think I see a cry for help. My heart thuds, louder than the music pumping through the nightclub's speakers. I'm probably not the right person to help him. I just met the guy. The only things I know about him are what he's posted on the internet.

But I also can't ignore what's in front of my very eyes.

I grab the two chairs we were sitting in and drag them over to the wall. If he feels better over here, then that's where I'll meet him.

"Thought you might like to sit," I say, setting the chair down next to him.

He looks at it for a moment, like he's trying to decide whether he should accept the favor. Then slowly, he lowers himself into the chair. I put the other chair down right beside him and plop myself on it.

Neither of us speaks for a moment. Then Hayden leans over.

"Thanks," he says, almost too quiet to be heard over the music.

I smile, proud of myself for making the right choice. "No probs, dude."

CHAPTER
FIVE

HAYDEN

Consciousness comes to me slowly. It's hazy at first, fuzzy around the edges like a dream. But gradually, light invades the dark corners of my room and sounds solidify into car horns and sirens in the distance.

There's a split second before I'm fully alert when my brain hasn't quite remembered the shit I've been going through lately. In that fleeting moment, I feel like my old self again, filled with excitement over the potential of a brand-new day. But then my brain powers all the way up and that positive, optimistic feeling vanishes.

I open my eyes and groan. Fuck, I'm tired. I haven't felt this tired in… actually, I don't know if I've ever felt this tired before. We didn't even stay out that late. And I only had a couple drinks. There's no reason why I should want to curl back up under the covers, but I really, *really* do.

Last night comes back to me in stages. It was fine at first. Great, even. But by the time food was served at dinner, everything started falling apart.

The ache in the middle of my chest. The invisible heaviness weighing me down. The distance between me and everyone else. Like I was watching them through a thick pane of glass. Like I was drowning on one side while they all continued with their evening on the other.

It only got worse at The Bronzed Rail. Everyone was having so much fun. They all looked so happy. I should've been in the middle of it, smiling and laughing along with everyone else. But the more I watched them, the more the ache tried to swallow me up and the heaviness tried to crush me. And then there was the voice.

I mean, it's not really a voice. Like, I'm not hallucinating and hearing things that aren't actually there. The voice is just me, but it's putting words to thoughts I've never had before. Like, they're coming from me, but they're not really mine.

No one wants you here. You're only here because they need someone to bring Santino to the restaurant. You could get up and leave and no one would notice you were gone.

I didn't think any of that was true, but the voice wouldn't stop repeating it over and over and over. At one point, I wanted to cover my ears and scream just to drown it out.

But then someone did notice. Someone saw I was standing against the wall, trying to focus on anything else but those ugly, negative thoughts. Someone came over and sat down with me. Someone made sure I wasn't alone.

Santino. The new guy.

God, how embarrassing. He must think there's something wrong with me. I mean, I guess there *is* something wrong with me. But *he* didn't need to know that. Not when he has to live with me for the next few weeks. The least I could've done was pretend I was normal.

But nope. He saw me hovering on the edge of freaking out. He reached out and threw me a lifeline. He reeled me in and made sure I didn't float away.

How was he able to see me when no one else could? How did he know I needed someone to sit with me? Who is this guy?

Something stirs in my chest. It feels a little frantic, a lot desperate. It wants to latch on to Santino as if he'll be able to save me from whatever's wrong. As if one small act of kindness means he has the answer to all my problems.

Life doesn't work that way, though. People don't waltz into your life and magically fix everything that's wrong. He didn't come here to fix me anyway. He came here to work on the documentary. What right do I have to ask him to help me?

Besides, he probably thinks I'm a freak now.

I stab my fingers through my hair and force myself out of bed. I should stay away from Santino. Let him enjoy his time in the city. Let him focus on the documentary. He doesn't need me and my issues distracting him from why he's really here. And when he's finished, he can go home with happy memories of his time in New York. He's only here for a few weeks. I can hold things together for that long—I hope.

In the kitchen, I open the fridge door and stare inside. I'm running low on food, but there's still more than enough for a decent breakfast. I could do breakfast burritos, BLT bagels, straight-up omelets. But I don't really want to do any of that. I want to crawl back into bed and sleep for another hour or two or three.

Behind me, Rhys's door—no wait, *Santino's* door—opens. He comes out wearing boxers and a t-shirt. His thick, dark hair stands up on end and his eyes are barely open. He rubs a hand over his head. "Morning," he mumbles.

My heart does this weird lurching thing in my chest. He looks adorable. All warm and soft from having just woken up. I wonder what it would feel like to pull him into my arms and lose myself in all that warmth and softness.

I spin away, heart aching with just how much I want that. But it's ridiculous. I don't know the guy. I can't maul him first thing in the morning before he's fully awake. Instead, I put on the cheeriest voice I can muster while I'm still kind of groggy. "Morning! Want some breakfast?"

Santino leans against the counter as if he needs help staying upright. "Coffee?"

"Coffee! Yep, I can definitely do that."

Santino's face is all scrunched up as he eyes me with suspicion. "Lemme guess. You're a morning person?"

I open my mouth to say yes, but stop short. I don't know if I'm a morning person. Old Hayden would've been up hours ago, whereas I barely managed to force myself out of bed. I want to be a morning person again, but that feels so impossible right now. "Sometimes?"

Santino groans and rubs his hands over his face. "Bellamy's a morning person too. Always up at the crack of dawn. It's inhuman, bro."

His grumpiness is endearing and I find myself smiling a little as I fill the kettle and prep the French press. "Rhys is like you. He hates mornings. Never gets up before ten o'clock."

"See? Cool people don't wake up early. I knew I liked the guy. He knows what's up."

A wave of nostalgia hits me. God, I miss Rhys. He always made the apartment so lively and vibrant. He loved to hang out and catch up while cuddling on the couch. I even miss the bad things, like when he left dirty dishes in the sink or his long hair all over the bathroom floor.

The apartment was so empty when he moved out. It was so quiet—too quiet. I'd wander from the living room to the kitchen to Rhys's empty room to the bathroom and back again, never knowing what to do with myself in such a big place. I ended up cooking way too much food. I had no one to talk to. I know he's happier than he's ever been living with Angel and I want that for him, but…

What about me?

Guilt hits me like a train as the question echoes through my mind. What *about* me? I'm fine. I've got a great job, great friends, great life. So, the apartment feels too big for just one person. Find a fucking roommate.

Suck it up, loser. Deal with your own shit. Don't dump your problems on other people. They have their own lives. They don't have time to coddle you because you're feeling a little lonely.

"Hey."

I startle at the hand on my arm, spinning around to find Santino standing right next to me. He's close enough for me to feel the heat of his body and smell the scent of cinnamon on his skin. His hair is still mussed and in disarray. There's still some crusty white stuff around his eyes.

"Are you okay?"

The three simple words are like a knife, cutting through the delicate ties holding me together. I can feel myself falling apart, chunks of myself dropping away as my fragile defenses crumble.

No, I'm not okay. I want to scream it from the tops of my lungs. I haven't been okay in a long time and I don't know what to do. I can't tell anyone. I don't want the guys to worry about me. But I don't know what's wrong with me and nothing I do is working.

Maybe I could just tell him. I could let it all spill out like emotional projectile vomit. Maybe he'll know what to do. Maybe he'll be able to help.

But no. I can't do that. I've known the guy for less than twenty-four hours. He'll just think I'm crazy and run as far and as fast as he can. That's what any normal person would do.

That's what all your so-called friends have done, isn't it? You've chased them away with all your bullshit. You'll just chase this guy away too.

Is that true? Have I chased away all my friends? Is there something wrong with me? Did I do something to hurt them and didn't even realize it?

I can't do that to Santino. He's a guest. He's here to be in the documentary. He doesn't deserve to be saddled with me just because I've got an empty room for him to stay in. He's only being nice. He doesn't actually care if I'm okay. Why would he care? He doesn't know me.

I force a smile onto my face. "Yeah, I'm fine. Just, you know, mornings. Do you take milk or sugar in your coffee?" I spin away to dig out mugs from the cupboards.

"No, just black." There's a hint of caution in his voice, like he's not buying my act.

So, I try to smile bigger. "Nice. This coffee is from a local roaster. They get their beans directly from farmers in

Colombia. You'll really taste all the flavor notes when you drink it black." My hand shakes when I reach for the kettle and I have to use both hands to pour the boiling water into the French press.

Santino doesn't say anything, but I can feel the weight of his gaze on me. He's too observant. He sees too much. When I risk a quick glance in his direction, his eyes follow my every move as if I might spill boiling water on myself or drop the mug on the floor.

I don't think I can stay out here any longer. I can't hold myself together under his scrutiny. "Okay, so, um, you'll want to let this steep for a few minutes. Then push down this depressor thing to filter out all the grinds—sorry, you know how to use a French press. Obviously. Anyway. Um, yeah. Help yourself to whatever in the fridge."

I make my escape and run into my bedroom, just barely stopping myself from slamming the door shut behind me. I perch on the bed, gripping the edge with both hands. My heart is racing like it's trying to beat its way out of my chest. My mind races, jumping from one thought to another faster than I can follow.

Wow, that was embarrassing. You're such a loser. Santino's gonna think you're a lunatic. Everyone thinks you're a lunatic. Nobody likes you. That's why Rhys left. That's why they all left.

In the small, rational part of my brain, I know none of this is true. My friends love me. Rhys loves me. I'm not a loser. I'm not an embarrassment. But the voice is louder than my reason. The voice blares on repeat in my mind until there's no space for any other thoughts. It's like a parasite that's lodged itself inside my skull.

I dig my fingers into my hair and pull. I bang the heels of my hands against my head. I grab a pillow and try to suffocate myself with it, trying to block out the voice. But how can I block out something that's in my head?

I need it to stop. I need it to go away and leave me alone. I just want to be happy again. Is that so much to ask? I just want to be the person I used to be before this all started happening. I just want to be normal.

CHAPTER
SIX

SANTINO

Um… what just happened? Hayden went from totally cool —or at least, he looked fine—to so incredibly sad I could feel it radiating off him, to freaking out and running away.

I hope it wasn't something I said. Maybe I shouldn't have asked for coffee?

I scan the empty kitchen and out toward the empty living room, feeling like an intruder in someone else's home. Hayden said I could help myself to whatever, but that feels wrong. Like, the dude is dealing with something and I'm supposed to just make myself at home in his apartment? That's like, rude, right?

Should I check on him and make sure he's okay? Maybe there's something I can help him with. Maybe I should call one of the guys, just in case.

Or maybe I should mind my own fucking business. I've known the guy for like, what? Eighteen hours? What the hell do I know about what he's going through? Maybe he's already getting all the help he needs and the last thing he wants is another person invading his privacy. I'm already intruding on his space, the least I can do is give the guy some room to breathe.

I pour myself a cup of coffee from the French press, take a sip, and let out a moan. Hayden was right. This is really damn good coffee. Rich and fragrant and the perfect hit of caffeine.

Coffee cup in hand, I wander out to the living room. The two big windows overlook the street. One of them has an air conditioning unit installed, but the other window opens easily when I tug on it. It opens onto a fire escape with a metal staircase running diagonally up and down to the other floors.

I squeeze myself through the window and take a seat on the stairs. The morning air is starting to turn warm and muggy with the rising sun. The sounds of birds chirping and dogs barking mix with the car traffic and sirens. Pedestrians powerwalk along the sidewalk below me.

The city feels alive all around me, the air vibrating with energy and possibility. My stomach twists with nervousness and hope. I really, *really* want this trip to work out.

This documentary isn't the type of thing The Camboy Network usually does, but that's okay. I'll take whatever I can get. And if I can manage to impress them, maybe they'll ask me to do the other type of project too. Maybe I could become one of them, one of the camboys.

The idea is as terrifying as it's exciting. I've done a few videos on my own before. Nothing fancy. Just jerking off while pointing my phone at my dick. I've never shown my face or anything—I was too nervous to do that. But there was something about recording myself and knowing other people would see that had me nutting in seconds. I wonder if it'll feel the same with a full-on video with another guy.

My brain immediately conjures up an image of me and Hayden. Naked. Sweaty. His cock deep inside my ass. I've seen enough of his videos to know he's hung. I mean, he's a big guy, so that isn't surprising. I'm usually pretty *meh* about bottoming, but I'd bend over for that snake of his. In a heartbeat.

I peek back through the window. No sign of Hayden.

Even if I can convince Sebastian to put me in a porn video, I doubt he'd match me with Hayden. Hayden's one of the originals. He's too big a deal to waste on a video with me. Sebastian would probably want me to do a solo video first. See how I do on my own before pairing me up with someone.

It's a little disappointing, to be honest. I'd be lying if I said I didn't have a crush on Hayden. Can you blame me? Just look at him with his sculpted body and blond hair and green eyes. And that was before I even met him. Now that I know about all the library books stacked around the apartment, the fully-stocked kitchen and fridge filled with ingredients I've never seen before in my life, the gourmet coffee made from locally roasted, Colombian fair-trade beans… he's so much more than a pretty face. Come on, how can I resist?

But I need to set my expectations realistically. Sure, it's nice to daydream about getting railed by Hayden, but I shouldn't ask for too much. I'm new here. I need to prove I'm worth their time.

And also… the guy might not be okay. So maybe face-casting him with his dick in my ass isn't really that appropriate.

I finish the coffee and climb back into the apartment. In my room, there's a notification on my phone's home screen. It's a voice message from Mom. My stomach sinks. Shiiit.

She's going to be so upset when she finds out I took off to the other side of the country without telling her. She's going to take it personally, like I didn't want her to know because I'm trying to run away from her. But it isn't like that at all.

I wanted to tell her. I'm terrible at keeping secrets and I'm an even worse liar. But she wouldn't understand why I need to do this.

My whole family has always lived within a twenty-minute drive from each other. My parents, my two older sisters, grandparents, uncles, aunts, cousins and so many nieces and nephews, I've lost count. Half of them have worked for my dad's pool maintenance company at one point or another. None of them has any desire to move away or try anything new. They're all content with living the same life as everyone else around them.

I don't want that though. I want something more. Something bigger.

I tried explaining it to Mom once and she accused me of wanting to abandon her. She's never really dealt with loss well, but it got a lot worse after Grandma died. After that, Mom clings to all of us like we'll disappear into thin air if she doesn't see us at least once a week. I mean, I get it. None of us wants to relive that year when she was deep in depression. But like… does that mean I don't get to live the life I want either?

My phone buzzes again. Mom with another voice message. Fuck. I can't listen to it right now, not when it's still ass-crack early on the West Coast. She'll see I read the message and she knows I would never be up this early at home. Hell, I'm surprised I'm up this early right now.

A bang comes from Hayden's room. Like he tripped and fell or dropped something heavy. I'm at his door before I can think better of it, my protective instincts overriding whatever I've told myself about giving the guy space.

"Hayden?" I call out while knocking. "You okay?"

There are a few muffled curses before he responds. "Yeah, I'm fine."

I hesitate. My gut tells me something's wrong. "I heard a loud bang. Are you hurt?"

I hear him scrambling on the other side of the door and then it opens. He holds onto the edge, leaning on the door as if he needs the support to stay standing. There's a haunted look in his eyes and he can't quite keep my gaze. His eyes flick up to mine, then away, then back, then away. He's smiling, but the expression looks strained, like he's putting it on for my sake. Like he's putting on a brave face.

"Sorry. I just, um, hit my toe against the… thing." He waves vaguely behind him. "But I'm okay. Seriously. Thanks for checking on me."

I cock an eyebrow. "Do you want me to scold the… thing for you? For being in the way of your toe?"

He blinks, staring blankly at me for a moment before he catches on that I'm teasing. His smile softens and the corners of his eyes crinkle just a bit. His chin drops to his chest in an adorably shy move. "No, it was my fault. I left a bag of books in the middle of the floor. It's not like it could grow legs and move out of my way."

My worry eases as he plays along. "Ugh, those books

are so inconsiderate. They *should* grow legs and move out of the way. Who do they think they are? This is *your* bedroom, amirite?"

He chuckles, barely audible, but a subtle vibration travels across the distance separating us and makes my skin tingle. My breath catches as he finally meets my gaze. His eyes are so green, I could stare into them all day.

"Thank you," he murmurs quietly.

Maybe it's just my imagination or perhaps it's wishful thinking, but it feels like more than a simple show of gratitude.

"Yeah, no problem," I reply, my voice a little breathy.

We gaze into each other's eyes for a moment longer and it feels like yesterday afternoon in the kitchen when I thought Hayden was going to kiss me. Like there's some invisible force nudging us toward each other. I thought maybe I'd imagined it, that my crush on the guy had me reading into things that weren't there. But I don't think I was. I think there might be something there.

Hayden breaks eye contact first. "Did you… um, I know you said you only wanted coffee earlier, but would you like something to eat now?" There's a note of uncertainty in his voice, like he's bracing himself in case I turn him down.

I smile, my heart skipping a beat at his adorableness. "I heard you're famous for your cooking."

His eyes flick up to mine, wide with surprise, before he ducks his head again. "No, I mean, I can cook. I like cooking. But I wouldn't say I'm famous for it."

"That's not what the guys say."

Hayden seems to let that absorb for a moment, like he's not sure if he believes me or he doesn't think the guys would say something like that. Then he flashes me a hesitant smile and squeezes past me to head to the kitchen.

"Savory or sweet?" Hayden asks as he opens the fridge.

I don't even need to think about it. "Sweet. Always sweet. Except if there's bacon involved. Then always bacon."

Hayden laughs softly and it makes me wonder what he would sound like when he really laughs. Like full body, throwing head back, laugh out loud without caring who hears. I have a feeling it would be awesome. Like a happiness bomb going off, sprinkling everything with glittery joy.

"Sweet and bacon. I can do that." He starts pulling ingredients out of the fridge and the cupboards.

I recognize the flour, milk, eggs, and bacon, but I'm not entirely sure what everything else is. "What are you making?"

"Brown sugar bacon waffles," he says as he lays out thick slices of bacon on a metal tray, as if this is something he makes every day.

"Brown sugar bacon waffles?" I repeat. "Have you made this before?"

Hayden shakes his head while sprinkling brown sugar over the bacon. "No, but I saw a recipe for it once. It was really simple."

Simple. Right. Yeah. Except I absolutely cannot follow what he's doing. If this is a simple recipe, with a dozen ingredients and multiple mixing bowls, I can't imagine what a complicated recipe would look like.

He pops the tray into the oven and within a few minutes, the fatty scent of bacon starts filling the air. My stomach growls loudly in response. Hayden looks up from the big bowl of batter he's mixing, eyes sparkling with amusement.

I give my stomach a loving pat. "Bro, you're making bacon. My stomach is excited."

He laughs a little louder than before and I feel like a fisherman with a tug on his line.

"What else makes your stomach excited?" he asks.

"Meat," I answer immediately. "Any kind of meat. The greasier the better."

Hayden shakes his head like he was expecting me to say that. "No veggies?"

"I mean, if you can make them taste like meat."

He peeks up at me again, just for a second, as a smile flirts at his mouth. "You like the taste of meat, huh?" His gaze darts back up to me, like he's checking if I got the joke.

Oh, I got it alright. Hayden Summers—looks like a Greek god, is a nerd at heart, and cracks dirty jokes like a twelve-year-old boy. "Mmm, especially sausages. Long and thick and juicy."

His eyes go even wider and his lips curl into a shy, sheepish smile, as if *I'm* the one who started the dirty joke train. I didn't, but now that I'm on it, I don't plan on getting off.

"I like to see how much of the sausage I can fit into my mouth at once," I say, fighting back the giggles.

Hayden's lips twitch and his smile grows wider. "What about meatballs? You like those?"

"Oof, I get real messy with meatballs. I get them all over my face, you know? On my cheeks, on my chin, on my nose."

Hayden snorts a laugh as I continue.

"But sausages and meatballs together. Now we're talking. That's a full-ass meal."

Hayden slaps a hand over his mouth as laughter threatens to burst free. His shoulders shake as he tries to keep it in. I wish he didn't do that. I wish he'd let it all out. I wish I could hear that bright, beautiful sound.

"A full-ass meal," he repeats, wheezing. "Oh my god."

"Mmhmm, if you're cooking it, I'll eat every damn bite."

CHAPTER
SEVEN

HAYDEN

I didn't accidentally stub my toe on the bag of books in my room. The bag wasn't even in the middle of the floor. It was sitting in the corner where I always put it. I went and kicked the damn thing because I couldn't take it anymore. I was going out of my mind. I needed the pain pulsing in my foot to distract me from the nonstop drone of the voice in my head.

It didn't work. The voice just had something new to berate me about. *What kind of idiot goes and kicks a bag of books on purpose?*

But then Santino came to check on me. And then he teased me. Then somehow I ended up cooking for him while we made dirty jokes like teenage boys. I don't know how he did it, but he managed to pull me out of the endless downward spiral that was killing me. And as long as I didn't let my mind wander, as long as I stayed focused on him, everything was fine. Good, even. Maybe a little bit great. I haven't had that much fun cooking in months.

Santino is so funny. I didn't expect that, for some reason. I mean, the dad jokes are corny and the dirty jokes are silly, but there's something absurd and ridiculous about his humor that makes my problems feel less bad. Like, here, have a joke, you don't have to take life so seriously. You can spare a couple laughs.

Watching Santino eat is about as hot as watching one of our Camboy Network videos. He's so expressive, moaning and groaning with every bite he takes. I mean, the brown sugar bacon waffles are good, but you'd think they were laced with cocaine from the sounds he makes. Now I want to feed him all sorts of delicious things so I can watch him eat all the time.

After we finish breakfast and clean up the kitchen, we have just enough time to get ready before leaving for Noel and Bellamy's apartment. Santino is nearly bouncing off the walls as we step out, barely able to contain his excitement. His smile is so wide. His eyes are so bright. There's an energy radiating off him that's utterly contagious.

I recognize the feeling. The anticipation at the start of a project. Eagerness to jump in and create something shiny and new. But I haven't felt that rush, that thrill for a while now. And certainly not over this documentary project.

The truth is, I've been kind of dreading it. I mean, I'm happy for Noel and Bellamy. I really am. They couldn't be more perfect for each other. But do I want to spend the next few weeks documenting just how ecstatic they are to get married? Not really.

It's selfish of me, I know. But I don't really want the constant, in-my-face reminder of how my friends are moving on with their lives and leaving me behind.

I don't have a choice though. Sebastian needs an extra

pair of hands to help with the cameras and I'm the most obvious person to ask. It would've been a real douchebag move for me to say no. No matter how I'm feeling, no matter how much I don't want to, when my friends need me, I'll be there.

Seeing how enthusiastic Santino is to get started on the documentary, it's hard not to get excited too. His smile is infectious. His laughter is irresistible. And by the time we're walking into Noel's building, I feel like maybe this won't be as bad as I expected.

The doorman is waiting for us and when we arrive, he ushers us directly into the elevator. Noel lives on the top floor of a Lower East Side building, in a penthouse loft that looks out above the roofs of the surrounding neighborhood. The apartment looks like it's been taken straight out of some interior design magazine, with a sleek stainless-steel kitchen, a large U-shaped leather sectional, and a rustic dining table that seats ten.

Bellamy answers the door and when he steps back to let us in, Santino's jaw drops. Laughing, Bellamy throws an arm around Santino's shoulders. "Sick place, right?"

"Uh huh." Santino's jaw is still on the floor. "You live here?" he whispers with a look of awe in his eyes.

"Yes," Bellamy says, matching Santino's volume. "Why are we whispering?"

"I don't know."

Bellamy gives him a light, playful shove, then continues in a normal voice. "Come on, let me show you around." He guides Santino toward the windows and I find myself hovering awkwardly in the middle of the room.

My body wants to follow Santino to the windows. My

brain reminds me I shouldn't be so clingy. There's something so light and refreshing about Santino, like he's able to clear the air around him of anything bad or heavy or dark. An irrational part of me gravitates toward that, wanting to stay in his bubble of safety for as long as I can. But logically, I know I can't. I shouldn't. I'm bad for him. I'll contaminate him. He should stay far away from me. He should run and save himself before I end up hurting him.

"Hayden!" Sebastian waves me over to the large dining room table where he's laying out black binders. "How's it going with Santino?" he asks, skipping over pleasantries.

"Um, okay?" If I don't count him seeing me struggling at the club last night. Or my freak-out this morning. Or me kicking a stack of books that had him running to make sure I was alright.

At my less-than-enthusiastic answer, Sebastian glances up from straightening a binder and casts me a questioning look.

Squirming, I put on the smile I know will put him at ease. "It's been great, actually. He's a really cool guy. He's not a morning person. He drinks his coffee black. I made waffles for us this morning and added bacon because he likes bacon." I stop myself from rambling as Sebastian's expression goes from amused to concerned.

He opens his mouth and I brace myself for questions I don't want to answer, but Bellamy interrupts just in time.

"You guys want anything to drink?" Bellamy asks, heading to the kitchen. "We've got beer if we're day drinking. Otherwise, soda, LaCroix, water…?"

"Whiskey!" Noel shouts before appearing from the hallway that leads to the bedrooms.

"No day drinking!" Sebastian shouts back and Noel

rolls his eyes. "I need everyone alert and focused for this meeting."

Bellamy grabs an armful of LaCroix cans from the fridge and brings them over to the dining room table.

"Don't forget the coasters!" Noel calls out.

"Yeah, babe, I've got them." Bellamy sounds equal parts exasperated and indulgent. He places cans down on the thick glass coasters already set out in front of each chair.

"Alright, let's get started," Sebastian says. "I've made custom packages for everyone, so please find the binder with your name on it and sit in your assigned seat."

Noel rolls his eyes again and Bellamy backhands him lightly on the arm. Noel sticks out his bottom lip in a pout as he rubs the sore spot.

Sebastian takes the seat at the head of the table, with Noel and Bellamy on either side of him, facing each other. Then Santino and I are in the next seats down, also facing each other.

The moment we're seated, Sebastian starts. "If you open your binder, you'll find a table of contents. This will help you locate whatever information you're looking for. We'll go through the binder one section at a time."

Across the table from me, Santino's jaw is slack as he flips quickly through his binder. "Whoa…" he murmurs under his breath.

It's always fun watching someone experience Sebastian for the first time and Santino's response is perfection. He sneaks a peek at me, as if asking whether this is for real and I give him a little shrug. Yeah, this is for real for real.

Sebastian takes us through the binders' daily and hourly breakdowns of the shooting schedule, including location details, a list of equipment needed, costume requirements for those in front of the camera. He's outlined each scene with key dramatic moments, preliminary dialogue prompts, and suggested camera angles.

He's got us scouting wedding venues and doing tuxedo fittings and cake tastings. There's a weekend-long bachelor party, and then the actual wedding. The only thing we're not doing on camera is signing the damn marriage certificate—Noel and Bellamy are doing that in a more private ceremony with Bellamy's family in Ohio.

Santino looks stunned through it all. The rest of us are used to Sebastian throwing a truck ton of information at us all at once, but I'm not sure how much Santino is actually absorbing. When Sebastian pauses to ask if there are any questions, Santino sits back in his chair, a dazed look on his face.

Bellamy suggests we take a break and after a moment of hesitation, Sebastian agrees.

Santino is up and out of his seat before the rest of us can push our chairs back. He immediately pulls Sebastian away and I watch as they migrate to the other side of the room.

What are they talking about? Is Santino backing out of the project? The binders are pretty intimidating. Maybe this isn't what he thought he was signing up for.

Or maybe it's me. He doesn't want to stay with me anymore. He feels uncomfortable around the strange dude who goes around kicking things because he hears a voice in his head.

From across the room, Sebastian shoots me a quick, examining look before turning back to Santino.

Yeah, it's probably you.

Doubt slithers through my mind, twisting everything that's happened in the past day into a darker, more menacing version of what I remember. Santino only ate my waffles because he felt bad saying no. He only came to sit next to me at the club because he was tired. He only checked in on me when I kicked the books because I was making too much noise. Everything takes on a sinister, shadowy hue until I don't know what's true anymore.

I hurry to the bathroom as an ache blossoms in my chest. I don't know what I'm doing here. I'm going to ruin this project. I'm the last person Santino should be staying with. They would all be better off without me.

The ache expands across my chest, rising up to my throat until it feels like I'm suffocating. I huddle on the bathroom floor, wishing I was at home, in bed, curled up under the covers. I never should've come today. I never should've agreed to let Santino live with me. I'm so dumb. I'm so stupid.

A knock on the door makes me jump. "Hey, Sebastian told me to tell you we're starting again," Noel calls through the door.

I suck in a lungful of air and my head spins. I can't tell up from down anymore. I can't tell left from right. Everything feels so mixed up, like I'm being tossed in a current and buried under several feet of water.

Noel knocks again. "You hear me?"

"Yeah, one sec," I croak, pushing myself unsteadily to my feet. My hand shakes as I turn on the faucet and splash cold water on my face. When I look in the mirror, I don't recognize the man staring back at me.

He looks like me. He has my hair, my eyes, my nose.

But he doesn't feel like me anymore. I feel like I'm someone else masquerading as Hayden.

Noel's still there when I open the bathroom door. He gives me a strange look, like he's wary of what I might've been doing in his bathroom. "You good?"

I force my face into a smile and hope it's good enough to fool him. "Yeah, I'm good."

I don't know if he believes me.

When we get back to the dining table, Sebastian and Santino are already seated.

"So, *small* change in plans," Sebastian says. "Hayden, how do you feel about performing with Santino?"

CHAPTER
EIGHT

SANTINO

Oh, shit. Would it be bad if I crawled under the table to hide?

I didn't realize Sebastian was going to bring this up right *now*, in front of *everyone*. I thought he'd at least give it some thought first. I thought he'd pair me up with someone less high profile than Hayden.

What if Hayden doesn't want to do a video with me? What if he's like, ew, with Santino? Nah, bro! How fucking embarrassing would that be?

Or worse. He agrees to it but only because I'm sitting across the table from him and he feels bad rejecting me in front of everyone. The last thing I want is to force Hayden into something he doesn't want to do.

I swear to god, I didn't mention Hayden's name when talking to Sebastian just now. When I saw the binders and all the work Sebastian had put into preparing for this documentary, it cemented things for me. This dude knows his shit. He's a serious professional. If he can't help me get my life on track, then no one can.

I just said I was open to doing camming stuff if there was an opportunity for it while I was here. Then Sebastian asked if I only wanted to do solo videos or if I was open to performing with someone else. I mean, my mind immediately went to Hayden, of course, but I didn't say that out loud! I was just like, yeah, sure, I'm open to whatever!

Then Sebastian got a look in his eye and suddenly he's at the table asking Hayden if he wants to have sex with me on camera.

Fuuck. Kill me now.

Hayden looks horrified. Like Sebastian just asked him to have sex with a subway rat or something. Then his gaze darts to me like he's trying to figure out if this is a cruel practical joke.

"Hear me out," Sebastian continues when the dead silence at the table goes on for a beat too long. "The storyline of the documentary is Bellamy and Noel are planning their wedding, right? And Santino's come in from out of town to help. While he's here, he spends a lot of time with Hayden, who's also helping with the wedding planning. You're both hot. Both available. Feelings develop. Etcetera."

"I don't get it. Where does the sex come in?" Noel asks. He's been slouched in his chair all day like he's bored out of his mind.

"Are you adding it to the documentary?" Bellamy asks, equally confused.

I'm confused too. I never suggested adding sex scenes to the documentary!

"No, not like that," Sebastian waves his hand dismissively. "You guys have to think of this as a movie, okay? The main plot is Bellamy and Noel planning their wedding. The sub-plot is Santino and Hayden meeting and falling in love. You know, like those wedding romcoms where the bridesmaid and the groomsman fall in love. We'll release the sex videos separately, but like, there's a cross-promo opportunity here!"

Sebastian gives us a look like the explanation is so obvious, a five-year-old would've understood. Except, I'm not sure we do.

But then Hayden finally speaks up, still looking like he's in shock. "Videos?" His voice cracks a bit when he emphasizes the "s".

"Yeah, at least two, I think." Sebastian's gaze goes a little distant, like he's not really with us anymore. He's off in some other dimension, dreaming up ways to take over the world. "Maybe we can use the roommate scenario too…"

He pulls out his phone and his thumbs start tapping away. The rest of us exchange glances, not sure what to do. I mean, Hayden hasn't even agreed to anything yet!

"You don't have to do this if you don't want," I say, even as a small part of me can't help but hope. Me and Hayden Summers? That's too good to be true, right?

"It's a good idea, though," Noel chimes in.

I want to tell him to shut the fuck up and hug him at the same time.

"It is," Bellamy agrees. "But we don't have to decide on this today, do we? Give the guy a day or two to think about it? We still have time to tweak the script."

Sebastian's not listening. He's lost in his own little world with his head bowed over his phone.

"I'll do it." Hayden's voice is so quiet I'm pretty sure I imagine it. But then he lifts his gaze and it crashes into mine, knocking the breath out of my lungs. The look in his eyes makes my heart skip a beat, like I'm the one he's been waiting for his whole life, like there's no one else on the entire planet but me…

"Yes," Sebastian says in a hushed voice. "See the chemistry? The fans will go batshit over this."

Hayden breaks eye contact first, dropping his gaze and shifting in his seat.

"So yeah? We're a go?" Sebastian asks again, just to be sure.

Hayden nods, bottom lip caught between his teeth. "Yeah, we're good."

"Excellent." Sebastian flips through his binder, which is about twice as thick as the rest of ours. "I'll start working on the script changes today and will get you new copies by Monday. Santino, you'll need to sign another set of contracts and waivers. Oh, and get tested. Are you on PrEP?"

"Uh…"

Sebastian's moving so fast, I can't quite keep up with him.

"Don't worry about it. We'll get it sorted out."

The rest of the meeting goes by in a whirlwind and if I'm honest, I don't really catch much of it. My mind is still stuck on the whole, I'm going to have sex with Hayden on camera business.

I can't decide if I'm ecstatic or terrified. Both. I'm definitely both.

Hayden is a professional porn star who's done dozens of these videos with other professional porn stars. I'm just some random dude who recorded himself jerking off a couple times. What the fuck do I know about performing? What if I suck at it? What if I'm so bad they want nothing to do with me ever again?

By the time we're done and ready to head home, I'm seriously debating telling Sebastian I've changed my mind. But Sebastian's already talking to Noel about locations where they can shoot the video and adjusting the documentary schedule to accommodate the new project. I'm the one who said he was open to whatever. Well, this is whatever, I guess.

Hayden and I are mostly silent on the way back to his apartment. When we get off the subway and out of earshot of bystanders, I blurt out the question that's been nagging at me.

"Are you sure you're okay with this?"

He shoots me a sideways glance, as if he's trying to assess what kind of answer I'm looking for. Then he drops his gaze to the sidewalk, staring at his feet as we walk. "Yeah, totally," he says. His voice is oddly neutral, like he's trying to sound upbeat but it fell flat.

"I didn't know Sebastian was going to drop it on you like that. If you want to back out of it, I'd completely understand." I mean, I'd be devastated, but I'd understand.

"Sebastian's really good at this stuff. If he thinks it'll work, then it'll work," Hayden says, which doesn't answer my question at all.

I've heard Bellamy say that Sebastian's a genius too, which like, great, but Hayden doesn't say it with nearly as much conviction as Bellamy did.

"Are *you* okay with this?" Hayden asks suddenly.

The question catches me off guard. Me? Who the hell cares about me? "Yeah, I am. It was my idea. I mean, not really. I just told Sebastian I was open to, you know, performing, and he came up with the rest."

Hayden nods like that's something Sebastian does on the regular. "But you didn't come to New York expecting to do this."

What is he trying to say? Does he think this is a bad idea? Like, this isn't what I was invited to do, so why am I trying to push my luck? "No, I didn't, but…"

How do I explain this in a way that doesn't sound pathetic? I don't know what I'm doing with my life. I'm going nowhere fast and if I don't come up with something soon, I'll be elbows deep in chlorine for the rest of my life. This trip is my last chance to climb out of the rut and I'm fucking desperate.

"Sebastian can be hard to say no to. He tends to get his way a lot. But that doesn't mean you always have to do what he says." Hayden's hands are stuffed into his pockets. His gaze is locked onto the sidewalk in front of his feet. He sounds tired, like he's sharing wisdom he's learned the hard way.

I can't really tell if he's speaking to me or to himself and my heart aches a little at the thought. Has he done things he hasn't wanted to do? Is that why he seems so sad sometimes?

"As long as you're not being pressured into it or anything, it should be great." His voice is tight, like he's struggling to be encouraging. His lips are curled into a smile, but it looks forced.

"I'm not," I say cautiously, feeling like I'm walking through a minefield for some reason. "Are *you*?"

There's a slight flinch around his eyes, but his smile doesn't budge. Like, not even the smallest twitch of muscle. "Nope."

"Good."

"Great."

"Awesome."

So why does it feel like there's a gun pointed at our heads? The feeling of being both the gunman and the hostage follows me for another couple blocks. I feel like I've set something in motion that I can't stop. That things are about to change, but I don't know whether they'll change for the better or for the worse.

But this is what I wanted, isn't it? This is why I came to New York. To do something different. To take a risk. But now that I'm here, now that it's actually happening, I can't help wondering if I'll end up regretting everything.

I'm so caught up in second-guessing myself, I don't notice where we're going until we're in the middle of what looks like a giant park.

"Uh… is this the way back to your place?"

Hayden blinks like he's surprised to find himself here too. "No, it's a park not far from my place. I… sorry. It's this way."

He turns to head down another path, but I grab his arm to stop him. "Hey, wait."

Hayden freezes, eyes flicking to my hand on his arm. I let go, hand still floating in midair.

"Sorry, I just…"

Hayden lifts his gaze and when I look into his eyes, all my words fail me. The emotions swirling around those emerald greens are so vast and complex. How can one person hold all those emotions inside them at the same time? Sadness and fear, hope and want, and a dozen other ones I can't tease apart. Like there's a battle raging inside him and it's too early to tell which side will win.

"It's a nice day," I say, gesturing vaguely around us. "Maybe we can hang out a bit?"

Hayden scans the park like he's seeing it for the first time. The trail we're on winds through giant fields of grass dotted with stands of mature trees. Groups of picnickers are scattered across the lawn, lounging on blankets or tossing frisbees around. Moms with strollers mix with other pedestrians as joggers weave in between us to get past. There's a light breeze that cuts the heat, making it actually comfortable to sit out in the sun.

"Yeah, sure," Hayden says, even though he sounds anything but sure.

I lead the way off the paved path and to a shady spot under a tree. We sit down and Hayden pulls his knees up to his chest, wrapping his arms around his shins. His gaze wanders across the lawn in front of us, stopping at each group of people like he's trying to see if he knows them. Then he drops his chin to his chest, chews on his bottom lip, and rips a few blades of grass from the ground.

I wish I hadn't brought up camming with Sebastian today. I could've waited until we started shooting the documentary to broach the subject with him. Maybe then he wouldn't have roped Hayden into this. Maybe then Hayden wouldn't look like his world was falling apart.

CHAPTER
NINE

HAYDEN

"How did you get started with camming?"

Santino's question isn't unusual. I get asked it all the time. It's the standard icebreaker in the industry and I have a canned response I've perfected over the years. It's short and witty, just enough to satisfy their curiosity without revealing too much.

But there's something about the way Santino asks that's different. It doesn't feel like an icebreaker or him being nosy. It feels like genuine interest and more than a little concern.

It's because of Sebastian's suggestion during the meeting today. About me and Santino doing a few videos together while he's here. I have to admit the idea is genius. But then, Sebastian's ideas typically are. But Santino's too observant for his own good and he's probably noticed I'm being weird.

It's not that I don't want to do videos with him. He's really cute with a strong brow and the tiniest bump on the bridge of his nose. His lips are wide and pouty and his jaw is covered in scruff that looks just this side of unkept. His dark hair is thick and full and I bet it'll be silky soft when I run my fingers through it.

It's not Santino. It's me.

I haven't felt very… sexy in the past little while. And I haven't done a video recently, so it hasn't been a problem. But… it's kind of difficult being a camboy when I can't get it up.

Yeah, that's right. Not only are you crazy, you're also defective.

"You don't have to tell me if you don't want to," Santino adds when I take too long to respond.

"No, sorry. I mean." I shake my head, trying to dislodge the voice, and take a deep breath. "I grew up in New Jersey." I'm not sure why I started there. It has nothing to do with why I started camming. But my normal response to the question doesn't feel quite right. "My family was pretty poor. My dad was a truck driver, so he was never around. My mom had a drinking problem, so when she wasn't working at the grocery store, she was usually passed out somewhere. My sister ran off with her boyfriend when she was seventeen. I wanted to get out of there too."

I pinch some grass between my fingers and yank. The tension and release of the blades ripping is strangely calming, like I can somehow channel the chaos of my emotions into that smallest act of destruction.

"Camming was your way out?" Santino asks when I don't continue.

"I tried going to community college." I shrug. "It wasn't for me. But I was in class one day and I overheard someone else talking about camming. How they were paying their tuition from what they earned. So I figured I'd check it out, give it a shot."

Santino casts me a sideways, amused half-cringe. "How old were you?"

I pause and give him a sheepish look. "Legally or…?"

Santino laughs, throwing his head back as the sound rings through the air. It's bubbly and bright, sending tingles down my arms. The dappled sunlight coming through the tree's foliage dances over his face and the distinct bump of his Adam's apple.

He looks like he's glowing. The air around him seems to sparkle. He's got a dark complexion, but it feels like there's a brightness coming from inside him, lighting him up from the inside out. I feel like I can breathe more easily when he's next to me. I feel less like I'm drowning when I'm next to him.

I would love to do a video with Santino. I'd love to see how he responds when I touch him, what kinds of noises he makes. Will he be aggressive and take the lead? Or would he rather be manhandled?

Santino lies down on the grass, folding one hand behind his head and planting the opposite foot on the ground. He sighs contentedly, gazing up through the tree's canopy. Shifting, I turn toward him and lean back on one hand, tucking my legs under me so my knees aren't in the way.

"Do you like your job?" he asks, glancing over at me. "Would you rather do something else?"

I don't answer right away. Even a few months ago, it would've been a no-brainer. But now, I'm not so sure. Theoretically, I love my job. There isn't anything else in the world I'd rather do for a living. But how can I love my job when I'm so miserable all the time? How can I say I love it when the thought of having sex with someone as hot as Santino gets absolutely no response between my legs?

"I like it," I say, trying to lie without really lying.

"What do you like most about it?"

I rip another handful of grass. At the moment? I have no freaking clue. It used to be fun. I got to have sex with a bunch of hot guys and get paid for it. I got to work with my best friends. The company we started took off and I got to do so many cool things I never would've thought were possible.

But now… none of that's appealing. But it's not just camming—nothing feels appealing at the moment. Not the documentary or going to see Rhys perform at The Bronzed Rail. Not even cooking or reading or playing video games or working out. These are all things I supposedly love to do… so why don't I want to do any of them?

"It pays really well?" I can't stop my voice from going up at the end like I'm asking a question. It's not an answer I ever would've given before, but it's the most common one in the industry.

"Is that why you do it? For the money?" There's no judgment in Santino's voice, more like confusion, like that wasn't what he expected me to say.

"No, it's not for the money. I…" I don't know how to have this conversation. I don't know how to reconcile what I used to feel with what I feel now. I don't know how to give the answers I know are true, but feel like a lie.

"It's okay, you don't have to tell me." Santino's smile is carefree and relaxed. Understanding and earnest. His eyes drift shut. His free hand lies on his stomach, lifting and lowering with his every breath. "I shouldn't be prying anyway."

"You're not prying. It's just... I'm..."

A fucked-up loser who can't even answer a simple question.

The voice is so loud, I swear to god it sounds like someone is standing right behind me, shouting in my ear. I flinch, grateful that Santino has his eyes closed and doesn't see. But then the ache in my chest hits hard and fast, eating through me like it's trying to hollow me out. I turn away, hoping Santino doesn't notice, and struggle to breathe through the vise around my chest.

"Hayden? You okay?"

Fuck. No. Not now. I have nowhere to hide. Nowhere to run. I nod frantically, but it feels like my entire body is shaking with the movement. "Yeah," I gasp. "Sorry, I'm just—"

A. Fucked. Up. Loser.

Every dumb thing I've ever done comes flooding into my mind. Every time I've said something stupid or made a joke nobody laughed at. Every time I didn't understand what the guys were talking about and needed someone to explain it to me. The weight of all the memories comes crashing down on me like they're trying to grind me into pieces.

"Hey." A gentle hand settles on my shoulder, warm and solid.

I just barely swallow down the sob that threatens to escape, but I can't stop the bone-deep shudder that ripples through me.

The hand slides across my back until Santino's arm is wrapped around my shoulders. I resist the urge to lean into him, to take the comfort he's offering. It's not fair to him. This is my problem to deal with. He's my guest. I should be helping him, not the other way around.

"Sorry," I say again, hating how weak my voice is. "Sorry, I just, um… I'm okay. I'm fine."

I die a little more with each word I utter. I'm not okay. I'm not fine. Something's wrong with me and I don't know how to fix it.

"Are you sure? Do you want me to call someone?"

"No!" The single word rips from my throat. I can't let my friends know. Not Rhys. Not Sebastian. They'll worry about me. They'll feel bad and think it's their fault. They already have enough going on. I don't want to drag them away from their lives because I can't manage my own shit. "No, sorry, you don't need to do that. They're busy. This is nothing."

You're nothing.

I wince at the verbal attack and I'm pretty sure Santino sees it. "It's just something that happens sometimes." I let out a strangled laugh that makes me sound manic. "It'll pass. Don't worry. I'm good."

Santino's brows draw together like he doesn't believe me, but at least he doesn't try to argue with me. "Do you want to go home?"

Home. Yes. Home. Where I can close my bedroom door. Where no one can see me. Where I can curl up in a ball until the ache goes away, until the darkness recedes, until the voice goes silent.

"Yeah, I think I'm just tired. That's all." I sound like I'm trying to convince myself.

Santino jumps up and offers me a hand. I hesitate before taking it. I shouldn't need his help getting up. But his hand felt so nice when it was on my shoulder. I don't want him to think I'm weak. But the ache in my chest hurts so much.

I slide my hand into his and when his fingers close around mine, it feels like a lifeline. A buoy. All I need to do is hang on and he'll draw me in to safety.

He pulls me to my feet with a little too much force and I stumble into him. My chest presses against his, our clasped hands sandwiched between us. He steadies me with his other hand on my waist. Our faces are inches apart and he smells like cinnamon, warm and spicy. His lashes are dark, long and thick, framing deep brown eyes with golden specks that catch and reflect the sunlight. They're beautiful.

It takes every last ounce of strength I possess to step away from Santino. He's just being nice. He doesn't need me mauling him. I'm a grown man. I should be able to stand and walk home by myself.

The loss of his body heat is immediate and profound. I miss him. I barely know him, but I miss him already. How is that even possible?

I stuff my hands in my pockets to keep myself from reaching for him, then clear my throat before I speak. Even then, my voice is thick and groggy. "Sorry."

"Don't worry about it. You're good."

Filled with embarrassment, I turn down the path that will take us back to my building. Walking feels weird. Like my feet aren't really my own. And yet somehow, they manage to take step after step that lead me closer to home. Navigating around the other pedestrians helps distract me from the tightness in my chest. It's not quite so all-consuming when I have to move aside to let joggers pass, or when a dog on a leash comes over for a quick sniff, or when I need to speed walk around a group of loitering teenagers.

I can feel Santino beside me the entire way. Not quite touching, but close enough for us to brush up against each other every so often. He doesn't try to talk to me, doesn't tell me to slow down. He keeps up with the fast pace I've set, a steady presence by my side.

By the time we make it back, I feel silly. Ashamed. I can't believe I freaked out in the middle of the fucking park. I can't believe I needed Santino to comfort me, to keep me from spiraling completely out of control. What the fuck is wrong with me? What is this thing? Why is it happening to me? What have I done to deserve this?

The darkness that had retreated during the walk starts creeping back in. It's heavy and thick, sticky like sludge, clinging to everything it comes into contact with. It fills up the big, empty cavern the ache has left in my chest, drowning me, suffocating me.

I can't do this. I can't be here. I can't take it anymore.

I mumble some excuse about being tired and don't bother to wait for Santino's response. I beeline toward my room and shut the door firmly behind me. No one can see me here. No one will know.

I crawl into bed, hugging a pillow to my chest as if it'll relieve the pressure growing inside me, threatening to burst. It doesn't help. I squeeze my eyes shut as they sting with unshed tears. I hate this. I hate this so much. I just want it to end.

CHAPTER
TEN

SANTINO

This feels wrong. I feel it in my gut so strongly, my stomach is actually unsettled. Hayden's obviously going through some shit, except I think I'm the only one who knows. I thought these guys were all super tight, but no one else seems to be doing or saying anything to make sure Hayden's okay.

We're in this mansion. Like, a literal fucking mansion from the olden times. Wrought iron gates guard the house from the public. The front hall is lined with busts of famous dead people. The floors are marble and the ceilings are double height. Every room is lit by massive crystal chandeliers. The walls are covered with priceless art. The furniture is antique. The ceilings are trimmed with gold. This is supposed to be someone's house, but it looks more like they tried to cram every single expensive thing they could find into the building. Honestly? It's pretty ugly.

We're shooting the venue-scouting scene for the documentary, so I'm supposed to wander around the place with

Bellamy with my jaw on the floor, which isn't difficult because every room we walk into is worse than the last.

I've been given a GoPro to hold while we work our way through the house. Sebastian has another one, while Hayden's got the big fancy camera. He circles around us, head bowed and eyes focused on the viewscreen, stopping every once in a while to check camera angles with Sebastian.

I was told to ignore Hayden and pretend the camera isn't there. But my gaze keeps drifting in his direction, like a compass always pointing toward true north. I can't help it. This isn't sitting right with me.

Hayden seems okay on the surface. He's taking instructions from Sebastian and getting the work done. He's a little quiet, but I'm realizing that's just the way he is around the guys. He's the quiet one in the group. The one who lets his friends take the spotlight. But I'm getting really bad vibes, like there's a giant elephant in the room that no one else can see except me.

I've had the apartment almost entirely to myself the past couple days. Hayden's kept to himself, only coming out of his room to go to the bathroom or get something to drink from the kitchen. But he always immediately goes back and closes the door behind him.

I've tried to catch him on those rare occasions, tried to ask how he was doing, whether he wanted to grab something to eat together. He kept saying he wasn't hungry and he was tired, then he would disappear again. Unless he's got some stash hidden in his room, I'm pretty sure he hasn't eaten in almost forty-eight hours. He definitely hadn't showered. Hell, I didn't know if he would even show up to the shoot today.

But this morning, he emerged from his room, showered and dressed, a tuft of blond hair sticking out of the hole at the back of the backward baseball cap on his head. There were bags under his eyes and he looked a little gaunt, but other than that, there was no sign he'd been a fucking hermit all weekend.

He made coffee, had some toast for breakfast, and asked me how I was feeling about the first day of shooting. Like everything was totally normal. Like nothing had happened in the park that day.

But something did. I was right there. The dude was not okay. He was hyperventilating and shaking uncontrollably. I thought he was going to pass out or something. I'm not even sure how he managed to walk all the way home.

And he didn't want me to call his friends for help. Which kind of makes me think that they have absolutely no fucking clue that there's anything wrong with him. Either that, or having panic attacks in the middle of public parks is a normal occurrence for Hayden. I don't know, man… that doesn't feel normal to me.

"This is perfect," Noel announces as he turns in a circle in the middle of the ballroom. Giant gilded mirrors line the walls and three enormous chandeliers hang from the ceiling.

Standing next to him, Bellamy looks skeptical. "Seriously?"

"For the ceremony, yeah."

"Don't you think it's a bit…" Bellamy trails off.

"Ugly? Tacky? Gimmicky?" I offer a bunch of options and Noel shoots a murderous look in my direction.

"It's just not really my style, babe." Bellamy's way more diplomatic than I am.

"Why don't you guys have a beach wedding?" I ask. "You know, breeze coming off the water, ocean scent in the air, sun shining down on the warm sand."

"That does sound nice," Sebastian agrees.

"What happens if it rains?" Noel crosses his arms over his chest, glowering. "I don't want to resort to plan B. We're only having a plan A and plan A is going to be perfect."

This is all in the script Sebastian wrote for us, but Noel is actually really convincing. So either he's a much better actor than I thought he was, or he's genuinely this stuck-up in real life. I'd bet on the latter.

Bellamy sighs. He's wearing that amused and indulgent expression he has for Noel. Like he knows how ridiculous Noel is being, but he finds it endearing rather than annoying. He pulls Noel into his arms and waits until Hayden's in place to catch a close-up shot of them both. "You really like this place, don't you?"

Noel pouts a little, giving Bellamy puppy dog eyes as he nods. It looks hilarious on a guy who's always scowling, but it works because Bellamy fucking melts.

"Okay, fine, we'll do the wedding here." Bellamy sounds exasperated, but he looks completely smitten. Noel does too.

When they lean in for a kiss, it's full-on with tongue and everything. If I didn't know better, I would've thought they were going to strip down and fuck right then and there.

They're still going at it when Sebastian calls, "Cut!" They don't stop immediately either. They take their time, slowing to soft, lingering kisses that leave them panting.

"Hayden. Santino. You guys are up," Sebastian calls, gesturing for us to follow him down a long hallway. "Here's how it's going to work. Santino, you'll be looking at the art. Hayden, you'll be filming him. I'll be filming both of you."

"Do you want me to actually record?" Hayden asks, holding up his camera.

"Yeah, definitely. I might be able to edit some of your footage in with mine." Sebastian says. "Then Santino turns. You make eye contact. Hayden keeps recording as you guys flirt. Got it?"

Suddenly, my heart is racing. It wasn't beating this fast when we showed up this morning for the first day of shooting. It wasn't even beating this fast when Sebastian first called out action. This is it—just me and Hayden on screen and I'm going to have to sell it. If I fuck this up…

I glance over at Hayden to find him watching me. I forget to breathe. There's something in his eyes I don't recognize. Something soft and tender that makes me want to go to him and wrap myself around him. What's going on inside that beautiful head of his? What's he so desperate to hide from everyone?

"Save it for the camera, guys."

We break eye contact but I can still feel the weight of Hayden's gaze, the heaviness of whatever secrets he's got bottled up inside.

Sebastian shows me where he wants me to stand and I do my best to pretend I'm admiring the art when he calls out, "Roll cameras. Action."

Out of the corner of my eye, I see Hayden moving toward me. I wait until he's pretty close before glancing in his direction.

His head is bowed, staring into the viewscreen of the camera he's holding. Sebastian circles around us.

"Hey," I say, following the script.

Hayden lifts his head and meets my gaze. The portable light Sebastian's holding hits his face at just the right angle, making his eyes sparkle. They're so intensely green and I watch as the different shades dance and shift. He studies me like I'm one of the paintings on the wall. The smallest of smiles graces his lips, barely more than a tilt at the corners.

"Hey," he says back. His low, rumbling voice hits me right in the gut.

Heat gathers low in my stomach as my groin tightens and my dick stirs. My mouth goes dry and my knees go a little weak.

"You wanna see some of the shots we got today?" he asks, holding up his camera.

"Yeah, sure." The words come out breathy and I'm seriously a little lightheaded.

Hayden sidles up next to me, his body emitting so much heat, he feels like a furnace. I want to burrow into it, snuggle right up against him and rub myself on him like a fucking cat. I bet it'd feel amazing to fall asleep in his arms. Even better to wake up in them too.

When I manage to focus on the camera, he's actually got footage of me cued up. He hits play. There's no sound, but even then, I'm immediately drawn in. There's me with Bellamy, looking dumbfounded as we take in the front hall. Me and Bellamy again, this time with Noel and Sebastian too, climbing the winding marble staircase. We look tiny in comparison to all the stone around us.

Then just a shot of me sitting on a couch, testing the

bounciness of the cushions with my hands. Slapping a hand over my face, I laugh and groan at the overly serious expression I'm wearing, as if the firmness of the couch is going to make or break the wedding. Hayden is standing half beside me, half behind me and when he chuckles, the sound reverberates through my body. My skin tingles.

"I can't believe you got that." I'm not acting when I say that.

"It's cute," he responds and a part of me hopes he's not acting either.

The next shot is me standing in front of the window. I remember this one. The window overlooks Central Park and I was looking out, amazed at how big the park is. The heavy, velvet curtains cast shadows all around me, but the sun is shining brightly on my face. I look... ethereal. I didn't know I could look like that.

Then finally, a shot of me gazing directly into the camera. There's a look on my face that surprises me. It's way too revealing, too unguarded, all of my emotions on display: my crush on him, my worry for him, my confusion over what I should do. My heart skips a beat at the realization. He caught me staring at him when I thought he wasn't paying attention.

Hayden takes a breath and as his chest expands, it touches the back of my arm, my shoulder. I lean into the contact. I don't even do it consciously. My body is just drawn to him.

His hand settles on my hip, as if he's steadying me. Or holding me. I can't tell. But the touch is searing. It burns through my clothes until it singes my skin.

I don't breathe. If I take a breath, I might break the spell of this moment and I want this to last forever. I want Hayden's hands on me always.

"Cut." Sebastian's voice shatters the little bubble around us. "That's great, guys."

I blink as I look away from the camera Hayden's holding. I feel like I'm coming out of a trance, with my senses finally picking up signals from outside the little space between me and Hayden. Sebastian's actually standing really close, scrolling through the footage on his camera. I didn't even notice him there. I was totally engrossed in Hayden.

Hayden's hand drops from my hip and he takes a step back, but only by an inch or so. He's still close enough for me to feel his body heat, to hear the heavy inhales and exhales of his breathing.

I turn my head to glance over my shoulder. He's watching me. Bottom lip caught between his teeth. He's always abusing the poor thing.

Without thinking, I reach up and use my thumb to tug his lip free. It's red and bruised and all I want to do is kiss it better. Hayden lets out a breath and the warm air blows over my skin.

I really, *really* want to kiss him. My lips tingle with how much I want to press them against his. I want to thread my fingers into his always messy hair. I want to feel the hardness of his body flush against mine.

My dick is hard, straining against the zipper of my shorts. My nipples are sensitive, burning where they rub against the fabric of my t-shirt.

I could do it. I could kiss him. He's so close. I'd just need to lean in, tilt my chin up, and we'd be kissing.

Something flashes in Hayden's eyes a split second

before he spins away from me. It's so abrupt that I actually stagger backward a little.

"Sorry, I shouldn't have… I need to…" Hayden shakes his head, almost like he's trying to clear something from his mind. "Sorry."

He stalks off, leaving me standing alone in the middle of the long, freaky hallway.

No, actually, I'm not alone. Sebastian is still here. With his camera pointed at me. Secretly recording us.

He lowers the camera and gives me a look that makes me pause. It's not an unkind look, but it's also not understanding or sympathetic. It's guarded, almost calculating.

Shit, I probably shouldn't have done the lip thing. There are strict rules about not touching without consent. It was all laid out in the paperwork Sebastian had me sign.

"Sorry, I didn't mean to—" I wave vaguely at my own lips, hoping he knows what I mean. "It won't happen again. I promise."

Sebastian studies me for another second, expression unchanging. "It's okay," he says before turning to leave.

My stomach sinks. I hope I didn't just fuck everything up.

CHAPTER
ELEVEN

HAYDEN

I feel like I'm on a rollercoaster I can't get off of. Every time I think the ride is over, it blows right past the platform and starts cranking up the incline. The darkness creeps in, blurring the edges of my mind, and the pressure inside me builds. Then I crest the top and free fall. The ache in my chest consumes me. I feel like I'm dying. The voice shouts incessantly in my head.

You're worthless. You're pathetic. No one likes you. You're a burden. You should leave. No one would miss you.

In some deeply-buried rational part of my brain, I know it's all lies. But the voice is so loud and so constant I can't separate its lies from my own thoughts anymore. They're becoming real. I'm starting to believe them.

Then I'll cross paths with Santino. A look. A touch. A kind word. And I feel like maybe I can fight my way out of this darkness. Maybe if I latch onto Santino tightly enough, he'll save me from the ugliness that's taken up residence inside me. For a few fleeting moments, the ride starts to slow and I think I'll be able to get off. I think I can go back to being Old Hayden.

But then the cycle starts all over again.

I've been pretty good at keeping my mask on in front of the guys. Happy. Cheerful. Easy-going. That's the Hayden they know and love. I don't think any of them suspect.

It's harder to hide from Santino, though. I'm around him way too much. My mask doesn't work as well when I have to wear it for so long. Especially at home, when all I want to do is barricade myself behind my bedroom door. I'm pretty sure he thinks I'm a fucked-up weirdo.

I've tried to avoid him as much as possible. It's best to limit the amount of crazy I subject him to. But every time I see him, I feel like a moth drawn to his flame. With his lopsided smile and silly jokes, it would be so easy to latch onto him and never let go. It would be so easy to take everything he has to offer and still want more. It would be devastating when he eventually goes home and leaves me even more broken than I already am.

I think he was going to kiss me that day at the mansion. He had that look in his eyes and he'd started to lean in. I wanted to kiss him too, to give in to this magnetic force that keeps pulling me toward him.

But that's also why I couldn't let him. I need to keep our contact strictly professional. Only when the camera's rolling and we're both in character. I can't risk blurring that line between work and real life.

We're supposed to shoot our first video together tomorrow and I don't know what I'm going to do. I haven't told Sebastian about my problem. He thinks everything is fine. But I've tried to get myself hard a few times over the last couple days, even letting myself fantasize about Santino, but it hasn't worked. My mind is broken and apparently, so is my dick.

There are ways to get around this problem—not every porn star can get hard and stay hard on demand. But I've never had to use any of those methods before and I'd really rather not start now. I don't know what I'm going to do when Sebastian calls action tomorrow and I'm still a limp noodle.

There's a firm knock on my door—not hard enough to break it down, but definitely not timid either. "Hayden? You got a minute?"

I sit bolt upright in bed, my heart pounding, and I frantically survey my room. Clothes are everywhere, dirty ones mixed in with the clean. A pile of glasses is growing on the floor beside my bed. The air probably smells rank since I haven't been showering every day and I haven't washed my sheets in weeks.

"Uh, one sec!" I grab the first pair of sweatpants I can get my hands on, hoping they're somewhat clean. Then the first t-shirt I can find that doesn't have massive sweat stains around the armpits. I stab my fingers through my hair a few times, then take a deep breath before cracking open the door.

On the other side, Santino takes a step back when he sees me, his brows knotting together. My chin drops to my chest and I wrap an arm around my middle. I keep myself wedged between the door and the jamb so he can't see the disaster inside my room. "What's up?"

Santino gives me a once-over and I can't help but cringe at what he must see.

Pathetic. Loser. Slob.

"I wanted to talk to you about tomorrow, if that's okay?" He points to the living room behind him with his thumb.

My stomach sinks at the gesture. He wants me to go out there? Sit on a couch next to him and talk? I don't know if I can do that right now.

"I just have some questions about how it all works and everything."

Then it hits me. This'll be Santino's first video with another guy. He's probably nervous and scared, while I'm over here throwing myself a giant pity party.

You're such an asshole. Inconsiderate. Selfish.

"Oh, yeah, sure, lemme just…" I shut the door in his face and take a few deep breaths. The voice cackles at the back of my mind.

This is going to be good.

There's a relatively clean hoodie hanging on the back of my door that I slip on, pulling the deep hood over my head. It isn't burying myself under the covers of my bed, but it'll have to do.

When I reopen the door, Santino hasn't moved. He looks worried and guilt snakes through me at how rude I've been. I should've been more attentive and made sure I addressed his concerns. I should've been more present and available to answer his questions.

I make sure to shut my bedroom door firmly before following Santino to the living room. I curl myself into the end of the couch, knees drawn up to my chest, hood still pulled low over my head. "So, um, how are you feeling about tomorrow?"

Santino sits in the middle of the couch instead of on the other end. His one leg is folded up so he can sit facing me, arm resting across the back of the couch. There's maybe a foot of space between us. "Oh you know, a little nervous, but also excited. I've been looking forward to it."

"You have?" I stare at him, but he doesn't look like he's lying.

His eyes are soft as he gazes at me. His lips are curled in that lopsided smile. He's leaning toward me like he wants to crawl over and cuddle up beside me.

"Yeah." He chuckles softly, dropping his gaze to the couch cushion before it drifts back up to me. "I kind of have a crush on you. I hope that's not like, weird or anything, but I've watched your videos and…"

I gulp. My stomach twists into knots. That's not really me in those videos. Not the current me, at least. All of those are Old Hayden and he's been gone for a while now.

"I'm really glad my first video is with you," Santino says.

More guilt crawls through me at the sincerity and trust I hear in his voice. He shouldn't be glad about that. He shouldn't trust me.

"How are *you* feeling about tomorrow?"

My eyes snap to his face at the unexpected question and I'm caught in his gaze. He knows. He knows everything. I can see it in the wariness around his eyes, the way his smile falters with uncertainty. The question hangs in the air between us, asking so much more than the meaning of the words themselves—am I up for this? Am I going to fuck this up for him?

"Um, good?"

His brows draw together in disbelief. "Really?"

I want to lie and laugh it off, pretend everything's

great. What darkness? What voice? I don't know what you're talking about. Everything's *fine*.

But Santino will see right through it. He's too observant. He doesn't buy my wide smile and cheerful voice. I can't fool him. My chin hits my chest as panic seizes my lungs. My chest is tight, my stomach cramps, and the ache sits like an anchor right on my sternum.

The couch cushions dip and before I can react, Santino is there. His hand is on my shoulder. It slides around to grip the back of my neck. He shifts closer, settling his other hand on my shin. His touch is so solid, so sure—even through the layers of my clothes. They feel grounding, like if he's touching me, I can't spiral out of control.

"I don't want to do this if you're not cool with it," he says softly.

"I am cool. Totally cool," I croak, convincing no one.

"I know we just met and like, I don't know anything about you, but..."

But we both know I'm not qualified to do the video with him. "I can call Sebastian. He can find someone to replace me last minute. He's done it before. It shouldn't be too hard."

Disappointment—more than I thought I'd feel—spreads through me. I don't want Santino to do his first video with someone else. I want him to do it with me.

The hand on the back of my neck goes slack for a second before tightening again. "That's not what I meant."

I force myself to suck in a breath as my lungs burn from lack of oxygen. "It's not?"

"No, I..." Santino tugs lightly on my hoodie. "Can I?"

I peek up at him through the hair falling in my eyes, past the edge of the hood obscuring my face. He looks so earnest, so eager. His golden-brown eyes are filled with so much compassion and hope. He looks like he wants to help me. He looks like he's afraid I'll say no. My willpower crumbles.

I push the hood back, feeling like I'm peeling off layers of skin and tissue until I'm exposed, raw and vulnerable. Santino's lips curl in a soft grin as his gaze dances across my face. I don't know what he sees when he looks at me, but I can't imagine it's very attractive.

"So, um, I'm not like, a mental health professional or anything," he starts, growing a little shy and sheepish as he speaks. "But, um, my mom went through a rough patch when I was in high school. My grandmother died and my mom didn't take it well. She fell into this depression that was… pretty bad. And like, I don't want to overstep or anything, so you can tell me to fuck off if you want, but um, you kind of look the way she did back then."

My brain short-circuits. I stare at Santino, unable to speak, unable to move, unable to even breathe. It feels like my heart stops beating for a couple seconds.

"I'm not saying you're depressed or anything!" Santino hurries on. "Like I said, I'm not a mental health professional. I'm just saying, you look like you're struggling and like, it doesn't seem like any of your friends know?"

Everything rushes back at me all at once. Oxygen pours into my lungs, making my head spin. My heart trips over itself trying to make up for lost beats. A million thoughts and emotions ricochet through my mind until it feels like my brain is going to explode.

Santino thinks I'm depressed. He thinks I have depression.

CHAPTER
TWELVE

SANTINO

Oh fuck, oh fuck, oh fuck. Why did I say that? Why did I bring up the D-word? I don't know if he has depression! I don't know how to diagnose someone. Maybe he's just weird! Weird isn't bad. Weird is okay.

Hayden stares at me like I've lost my fucking mind. And honestly, I probably have, because who the fuck goes around telling people they're depressed?

Except there's no way I would've been able to go into tomorrow pretending everything's okay. Not when it's so obvious to me that Hayden's dealing with some shit. Maybe it's not depression. Maybe it's anxiety or panic attacks or I don't know, whatever. But I'd be a real shitty person if I didn't at least check.

With his chin to his chest, Hayden inhales and exhales a few times like he's trying to catch his breath. "I'm sorry," he mumbles so quietly, I can hardly hear him.

What? He's apologizing? What the hell for?

"I'll call Sebastian right away." He moves to stand, but I grab him and hold him in place.

I feel like we're having two different conversations. "Why are you calling Sebastian?"

"To ask him to find you another scene partner," he says matter-of-factly, as if this is something we've already decided together.

But that isn't at all what I was trying to say. "Wait, let's just—" I tug him backward until he's settled on the couch again. "I don't want another scene partner. I want to do the scene with you." I pause, trying to communicate telepathically how much I want to have him fuck me on camera. "But only if *you* want to do the scene with *me*. I'd feel terrible if you felt pressured into something you weren't up for."

He blanches a little and almost buries his face in that little space between his chest and his knees. Under my palms, I can feel him tensing up, his shoulder inching up toward his ears.

"Do you want to do the scene with me?" I hold my breath. I'm pretty sure I know the answer and that would be totally fine. If he's going through something and doesn't feel ready, then he absolutely shouldn't. And if it's just me he doesn't like, well then, he shouldn't be forced to fuck me either. But I can't help a pre-emptive hit of disappointment in my heart.

"I do. I just..." Hayden takes in a shaky breath, sounding like he might be on the verge of tears.

Squashing my disappointment, I shift away from Hayden, pulling my hands away. He doesn't want to perform with me and that's fine. It doesn't matter what his reasons are. I'm not going to force myself on him.

But instead of sighing with relief that I'm finally leaving him alone, he follows me. His hands snap out and grab hold of mine. He kind of looks like he wants to crawl into my lap.

"I do," he says again, with so much conviction it's kind of staggering. "You have to believe me. I just…" He drops his gaze to our clasped hands. "My… body… hasn't been cooperating lately."

Oh. Ooohhh. I… that was *not* what I was expecting him to say.

Hayden draws away from me, curling himself into a ball that should be too small for a man of his size—I mean, height. His face is mostly hidden now that he's tucked it behind his knees, but the parts I can see are filled with so much pain. Like, sooo much. Which makes me wonder whether this is only about erectile dysfunction or whether that's just one part of something bigger. Because like, they have pills for stuff like that, right?

I scoot closer again, placing my hand back on his shoulder. He stiffens at first, but then leans into the touch. That small surrender tugs on my heartstrings with way more force than it should. I don't know if he's hurting because his junk doesn't work properly anymore or if it's because of something else, but the one thing I do know is that Hayden is hurting. And my heart hurts for him.

I mold myself around him, wrapping one arm over his back and the other over his shin. I lean in and rest my head on his shoulder. Hayden sniffles a few times before he shifts his weight, relaxing into my embrace.

I hold him as pain and sadness pour off him in waves. I try to absorb as much of it as I can, as if I can siphon it from his body and into mine. I hold him as his sniffles morph into quiet hiccups. I hold him until his trembling slows and his breathing evens out.

I don't move away when he lifts his head. His eyes are red and puffy. His cheeks are tearstained and splotchy. His bottom lip is bruised and swollen. He ever so slowly lifts his gaze to mine and I fall into the clear green of his eyes. They're so expressive. So open and honest. And I feel incredibly humbled that Hayden would let me see him like this.

I'm not sure who moves first, or maybe we both move at the same time. But the next thing I know, our foreheads are touching, then our noses. The puff of his breath blows across my cheek, then our lips are touching too.

That's all it is. Just the press of lips against lips. But it's also so much more than that. It feels like two souls meeting for the first time. It feels like two hearts being drawn together from opposite sides of the country.

Hayden breaks the kiss, gasping lightly. I open my eyes to find him looking startled. His brows furrow and his lips part, disbelief written all across his face.

"What is it? What's wrong?"

He shakes his head. "I think I felt something."

My eyebrows shoot up and my lizard brain comes hobbling to the fore. I give his lap a pointed look. "Down there?"

He winces and shakes his head again. "Not really, but something more than I have in a while."

Alright, you can't say something like that to a guy and not expect his ego to take over. I wiggle my eyebrows exaggeratedly and preen a bit. "Maybe I have a magic kiss." I'm only mostly joking.

Hayden's lips twitch and that feeling of doom and

gloom around him dissipates a little. "Can we test the theory?" he asks shyly.

By kissing again? Hell yeah, we can test that theory.

I'm the one who moves this time, easing in gradually to give Hayden plenty of opportunity to push me away. But he doesn't. And when our lips touch, electricity crackles in the air and fire races through my body.

Hayden almost immediately takes control, tilting his head to fit his mouth against mine more snugly. I gasp as he licks across the seam of my lips and a shudder runs through me when he slips inside. Our tongues touch and my dick roars to life. He nibbles lightly on my bottom lip and my balls start to ache.

Christ Almighty, I've never gotten this close to coming, this fast, from something as simple as a kiss.

But this isn't just any kiss, is it? This is a kiss from Hayden Summers. The guy's a professional. He knows what he's doing. And even if his dick won't get hard, the rest of him definitely still works.

Hayden unfolds himself from his fetal position and I lie back on the couch. His thigh comes in between mine and I arch up into him, grinding my hard-on against his quad. He lies down on me, letting me take his delicious weight, and my hands roam up his back and down to his ass. He groans when I squeeze the two globes of his ass and the vibration travels from my lips to my nipples to my groin, where my dick pulses, hot and heavy.

His hand slips under the hem of my t-shirt and when he flattens his palm against the skin of my waist, I gasp. It's searing. A scorching brand that melts my insides. He slides his hand up my stomach, my chest, until he finds a nipple and pinches it between his fingers. Pleasure zings from the top of my head to the soles of my feet, zapping every cell in between.

Hayden kisses along my jaw and worries my earlobe with his teeth. I cradle the back of his head, threading my fingers through his hair, holding him to me like I never want to let him go.

Because a part of me doesn't. It's not realistic, I know. It's completely delusional. Hayden's not mine to keep. He's Hayden fucking Summers and I'm just some rando who's crashing in his spare room for a few weeks. I don't know what I'm doing after I finish these projects with The Camboy Network, but unless some sort of miracle happens, chances are I'm going back to California.

But I like Hayden. I really like him. Not just his Greek-god level of gorgeousness. But also the very human and imperfect beauty inside. I want to help him. I want to protect him. I want to see him happy and healthy and whole.

I drag his mouth back to mine and slip my tongue between his lips, drinking him in. My leg hooks around the back of his and he angles his thigh so it's one solid block of muscle right between my legs. I thrust my hips forward. I shift them side-to-side. No matter what direction I move, my dick and balls rub hard against Hayden, over and over until I tip over the edge.

Cum fills my underwear as I ride the waves of my orgasm. Aftershocks ripple through me as Hayden maintains the pressure on my cock with his thigh. The pleasure settles into a blissful hum as I float down from the high.

Hayden's still above me, his face pressed against my neck. I can feel his heavy breaths against my damp skin. It dawns on me suddenly that he just made me come, but what about him?

"Did you…?" I don't even know how to ask the question, but he doesn't need me to voice it out loud.

He shakes his head and my heart sinks. Guilt ruins what's left of my buzz, making me feel kind of icky and gross.

"Shit, I'm sorry."

He rolls to the side, wedging his big body between mine and the couch cushions. His face is still hidden in the crook of my neck. His arm is still slung over my waist. "That was… more than I've felt in a long time. Thank you."

If anything, his show of gratitude only makes me feel worse. I didn't actually do anything but hump his leg and come in my underwear. And apparently, he didn't even get hard.

"It's okay if you want to back out of the video tomorrow," I say. In fact, maybe I should tell Sebastian to call the whole thing off. What kind of camboy can't even get his scene partner aroused? A shitty one, that's what.

"No, I…"

I can almost hear Hayden thinking, so I wait for him to gather his words.

"I think I can do it. I want to do it."

I pull my head back so I can see his face. "You're sure?"

Hayden blinks at me with a new resolve in his eyes. "Yeah, I'm sure."

CHAPTER
THIRTEEN

HAYDEN

I've never done anything like this before and I'm not just talking about the erectile dysfunction drugs. I've never been so selfish before, just taking what I want, who cares how it impacts anyone else.

I should back out of the video altogether so Santino can have a partner who's not broken. That would give the video the best chance of succeeding. But I don't want to back out. I don't want to see Santino with some other guy. I want to be the one he's with in front of that camera.

I want to be the one he's kissing, the one he's touching. I want to wrap myself around him and lose myself in him. He was joking about magical kisses, but I think there's some truth to that. Because when I'm with him, the darkness doesn't feel as dark and the heaviness doesn't feel as heavy. And my body comes alive in a way I haven't experienced in a long time.

His kisses were so soft and sweet. He made the most delicious sounds. It was so easy for me to lose myself in him and for those few fleeting moments, I was Old Hayden again. Happy, confident, carefree.

It didn't even matter that I couldn't get fully hard. I still felt something—a lot of something. Heat in my stomach, tingling along my skin, shudders of pleasure down my spine.

He doesn't owe me anything. It's not his responsibility to make me better. If I were a good person, I would push him as far away from me as possible. But I'm not a good person. I want Santino. And now I'm going to do something I know is wrong just to keep him.

I message Sebastian.

> HAYDEN
>
> Hey, do we have those 💊 ?

Sebastian responds immediately.

> SEBASTIAN
>
> You mean sildenafil?
>
> Why? You need them?

My hands shake as I type.

> HAYDEN
>
> Yeah, those. Do we have them?

> SEBASTIAN
>
> We do. Why do you need them?

> No reason. Just in case.

> Just in case of what?

I don't know how to do this. I don't know how to be

nonchalant and cool and just take what I want without caring what other people think. I'm not Noel.

My phone starts vibrating and I'm so startled by it, it slips out of my hands and lands on the floor. I rush to pick it up, only to find Sebastian's name across the screen. I don't want to talk to him. He'll ask questions I don't know how to answer.

My throat starts tightening and dread settles into an ache in my chest. How did I get here? Afraid to answer the phone because one of my best friends is calling. Being super sus while asking for drugs like I'm some sort of addict. This isn't who I am. I'm better than this.

Are you sure about that?

I shove my phone under my pillow and run out of the room, slamming the door shut behind me.

The window in the living room is open and when I bend down to peer through it, I find Santino sitting on the fire escape, a mug of coffee cradled in his hands. Just seeing him sends a wave of calm through me and my feet automatically carry me to the window.

I climb out and when Santino sees me, he spreads his knees so I can sit between them on the step below him. He leans forward, resting his chin on my shoulder so his cheek is next to mine.

"Want a sip?" he asks, holding out his cup.

I take the steaming mug and pour half of it down my throat. The scalding hot coffee burns and sets fire to my stomach. I wince at the pain, but it's a welcome relief compared to the chaos raging in my head.

Santino takes the mug back and silently plants a kiss on my temple. My eyes drift shut as I let myself be enveloped by his cinnamon scent mixed with the rich aroma of coffee. The tightness in my throat loosens just a bit.

"It's nice out here," Santino says. "I don't have a balcony in San Francisco."

I glance around the rusty old fire escape, then down to the trees lining the street below. The sun is just peeking over the buildings across the street. "I don't come out very often," I reply.

"Why not?"

I shrug. "It just never occurs to me."

"You should. It's nice."

I take Santino's arm and wrap it around my chest, then let out a breath as I lean back against him. He's warm and solid. And if I ignore all the shit going on in my head, I can almost convince myself I'm happy.

———

I wish we could've stayed out on the fire escape all day. But eventually, we climbed back inside and got ready to leave for the shoot. By the time we get to the fancy apartment Noel had found for us to use, I've almost forgotten about the whole... pill thing. *Almost.*

Christian lets us into the apartment after we ring the doorbell. "Sebastian's in one of the bedrooms," he says, pointing to the left.

Before I can follow Santino down the hall, Christian grabs my elbow and slips something into my hand: a pill packet.

"Just one, about fifteen minutes before we start," he murmurs quietly to me. "And Sebastian wants to talk to you."

My stomach twists at both his instructions and his warning. It must show on my face because Christian's expression softens with sympathy.

"Don't sweat it. It happens to me every once in a while. It used to happen to everyone all the time back in the day," he says, referring to decades ago when he first started in the porn industry. "And Sebastian's just worried about you. We all are."

He lets go of my arm and ambles off toward the corner where boxes of equipment and supplies are set up. I watch him for a moment, my stomach churning. It's one thing for Sebastian to be worried. But what does Christian mean by "we all"?

Heaviness drags at my feet as I search for Santino and Sebastian. I find them in the primary bedroom, Sebastian running Santino through his preliminary day-of checklist.

Sebastian glances up from his clipboard as I enter and there's an edge to his expression that makes me feel like a schoolboy called into the principal's office.

"Alright, cool," he says to Santino. He picks up a pair of folded boxer briefs and nods toward the en suite. "You can change into these. There are bathrobes hanging up in there."

Santino takes the underwear and casts me a wary look. He must pick up on the tension between me and Sebastian. He's too observant not to. I flash him a quick smile I hope is reassuring rather than alarming. His brows furrow a bit, but after a moment's hesitation, he goes into the bathroom.

"Hayden," Sebastian says the second the bathroom door snicks shut.

"Christian already gave them to me," I interrupt,

holding up the packet of diamond-shaped pills. My heart's in my throat and the darkness closes in around me.

He steps closer and lowers his volume. "I don't care about the pills. I want to know what's going on."

"I don't know what you're talking about." My voice is artificially high and borderline hysterical.

"I think you do."

I shake my head, the ache in my chest intensifying, and I resist the urge to rub on my sternum. "I'm fine."

Sebastian scowls at me. "You're obviously not fine. I should cancel the shoot today."

"No!"

Sebastian's eyebrows fly up at my outburst.

There's a vise around my chest and my heart is beating so hard, it almost feels like I'm having a heart attack. "No, don't cancel. Please. Santino's been looking forward to this."

He narrows his eyes, but before he can argue with me, the bathroom door opens again. Santino stands in the doorway, eyes flicking back and forth between me and Sebastian. I take advantage of the interruption and dart around Sebastian. Santino steps to the side so I can slip into the bathroom and shut the door behind me.

I hear voices on the other side of the door, but I can't make out what they're saying over the sound of my own breathing. Why did I think I could do this? That I could ask him for something I don't normally need and he wouldn't be curious why. That I could avoid answering his questions without him getting suspicious.

Because you're an idiot.

I gasp at the voice coming through loud and clear in my ears, so real it raises the hair on the back of my neck.

"Hayden?" A soft knock on the door behind me pulls me back from the brink. The doorknob turns halfway and only then do I realize I didn't lock the thing. "I'm coming in."

I step out of the way just enough for Santino to squeeze through. I want to grab him, haul him to me, and bury my face in the crook of his neck until the darkness recedes. But I don't trust myself not to completely fall apart if I do that. So instead, I wrap my arms around my middle and retreat to the far end of the bathroom.

Santino approaches me slowly. He's wearing a fluffy white bathrobe that falls to his knees. His legs are bare underneath, feet padding on the tiled floor. "Hayden, we don't have to do this."

But we do have to do this. I've already fucked things up so much and it'll all be for nothing if we don't shoot the video today.

"I'm fine," I somehow manage to squeak out.

Santino tilts his head with an unimpressed expression. "You don't look fine."

I turn away from him and catch my reflection in the mirror. He's right. I don't look fine at all. I look like a fucking lunatic with my hair all wild and my eyes totally manic. I squeeze them shut and force myself to take a few steadying breaths.

Soft footsteps on the tile bring Santino closer to me. "If you're doing this for me, you don't have to. We can reschedule. We don't even have to perform together at all. I can do a solo video if that's better. You shouldn't put yourself through… this."

I open my eyes in time to see him gesturing vaguely at

me. *This*. He means freaking the fuck out. Spiraling out of control.

"I just…" I shake my head. I *want* to do this. I really do. I used to love making videos and I don't want the darkness to steal away something I love. It's stolen so much from me already, I can't let it take this too. "I just need a minute."

I take two steps toward the counter and turn on the faucet. The shock of cold water hitting my face clears some of the haze from my brain. When Santino puts his hand on my back and starts rubbing it, a little more of the fog dissipates.

I can do this. I need to do this. I can't let the darkness win.

CHAPTER
FOURTEEN

SANTINO

I've already decided to call the whole thing off when Hayden straightens from splashing his face with ice-cold water. There's still something a little manic around his eyes, but there's also a steely determination that wasn't there a moment ago.

He turns toward me, water dripping from his chin and the tip of his nose. "You probably think I'm crazy."

I open my mouth to deny it, but stop when he gives me a pleading look.

"I think, maybe I am a little crazy," Hayden continues. "I don't know if I'm depressed or whatever…"

I cringe inwardly at how thoughtless I was throwing that out there. I should've been more careful. I should've let the fucking professionals hand out diagnoses.

"But I feel a little less crazy when I'm with you."

My heart expands in my chest, filling with something achingly sweet.

"I know we just met and I don't really know you, but

you're not like anyone else I've ever met. You're the one bright spot in my life right now."

Oh, this poor man. I'm definitely not the only bright spot—he has so many friends who care so much about him. Including Sebastian, who nearly chewed me out a minute ago, demanding to know what was wrong with Hayden.

"I want to do this. For you, but also for me. I need to do this for me," he says, his gaze dropping to the floor. The desperation in his voice is so clear it nearly chokes me up.

I don't know the specifics of what he's going through, but one thing is obvious. He needs to do this video to prove to himself that he can. In which case, I'm going to help him make the hottest fucking video these camboys have ever seen.

I nod. "Okay, then let's do this."

His gaze snaps up to me in surprise, like he was expecting me to put up more of a fight. But come on, sweet, adorable, gorgeous Greek deity Hayden Summers is practically begging to fuck me—I'd be a fool to say no.

I give Hayden a minute to get changed, then we head out to the kitchen where we're filming the scene. A couple big light boxes are perched on top of tripods and cameras are set up around the room. Sebastian is standing next to Christian, his arms crossed over his chest.

"We're canceling, right? Or at least rescheduling?"

I cast a quick glance at Hayden, who looks uncertain and yet determined at the same time. "No, I think we're going ahead."

Sebastian zeros in on Hayden. "Hayden?"

He straightens to his full height, shoulders back, head

high. There's a little tremor in his voice when he speaks, but his resolve is unmistakable. "We're going ahead."

Sebastian hesitates, looking back and forth between us like he's waiting for us to crack. But then Christian bumps him with his elbow and Sebastian sighs. "Okay, fine, but at the first sign that something's wrong…" His threat hangs in the air, but we all understand what he means.

Sebastian quickly runs through the plan for the scene and reviews the hard and soft limits we'd previously discussed. Then he comes around the large island separating the kitchen space from the dining area. "Santino, you're standing here. Hayden over there."

Christian takes our bathrobes, then goes around to double-check the camera settings.

"Everyone ready?" Sebastian asks one last time. "Cameras are rolling. And… action."

I lean back against the kitchen counter, wearing nothing but boxer briefs, cradling a mug of cold prop coffee in my hands. It suddenly hits me that I'm shooting my first porn video. With the whole thing with Hayden, I'd kind of forgotten what exactly we'd come here to do. Butterflies flutter to life in my stomach and my heart picks up speed.

The sound of footsteps, bare feet padding on the tiled floor, announces Hayden a second before he appears. He's got one towel wrapped low around his hips, showing off the two deep V lines on his stomach, and another towel slung around his neck.

I watch, breathless, as he approaches. He really is so fucking hot. Even knowing he's not in the best place mentally, I can't help ogling his chiseled muscles and mop of blond hair. The lights are set up to make his green eyes sparkle and he seriously looks like he's just stepped off Mount Olympus.

"Morning," he rumbles, tossing me a lazy, languid smile. It's a miracle I'm not a puddle on the floor.

"Morning," I croak back.

He comes right up to me and for a split second, I think he's going to grab me and kiss me. But then I remember the script.

"Excuse me," he murmurs, just loud enough for the mic on Sebastian's camera to pick up. He starts reaching behind me for the coffee pot before I have a chance to move out of his way.

"Sure," I say, a beat too slow. And when I shift sideways, our naked torsos brush against each other. I shudder as goosebumps explode across my skin. I'm not acting. I wouldn't even know how to fake goosebumps. My reaction to Hayden is one thousand percent genuine.

My dick fills, tenting the front of my underwear. I reach down to adjust it, not bothering to hide the motion.

Hayden notices—like he's supposed to—and gives me the filthiest look I've ever seen over the rim of his mug. If I weren't already naked, my clothes would have melted from the heat.

I have to clear my throat before I can speak. "Sorry, morning wood."

"Mmhmm." He lowers his mug to reveal a smirk that's worthy of Noel. "Must be hard."

I choke on the sip of coffee I was taking, spraying the liquid clear across the kitchen, getting some on Hayden too.

"Oh shit, dude, I'm so sorry!" I quickly set the mug on the counter and grab the roll of paper towels that just happen to be sitting right there. I bend down to wipe up the mess and pretend to bump heads with Hayden who bent down at the same time. He exaggerates his reaction and goes sprawling across the floor. "Oh shit!"

I rush over to help him up, but he's lying there, laughing. The sight has me sitting back on my heels, taking him in. He's beautiful when he laughs. I mean, he's always beautiful, but there's something extra when he lets himself go and just enjoys the moment. I can't tell whether this is an act or if it's real, but I wish I could see him like this every day.

"You okay, bro?" I ask, laughing along with him.

"Yeah, I'm good." He slowly pushes himself up so he's sitting with one foot flat on the floor, arm draped over the raised knee. The knot in the towel he's wearing has loosened, but the terrycloth still covers the important bits.

"Sorry, I'm not usually that clumsy."

Hayden's laugh trails off as he tilts his head and peers at me through his lashes. "It's cool," he murmurs.

The sound of his voice winds its way through me, ensnaring me. I sway toward him, feeling trapped under his spell.

He leans toward me too, closing the distance between us. My lips part as the air around us heats up and Hayden's chest rises and falls a little faster with each breath.

The moment our lips touch, I'm immediately transported back to yesterday. On the couch in the living room. Hayden's telling me why he's been hesitant about performing. My nervousness and excitement melt away until it's only me and him and the secrets he's been brave enough to share with me. I want to make sure he feels good and confident and like, he's totally got this.

I swipe my tongue along the seam of his mouth. He opens and lets out a low rumble when I lick inside. Holding his head in place, I shift onto my knees, then push him down on his back.

Hayden blinks up at me, eyes a little unfocused. I kiss the tip of his nose, the space between his brows, each eyelid, the middle of his forehead. He sighs, his hands going to my waist and squeezing. I kiss his chin, under his chin, his Adam's apple, the spot where his pulse is strongest. Then down farther to the dip at the base of his neck and across each collarbone.

His towel is still covering his crotch and I don't feel anything hard poking me in the stomach as I move down his body, but I'm not giving up.

Hayden lifts his head to watch as I lave each nipple, swirling my tongue around and around until they're hard little pebbles. His breathing quickens, his chest rising and falling under my mouth.

I latch onto the dip in his sternum. He sucks in a sharp breath and drops his head back with a groan. Under the towel, something stirs.

Using my tongue, I trace the lines of his abs, licking and kissing each block of muscle on his stomach. I tease at his belly button and he squirms. He's panting now, lips parted and eyes half-lidded as he gazes down his body at me.

I gaze back while bathing the points of his hipbones and lick at the sharp lines that point straight to his cock. There's definitely a bulge under the towel now. It stirs when I accidentally bump my chin against it.

Holding the corner of the towel, I wait for Hayden to give me a nod. Then I lift it away.

His dick is still a monster when soft and there's something kind of adorable about holding it in my hand as it slowly hardens. I lick along its length and swirl my tongue around the spongy head, marveling at how it changes as it grows. The veins fill out into juicy blue lines. The head expands until the glans is swollen and shiny with my spit. The shaft thickens into a rod of steel. A small bead of pre-cum forms at his slit and I'm quick to lick it off. Musky and dark, the taste of it makes my head spin.

Strong hands grab my arms and yank me upward. Hayden catches the back of my head and holds me still as he catches my mouth with his. I moan when he shoves his tongue inside. He hooks one leg around the back of mine and suddenly, I'm on my back with Hayden covering me with his body.

He regards me for a moment, looking so vulnerable. There's moisture in his beautiful green eyes. I cup his cheeks and tug him down to touch our foreheads together. Our noses brush against one another. He murmurs a nearly silent "thank you" against my lips.

He doesn't have to thank me for anything. I wasn't being entirely altruistic. I just got to lick half of Hayden Summers' god-like body and coaxed his dick to full-mast. I feel like I got a pretty good deal.

Hayden kisses me again and I moan into his delicious mouth. My whole body is warm and tingly. When he runs his hand from my chest down to my hip, he leaves a trail of fire behind. I'm not done kissing him yet when he pulls out of my embrace and sits back on his heels. He hooks his fingers into the waistband of my boxer briefs and in one swift motion, they're gone.

My cock stands straight up from between my legs, achingly hard and leaking. With a reverent look, Hayden carefully wraps his fingers around it. My dick disappears between his palm and his fingers, caught in a vise that can't possibly feel so good, but it does. He gives me a short, gentle stroke and pleasure explodes inside me.

"Oh my god!" My eyes are glued to the space where the tip of my cock pokes out of his closed fist. It doesn't feel real. It feels too good. It feels like a dream I'll wake up from at any moment.

Hayden shifts and brings his monster cock in line with mine.

"Oh fuck," I cry right before he takes us both in his hands. His dick is so hard and yet so silky soft. It's searing hot against mine. My hips take on a life of their own, fucking up into Hayden's fist, fueled by the exquisite friction of rubbing against his dick.

Hayden peers up at me, hand still a tight vise around us, and my breath catches. His chest is heaving, coated in a thin layer of sweat. His dick is pumping out pre-cum like a fucking faucet, the musky, dark scent of it filling the air.

I did this to him. Me. I made Hayden feel this good, this turned-on. I helped him when he felt like he couldn't be helped. An odd mix of power, humility, and gratitude settles inside me—a feeling I've never felt before in my life. Like I'm capable, important, significant. All because of Hayden.

He strokes us until I'm hovering right on the edge. "Hayden! Hayden, please!"

Popping to his feet, he holds out a hand to help me up.

I sway, lightheaded from the sudden change in altitude, and Hayden holds me to him. Chest to naked chest. Stomach to naked stomach. He gazes into my eyes like I'm the most amazing thing he's ever seen.

A movement at the very edge of my vision catches my attention. I clock Sebastian circling around us with a big black camera in his hand. A thrill rushes through me, followed closely by a stomach-twisting sourness. I'd forgotten we weren't alone. I'd forgotten that every single thing we're doing is being recorded and will be broadcast out to thousands of people—of strangers. They'll see what we're doing—everything I want them to see and everything I don't.

The conflicting feelings pull at me. Shame at exposing myself like this. Hesitancy over whether I want the world to see some of these ultra-intimate moments between me and Hayden. And exhilaration at doing something so taboo, at not having full control over what happens... I feel like I'm about to burst out of my skin.

But then Hayden's kissing me again and all the thoughts about cameras and audiences evaporate. He slides his hands down my back to my ass. With one palm on each ass cheek, he pulls them apart. I can hear Sebastian behind me getting a close-up of my hole.

I gasp into Hayden's mouth when his fingers dip into my crease, brushing over the sensitive, quivering ring of muscle. He pulls again, tugging on my hole from two sides like he's trying to open me up to the camera's view. A gush of pre-cum spills from my cock.

Hayden's fingers disappear for a second and when they come back, they're cool and wet with lube. He presses against the opening. Slowly. Oh so slowly. And the second I bear down, he slips right in.

Oh god, fucking hell. Shocks of pleasure burst from that one point of contact, turning my body into one giant quivering mass. I drop my forehead to Hayden's shoulder as thick, long fingers play with my hole.

Planting kisses on my neck and shoulder, Hayden fucks me with one finger, then two. "Is this okay?" he asks and the only response I can manage is a sobbing moan.

We shot past okay ages ago. This is way more than okay. This is coming-apart territory. This is flying-over-the-edge region. I'm about to come and he hasn't even gotten his dick in me yet.

He adds fingers from his other hand and I swear to god, I'm going to die. I think there are three? Four in me now? "Relax," he murmurs, lips moving against the shell of my ear. Then he pulls his fingers apart.

Holy fucking shit on a stick. He's opening me. I can feel cool air in places that aren't supposed to be exposed to cool air. I try not to tense up, not to clench around nothing. I latch onto Hayden's shoulder with my teeth, breathing heavily through my mouth.

"A little more," Sebastian instructs from behind me and Hayden pulls me open another fraction.

Jesus Christ. Sebastian's right there. The camera's right there. Can it see inside me? Will people be able to see parts of me I've never seen before myself?

"Fuck," I cry, but it comes out as a garbled sob. I can't take it anymore. I can't. My dick is so painfully hard every bit of friction against Hayden's stomach feels like I'm rubbing on sandpaper. "Please, Hayden. Please."

"I've got you, babe. I've got you."

Everything is a whir as Hayden extracts his fingers from my ass and turns us around so I'm facing the kitchen island and he's behind me. With one hand on my back and the other on my hip, he bends me forward and pulls my hips back.

The stone countertop is cold against my overheated skin. I extend my arms out to either side, laying my chest and cheek all the way down. Between my legs, my dick hangs in mid-air with nothing to grind up against, nothing to ease the awful ache.

Hayden pulls my ass cheeks apart again, but this time, instead of his fingers, I feel the blunt tip of his cock at my entrance. He goes slow. Too slow. Inching into me one fraction of an inch at a time.

I can feel my hole stretch and stretch and stretch. And when I don't think it can stretch anymore, the head of his dick pops in. A cry echoes against the counter. It's me, impaled on just the tip of Hayden's cock and already feeling so incredibly full. How is he going to fit the rest of it inside me? How could there possibly be enough room?

Hayden soothes me, rubbing circles on my hip, across my back. He rocks back and forth, pushing himself a little deeper each time. My body gives way to his breach. It surrenders to his invasion. I'm helpless as he claims my hole for himself.

I'm delirious by the time his hips are flush against my ass. I can't move. I can't think. I can barely breathe. Every cell in my body is tuned into Hayden's cock inside me. How thick it is, how long it is, how my insides feel like they're being rearranged to make room for him. He's so big. And I'm so very, very full.

Hayden slides his hands up my back, then under my

arms to my front. Carefully, he lifts me from the counter, pulling me up so my back is against his chest. I let out a series of high-pitched cries as he gently manhandles me. The movement changes the angle of his cock inside me. It rubs up against my prostate. I think I can feel it in my throat.

I'm standing on my tippy-toes. My head falls back against his shoulder. I'm holding onto his wrists with a death grip. And in front of me is Sebastian with his camera.

There's nothing between me and the camera's lens. Nothing to hide me from view. Nothing to obscure what the camera can see. Sebastian pans up from my feet and all I can do is hang suspended on Hayden's cock, waiting for him to finish.

He pauses at my crotch, at my dick that's engorged and purple, with a steady stream of pre-cum leaking from the tip. Then up my quivering stomach, taking in my hardened nipples. And finally, my face.

I look directly into the camera. I can't remember if I'm supposed to do that or not. I don't care. I can't tear my eyes away. The glass of the lens is close enough that it reflects my image back at me.

I look… Christ, I look wild, debauched, totally drunk on sex. My eyes are half-lidded, my jaw is slack. My hair sticks up in all directions. My chest rises and falls with each open-mouthed pant.

This is what they'll see. Hundreds. Thousands. Complete and utter strangers. They'll see me just like this, getting fucked by Hayden.

CHAPTER
FIFTEEN

HAYDEN

Santino is hot and tight and as I hold him against me, I feel like I'm coming apart at the seams.

God, the sounds he makes. Better than the sounds he makes when he eats and those are already so fucking good. I'm not sure he even knows he's making them. His head lolls back and forth and his eyes are wild with lust. He sounds primal and animalistic. They're pure instinct and reaction. No thought.

But he's not really this sex-crazed creature. There's so much kindness and consideration underneath it all. I nearly cried at how tender he was earlier, helping me get hard. It felt like he was worshiping me, carefully blessing every inch of my skin. I've never felt so cared for while performing for the camera. Like it wasn't just about what looks good for the audience, but that it matters how I feel.

I did take the pill before we started. But I doubt it would've helped if it wasn't for Santino taking the time to bring me all the way there.

I don't know why he did it. I don't know why he cares. I'm no one special. I'm not a super competent leader like Sebastian. I'm not a bad boy like Noel. I'm not super sensual like Rhys. I'm just a regular dude who happens to be above average in looks with a big cock.

But from the very first day we met, Santino's always seen me as more than that. He's always seen what no one else has.

Santino is strangely taut and yet lax as I hold him in my arms. I can feel every twitch of muscle in his body—inside his body. He keeps clenching down on me, as if he's testing the size and shape of my cock. He lets out a sobbing gasp every time, like he can't believe I'm all the way in there.

But I am. I'm seated to the hilt. Every single inch, hard as a rock, buried in the heat of his body. I'd go deeper if I could. Hell, I'd crawl right inside him and take up residence. I'd live here if I could.

Sebastian gives me the signal to continue, but I kind of don't want to. I want to stay right here and savor Santino on my cock, in my arms. I don't want to pull out, even just to thrust back in. I don't want this moment to end.

I can't actually get much leverage while we're connected like this, with me holding most of Santino's weight. So I rock my hips, pushing in more than pulling out. Santino whimpers and turns his face toward me. I press my cheek against his. His stubble is scratchy and it sends tingles across my skin. He smells all warm and spicy, the scent of cinnamon wrapping around me until I feel like I'm surrounded by him.

He reaches one arm back to bury his fingers into my hair. We kiss. Lazy. Messy. Sweet. It makes my head spin.

It sinks deep into my bones, into my marrow. It unravels me.

My eyes sting a little bit and tears start welling up. It's all just so much. Dealing with the darkness on my own for so long. Having Santino walk into my life and peel back all my protective layers. Finding out it's not so terrible when I let someone in.

Fuck. I break the kiss and bury my face into the crook of his neck. I can't think about any of that right now. I need to pull myself together. We're on camera. It's not sexy when a camboy suddenly bursts into tears in the middle of a scene.

"Hayden." Santino's voice is husky with arousal, but there's also a hint of awareness, like he knows what's going on in my head. He tilts his ass up and I sink in just a little bit deeper, then he clenches around my cock.

I gasp at the tightness and my breath comes out in a stuttered exhale. I can do this. I can finish this scene.

Santino reaches out to brace himself with one hand on the edge of the counter. I reluctantly loosen my hold on him so he can lean forward, giving me more leverage to thrust into his body. I take hold of his hips, pull myself out until only the head of my cock is inside, then I slam myself home.

"Yes!" Santino cries out. He throws his head back and reaches down to jerk himself with his free hand.

I set a grueling pace, fucking him hard and fast. Sweat gathers in the deep valley that runs down the middle of his back, glistening under the set lights. The scent of his arousal—of us combined—fills my nose. The sound of my hips slapping against his ass rings through the air.

"Yes! Right there! Right there! Just like that! I'm going

to come! Fuck, I'm coming!" Santino shouts right before his whole body seizes up.

I keep pounding into him, fucking him through his orgasm. I wish I could see his face right now. I wish I could see what he looks like when he hits that high. I'll bet he's beautiful, gorgeous, angelic.

Next time. Next time we'll do this face-to-face. So I can gaze into his warm brown eyes, so I can see what ecstasy looks like on him.

The thought of doing this again sends me right over the edge. I'm still inside him when my orgasm first crests and I have to force myself to pull out so I can come on his ass and back for the camera.

Next time I'll come inside him. I'll fill him up with my cum. I'll shoot so deep a part of me stays with him forever.

As my balls empty, I stumble backward, my knees not quite able to keep me upright. I collapse against the opposite counter, chest heaving while I catch my breath. Fuck, I don't remember the last time I came so hard.

A few feet away, Santino starts shivering. He wraps his arms around himself and his shoulders hunch forward. "Jesus Christ, it's cold in here."

Sebastian glances at me. "Hayden?"

But I'm already moving, pushing away from the counter and closing the distance between us. "Come here." I curl myself around him and he melts into me.

"Was it this cold the entire time?" Santino asks.

"It's not actually cold," I explain, rubbing my hands up and down his back. "Your body chemistry is all out of whack after the scene. It's basically an adrenaline crash."

"Oh, shit." Santino tilts his head back to look at me. "Are you crashing too?"

I shake my head. "Doesn't happen with everyone. I'm usually okay."

He nestles into me again. "Good," he says.

Suddenly, I feel like a puppy who's been told he's a good boy. I hold him closer. "Skin-to-skin contact helps the body adjust more quickly," I explain, nuzzling his hair.

"Mmm, I dunno." Santino slips his arms out from where they were pinned between us and slides them around my waist, plastering himself to me. "I think I'm gonna need a couple more hours of this before I feel adjusted."

My eyes close, a spark of something I haven't felt in a long time igniting inside me. Something that feels like peace, like contentment.

Eventually, we get cleaned up and put our clothes on. But we're never more than an arm's length away from each other. A hand on the waist, resting a chin on a shoulder, pressing into each other's sides—every touch feels essential to my very existence.

Sebastian catches us before we leave and my stomach sinks. But instead of trying to interrogate me again, he simply claps me on the shoulder. "You did a good job today."

I nod, not trusting my voice as big, unwieldy emotions well up inside me.

Santino and I cuddle on the car ride back to my apartment and we awkwardly squeeze in side-by-side as we walk up the stairs. When we get home, we head straight to the couch as if this is something we've been doing with each other every single day for the past decade. We lie down and curl up together, arms and legs tangled, faces so close our noses brush.

That's how we fall asleep.

———

It's dark when I wake up again. For a moment, I don't remember what day it is or where I am. Then it all comes back to me. The shoot. Santino. The couch.

Santino's sitting on the floor next to me, back against the couch. His face is illuminated by his phone screen as he scrolls through social media. I don't recognize the people in the photos, but a few of them look kind of like Santino. There's an older couple that could be his parents. Then two women in their late thirties with partners and children. Santino's in a few of the photos too.

Is that his family? Does he miss them? Is he homesick?

Guilt lodges itself in the middle of my chest. It dawns on me suddenly that I know next to nothing about Santino's life before he showed up in my apartment. I don't know if he's close to his family or if he's got friends waiting for him back home. Maybe he even has a boyfriend he hasn't mentioned.

All I've cared about is me, me, me. What can Santino do for me? How can he help me? I've never once stopped to consider he might have stuff he's dealing with. He might be going through his own shit too.

You're such a selfish prick.

I flinch at the voice and the movement catches Santino's attention. He looks over his shoulder and a soft smile graces his lips when he sees I'm awake. "You good?"

As good as I can be with the darkness always lingering at the edges of my mind. "Yeah." I nod toward his phone. "Is that your family?"

He glances at his phone again before dropping it into his lap. "Yeah, it is."

"Do you miss them?"

He chuckles dryly. "More like I feel guilty."

Defensiveness rises up in me at the thought of Santino feeling guilty about anything. "Why?"

He gives me a sheepish look. "They don't know I'm here. I never told them."

I turn onto my side to get more comfortable. Santino takes my hand and lifts it to his cheek. His stubble is scratchy against the back of my hand as he nuzzles it. The intimate touch pushes the voice back momentarily. "Why didn't you tell them?"

Santino scoffs lightly. "They would've freaked out and tried to stop me from coming."

"Why would they do that?"

He hesitates and when he speaks again, there's a wistfulness to his voice. "I'm the baby in the family. Like, literally the youngest cousin in my generation. My two older sisters are ten and twelve years older than me. My whole family is really overprotective, but my mom is the worst. She almost disowned me for moving to San Francisco and that's only a few hours away. She would actually disown me if I told her I was coming to New York. That or she'd fly out here and drag me back herself."

I blink in the darkness. I have no idea what that would feel like. My family couldn't care less where I live. I haven't spoken to them in years and I don't think anyone misses anyone else. "But you're only here for a few weeks. It's not like you're moving to New York." I nearly choke on the words as I say them. Santino's only here temporarily. Then he'll be leaving.

"Yeah," he says with a sigh. Although I think there's a silent "but" in there somewhere. His voice grows small and vulnerable. "My life isn't really going anywhere back home. That's why I jumped on the documentary thing when Bellamy called. It's why I asked Sebastian if I could do more while I'm here."

What does that mean? Does he want to stay in New York after he's finished these projects? Seeds of hope plant themselves inside me before I can smother them. It's not a good idea to dream about Santino staying here permanently. It'll only end in disappointment and hurt.

Nobody stays. Everyone leaves.

Then I'll be all alone again.

I swallow around the tightness in my throat.

"Do you think…" He sounds vulnerable in a way I haven't heard from him before. "Do you think our video will do well?"

I don't usually keep tabs on that type of stuff. Sebastian handles the business end of things. I just do what he says will work. But this time, I really, *really* want our video to do well. I want it to outperform every other video The Camboy Network has ever made. "I hope so."

"Do you think Sebastian will let me join The Camboy Network if it does?" Santino asks with his eyes downcast. His fingers grip my hand tightly, like he's bracing himself for my answer. But he doesn't need to worry.

"He will." I haven't been confident in myself for a while now—in my ability to perform, in my value to my friends. But I am absolutely certain about this: if Santino wants to join The Camboy Network, I'll do everything in my power to make it happen.

CHAPTER
SIXTEEN

SANTINO

I've been looking forward to today ever since I saw it listed in Sebastian's binder. Cake tasting day. Hell, yeah.

We've taken over this fancy bakery place. Like, they've literally closed their store to the public for our shoot. Me, Bellamy, Noel, and Sebastian are sitting at a table in the middle of the room. All around us are light boxes and cameras set up on tripods.

A waiter serves us slice after slice of cake, every single one with wild flavors I've never heard of before. Strawberries and cream, passionfruit and white chocolate, spiced coconut and papaya, pistachio and dark chocolate. Who knew cakes could come in all these different flavors? I feel like I've won the cake lottery.

"This one is champagne and crème de cassis." The waiter circles the table, setting a single serving of cake in front of each of us, explaining things like the texture of the crumb, the balance of flavors, and other random things I don't understand. All I know is every bite I've taken so far has been fucking delicious and I would like to take home one order of everything, please.

"Mmm," I groan around the bite in my mouth. "This one. This has to be the one."

Noel shoots me an unimpressed look. "That's what you said about the last three cakes."

"Yeah, 'cause I hadn't had this one yet!" I shovel another forkful into my mouth and Noel rolls his eyes.

"This one *is* very good," Bellamy says.

"Should I add it to the shortlist?" Sebastian asks.

"Yes, definitely," I answer before Noel can object.

"How many more do we have?" Noel asks, pushing his barely-touched slice away.

"Two more, sir," the waiter says dryly.

I wince. The guy's been perfectly nice to us the entire time and Noel's been nothing but a grumpy asshole to him.

Across the room, Hayden's been rotating between the cameras, checking angles and adjusting settings. I catch his gaze and we share a look. He's tried to explain that Noel is only this gruff on the outside and that he's actually a marshmallow on the inside. But I'll believe it when I see it.

He gives me a shy smile that's little more than a quick curl of lips. I wish he wasn't all the way on the other side of the room. I wish he was sitting with me at the table.

It's been a couple days since we shot our scene together. Since we sat in the dark, in the middle of the night, and talked. It's felt like a dream. We went on a walk and lounged in the park under the sun. He asked me what I felt like eating and when I said lasagna, he made the best fucking lasagna I've ever had—from scratch. He read to me from his books and we played video games late into the night.

A few times, I've caught him staring off into space with an air of sadness surrounding him. But he always seems to snap out of it pretty quickly. He smiles when I tease him. He laughs at my dad jokes. I know mental health isn't something that magically disappears on its own, but it doesn't seem to be bothering him as much. I hope I've made things a little easier for him.

Listen, I know this whole falling-in-love thing is only a story Sebastian's weaving for the public. It's supposed to be make-believe. It isn't supposed to be real. But it feels very fucking real.

We look like a couple. We're acting like a couple. We *feel* like a couple. So when does it stop being an act? Because I haven't been acting. I fell in lust with Hayden from the first moment I set eyes on him. Now I think I might be falling in love too.

Is it too fast? Yeah, it probably is. Do I know everything about him? Nope, definitely not. But sometimes you just know, don't you? In that place, deep in your soul, where reason and logic don't matter. Being with him feels right— and I think that might be enough.

The waiter brings out the last two flavors of cake: coffee-infused mocha and ginger and rum. I think they're winners, but based on Noel's reactions, they probably won't make the cut.

Sebastian scribbles a few final notes in his notebook before closing it. "Alright, that's a wrap on the cake tasting. I need Santino and Hayden for a few more shots, then we're done here."

I push my chair away from the table, lift both arms

overhead, and arch my back to stretch. My t-shirt rides up and I can feel the heat of Hayden's gaze on the strip of skin around my middle.

Despite us being all couple-y the past few days, we haven't done anything more than cuddle. No making out. No sex. We've even kept to our own beds at night. I'm not entirely sure why.

I mean, no, we're not officially together or anything. So it's not a given that we'd be intimate. And there's no camera trained on us, so there's no professional reason either. I definitely want to kiss him again, feel his naked body against mine, have his dick deep inside my ass. But neither of us has made a move and… I'm pretty okay with that for now.

"Santino?" Sebastian waves me over to a long table by the wall, filled with extra slices of cake. "Alright, pick a plate. Then wave Hayden over and feed him a bite. Got it?"

"Yup!" I search the table until I find the one that reminds me most of Hayden.

"Ready?" Sebastian asks, pointing the camera at me. "And action."

I dig my fork into the cake and take a bite, moaning nice and loud for the mic to pick up. "Hey Hayden! You've got to try this."

Hayden enters the frame. "What flavor is that one?"

"Spiced coconut and papaya." I raise a forkful of cake and feed it to him. His lips wrap around the tines of the fork and his gaze locks onto mine as he slides the cake off the silverware. Jesus, is it just me or did it suddenly get super hot in here? My stomach tightens with desire and heat pools in my groin.

"Mmm," Hayden hums, not breaking eye contact. "It's good."

"Uh huh," I murmur.

There's a bit of frosting at the corner of his mouth. Almost in slow motion, his tongue slips out to lick it up, but he doesn't get all of it. In a trance, my hand floats up and I wipe off the rest with my thumb. I meant to clean my hand on a napkin or something, but Hayden catches my wrist. Still staring into my eyes, he brings my hand back to his mouth.

I watch in a lust-filled stupor as his lips part, then close around the digit. I gasp. It's hot and wet and somehow, it feels like he's sucking on my cock instead of my thumb.

He scrapes his teeth against the fleshy pad, bites gently, then soothes it with his tongue. The camera can't see any of that, but that only makes it hotter. He's not doing it for the camera. He's doing it for me. Only me. And I sure as hell can feel it all over my fucking body.

I shudder and sway toward him. He steadies me with a hand on my hip.

When he releases my thumb, my hand falls to his chest. The muscle is hard, rising and falling with each of Hayden's breaths. I can feel his heart hammering against my palm. So fast, it's like he's just run an obstacle course.

Is that how he feels when he looks at me? Because it's how I feel when I look at him. Like I've jumped through all the hoops, climbed all the walls, crawled through all the mud just to be with him.

"Cut!" Sebastian calls.

I hear him, but I don't want to move. I don't want to step away from Hayden or stop staring into those incredibly green eyes. I want to get closer. I want to press myself right up against him and squeeze out every molecule of air between us.

A vibration in my pocket makes me jump and I scramble to dig out my phone. My stomach sinks when I see the name on the screen.

I managed to get out of family dinner last weekend with some food poisoning excuse. I only barely convinced my mom not to drive all the way to San Francisco to drop off soup. I felt awful for lying to her and I'm not even sure she believed me, but what else was I supposed to do?

I debate not answering, but I already ignored her call from two days ago and if I don't pick up this time, she'll send the fucking National Guard. Reluctantly, I hit the green accept button and move to a quiet corner of the store. "Hey, Mom."

"Tino, where are you?" Mom practically barks.

Panic explodes through me. What does she mean, where am I? She better not be at my apartment in San Francisco. She only sometimes shows up unannounced. "Uh, what?"

"Where are you? Are you at home? I need you to find something for me on the internet."

Relief douses the panic and the sudden spike and crash leave me a little weak. I slump against a wall, letting my forehead fall heavily against it. "No, I'm not home right now. I'm out with some friends."

"Which friends? Who are they? Do I know them?"

I bite back a groan. I shouldn't have mentioned friends. I know better than to voluntarily offer information she didn't specifically ask for. "No, you don't know them, Mom."

"Well, then who are they? What are you doing with them?"

Oh come on. Seriously? "It's, uh, Bellamy and some of his friends. You know Bellamy? My old roommate?"

Now Mom sounds annoyed. "Yeah, I know Bellamy. Why did you say I don't know them when I do?"

"I don't know, Mom. It doesn't matter. What do you need me to look up for you?" I try to keep the annoyance out of my voice.

"Insoles. The doctor says I need orthotics, but the custom ones are too expensive. So I want to get insoles instead. Can you get me some insoles?"

"Um…" My mind blanks. I've never bought insoles before. I wouldn't even know where to start. Why is she asking *me*? Why can't she ask my sisters who both live ten minutes from her house? "Can't Paola or Lucia get them for you?"

Mom tsks at me. "No, no, they'll get the wrong ones. You have to get them for me."

"I don't even know what size shoes you wear, Mom."

She doesn't skip a beat. "Size seven. And make sure they have good arch support. I can never find ones with good arch support."

"Um, okay?" I say, resigning myself to researching insoles later tonight.

"When will you be home?"

I don't know how to answer that question. Where even is home right now? San Francisco, where there's nothing and no one waiting for me? Santa Cruz, where my family is chomping at the bit to smother me? Or here. In Hayden's apartment. Where I feel more free than I ever have before?

"Um, I'm not sure," I say, choking on my words. "But I'll have the insoles delivered to your place."

"Good. Make sure to do overnight shipping. I love you, Tino. Muah."

Guilt makes my stomach feel as heavy as a rock. "Love you too, Mom."

When I turn back toward the room, Sebastian and Bellamy are packing up the equipment while Noel stands around looking bored. There's no sign of Hayden.

Sebastian notices me scanning the room. "He went home. Said he was tired and wanted to nap."

"Oh." Disappointment hits me like a truck. He didn't say goodbye before leaving. He left without me. We were going to go sightseeing with Bellamy and Noel this afternoon. He seemed okay earlier. Did I miss something?

"He said you should still go to Rockefeller," Sebastian adds, giving me a look that speaks volumes. Like maybe Hayden wants to be alone. Like maybe he doesn't want me around.

CHAPTER
SEVENTEEN

HAYDEN

We were supposed to go to Rockefeller Center with Noel and Bellamy. We were planning to go up to the observation deck on the Chrysler Building. Santino was really excited about it and I kind of was too. He hasn't done a lot of touristy stuff in the city—mostly because of me—and I wanted to take him to do something fun.

But then the darkness started creeping in.

It never really went away, but the day after our shoot together, I almost couldn't feel it at all. I almost felt like my old self again.

It didn't last though. The darkness inched closer and closer with each passing day. The voice got louder and louder. I tried to keep it at bay. I tried to ignore it and focus on all the happy, joyful things I was doing with Santino. But the ache in my chest just wouldn't let up.

I couldn't stop thinking about what will happen after Santino finished the projects he's working on. Is he going home? Is he staying? What if he doesn't like me as much as I like him? What if he's just humoring me because I'm giving him somewhere to crash?

The rational part of my brain understood that there was no point in obsessing over these questions. But the darkness didn't care and the voice was more than loud enough to drown out all reason.

Of course, he's leaving. If not for California, then at least to get away from you. Because you're a pathetic waste of space. You're a parasite. You're worthless. It's only a matter of time before all your so-called friends turn on you.

It was really bad when I got up this morning. I could barely get out of bed. I felt like I was trapped under an invisible blanket made of lead. I'm actually not sure how I managed to get up. It's a miracle I made it through the shoot and out of the bakery in one piece. My hands were shaking and every time I had to adjust a camera, I held my breath I wouldn't ruin the shot.

You totally did. Every single shot. None of it's usable. Because you're useless.

The ache felt like a pool of acid, eat, eat, eating away at my flesh, leaving a big, echoing cavern in its wake. I kept rubbing at my sternum where the pain was the worst and every time I did that, I wondered whether my fist would go right through the crumbling shell of my body.

The clincher was when we were shooting our mini-scene with the cake. He fed the piece to me, then wiped the extra frosting off my lip. I caught his hand and sucked his thumb into my mouth. The dazed look he gave me as we stood there, like he was under some kind of trance, sent the voice into overdrive.

See what you've done to him? How you've manipulated him? Taken advantage of him? He would be much better off living his own life, but no, you've brainwashed him into thinking you're worth a damn. You're so selfish. Narcissistic.

There was no way I could make it through an afternoon of playing tourist with Santino. And as much as I wanted him to come home with me, he shouldn't have to give up on a fun excursion just because of me. Haven't I stolen enough from him? Haven't I wasted enough of his time?

I mumbled some excuse to Sebastian and hightailed it out of there before anyone could stop me.

When I get home, I slam the door shut behind me and slide down to the floor, back against the wall. My heart is racing. Blood rushes past my ears. My lungs are burning.

You're such a fraud. You think you're cool enough to be one of the guys, but you're not. They only let you hang around them because they pity you. They feel sorry for you. They'd much rather you were gone. They don't really want you around.

I bang my head against the wall and shove the heels of my hands into my eyes. I know those are lies. I know I shouldn't listen to them. But it just. Doesn't. Go. Away.

You can't get rid of me. I'm a part of you. How can I be lying to you when I am you? You're the one doing the thinking. If you don't believe what I'm saying, why are you thinking it?

The ache is all-consuming—not just around my chest, but extending from the top of my head to the bottoms of my feet. I feel like I'm disintegrating into a pile of nothing.

Because you are nothing.

I curl up into a ball by the front door. A haunting, wretched sound tears from my throat. It hurts. So much. So much.

I can't take this anymore. I can't stand it. It's too much. It never stops. It never ends.

So end it.

My hands tear at my hair as another crying sob escapes.

Seriously. End it. If it hurts so much, there's an easy way out. Unless you're too much of a coward to do even that.

No, I don't want to die.

It's the perfect solution. You won't be in pain anymore. Your friends won't have to pretend they like you anymore. They can go on with their lives without you being a fucking stone around their necks. They can be happy. You want them to be happy, don't you? You don't want them to be miserable because of you, do you? Why do you have to contaminate them with your misery? Why can't you just let them be free?

Tears pour from my eyes. I'm being gutted. Everything hurts. I hate this. I hate myself. I hate the world. I hate everything.

You know what you need to do.

I lie on the floor, adrift in a sea of agony. Drowning. I can't get up. I can't move. I can't do anything but feel hurt and more hurt and more hurt.

At some point, I pass out. Exhausted. Drained. Shriveled up and dried out. A ball of unconscious flesh and bone in the front hall of the apartment. I don't know how long I'm there for. It could be ten minutes. It could be five hours.

When I come to again, every single muscle in my body is sore. Every joint has been frozen into one position. Sharp, stabbing pain shoots through me as I try to unfold myself. I have to use the wall to stand up. My feet have gone numb. My head is throbbing. My eyes are swollen half shut.

I'm a shell of a human being. The ache in my chest is

gone. So is the deep, abiding sense of hate. But I don't feel happy or light or carefree. I feel empty. Hollow. Dead on the inside. A ghost.

Somehow, I stumble my way to my bedroom and into bed. I don't change or even take off my clothes. I just climb in, pull the covers over my head, and bury my face into a pillow. I slip in and out of consciousness, willing myself back to sleep when it looks like I might be waking up. I don't want to be awake. Things are bad when I'm awake. The voice is too loud. It says things I don't want to hear. Things that hurt.

Far in the distance, there are sounds of movement. A door opening. Someone's calling my name. Footsteps that draw closer and closer. Then a knock.

"Hayden? You in there?"

The doorknob turns. The slight scent of cinnamon wafts toward me. I hold my breath and pretend to sleep. I don't want him to see me like this. Pathetic and broken and defective. I'm ashamed of myself. I'm ashamed of thinking I could ever be good enough for Santino.

He moves closer, feet padding on the floor. "Hayden?" he whispers, bending over me.

I don't move. Not an inch. Even though my heart is racing furiously in my chest.

You're more inept than I thought. You can't even face him. You can't accept the truth you're good for nothing, you don't deserve him, you're a poor excuse for a human being.

Just as quietly as he entered, Santino slips out. The door closes with a light snick. I suck in a breath as the ache returns in full force, a monster tearing me apart from the inside out.

Panic seizes me and my heart lurches like it's trying to

chase after Santino. Don't leave. Come back. I don't want to be alone. Please. I don't want to be alone.

But you're better off alone. You're better off dead and gone.

I clutch a pillow to my chest, as if I can stuff it inside me to fill the enormous empty cavern. Fresh tears spring to my eyes, gathering on my lashes. I turn my face into my pillow and let the pillowcase soak up the moisture.

A muffled moan escapes my throat. I can't let him hear. I can't let him know just how weak and pathetic and stupid I am.

I struggle to breathe, the darkness doing a better job of smothering me than the pillow. It's seeping into every crack and crevice of my body, expanding and growing inside me, blocking up my airway, choking me. It's consuming me, this ugliness, thick and heavy and greasy.

The door opens again. This time without any warning. I try to swallow down the anguish, but instead, I make a gasping, strangled sound. I try to be still, but I can't stop my body from shaking.

The door closes and a moment later, the bed dips. Santino climbs over the covers, scoots in close, and lies down behind me. He wraps himself around me with an arm and a leg thrown over my body.

He doesn't say anything. Doesn't try to ask me what's wrong. Doesn't try to tell me everything will be okay. Doesn't even say my name. He just holds me. Tight.

A solid weight. Real. Grounding. Sure.

The tears return and so do the sobs. They flow like some dam inside me has burst, the hurt and pain pouring out of me in sweet, terrible relief.

I'm not alone. Santino's with me. He saw me when I didn't want him to see. He came when I tried to push him away. I don't deserve him, but I want him. I shouldn't have him, but I don't want to let him go.

Santino holds me as I cry, as I empty myself in wrenching, heaving sobs. The pillow is soaked through with my tears and snot and spit, and not once does he pull away. If anything, he holds me tighter and squeezes me harder. He stays until I sink back into unconsciousness.

CHAPTER
EIGHTEEN

SANTINO

I don't know what's happening, but I know it's bad. Mom never looked like this. She was sad and tired a lot. But she never looked like she was getting axe murdered by some invisible demon.

I couldn't stop worrying about him all afternoon. At Rockefeller Center, when we checked out a few shops, when we went up the Chrysler Building. I was only half there, half registering the stuff around me. The other half was back home, wondering what Hayden was doing. Hoping he was okay.

Bellamy asked if I wanted to grab dinner before heading home. I said I was going to have dinner with Hayden.

The apartment was quiet when I let myself in and my heart sank. I'd kept telling myself Hayden just needed some downtime. That he would be in the living room reading or maybe in the kitchen cooking. That I was getting all worked up over nothing.

But the apartment was empty.

And not just empty, but like, eerily silent. It felt like there was some other presence in the space. Lurking in the corners. Making the air toxic. A shiver of fear ran up my spine and my stomach filled with dread.

Hayden was a lump in his bed when I cracked open his door. He looked like he was sleeping and I stood there for a few minutes, not sure what to do. My gut told me something was seriously wrong, but I didn't want to wake him up and demand he start talking.

For a moment, I thought about calling Sebastian. The others don't seem to have the slightest clue about anything, but Sebastian obviously knows there's more going on with Hayden than meets the eye. I just don't know why he hasn't done anything about it. I mean, they're all supposed to be close, right? Why aren't they helping him? Are they really too preoccupied with their own lives to watch out for him? To make sure he doesn't slip through the cracks? Why am I the only one who sees this?

I quietly stepped out to let Hayden sleep, but the moment the door closed, there were a bunch of muffled sounds. Kind of like he was suffocating. Like someone was strangling him and he was thrashing around, trying to escape.

I hesitated. Mom sometimes wanted us to leave her alone, even when we didn't think she should be by herself. Hayden was probably pretending to be asleep, so maybe he didn't want me to see him like this. I feel like I've gotten to know him pretty well over the past weeks, but maybe he's had too much of me. Maybe I should follow his lead and give him some privacy.

But I couldn't make myself leave. Not when the sounds got worse. Like he was in agony. Like he was dying. How could I ignore that? How could I leave him to suffer through that alone?

I couldn't.

So I went back in, climbed onto the bed, and held him until the crying slowed and he eventually fell asleep. The room was filled with so much sadness that the air felt heavy and sour. Every breath was anguish. Every cry was torture. I don't know why Hayden feels so sad. I don't know what happened today to trigger this break. But my heart hurts to see him so broken and defeated.

I doze on and off for a while. My stomach growls with hunger from the dinner we missed. There's probably food in the fridge, but I don't want to leave Hayden, not even for a second.

It's well into the middle of the night before Hayden stirs again. He groans and struggles to push the blankets off. Which I've made harder by lying on top of them. I roll away to give him room and he tenses when he realizes he's not alone.

He sits up, shoulders rising and falling as he takes deep breaths to gather himself. "I'm sorry," he murmurs quietly, curling in on himself as if he's expecting me to lash out at him or something.

I bristle. He has nothing to be sorry for. There's nothing he needs to be ashamed of. I hate that he feels he has to apologize. I might not know exactly what's happening with him, but I know that whatever it is, it's not his fault.

I put a hand on his shoulder. He tenses for a split second before leaning into the touch. I scoot closer to him and press my body against his. He melts into me, letting me wrap him up and hold his weight. "You hungry?

"Not really."

Not the answer I was hoping for because hell, *I'm* hungry. "Oh... well... I kind of am. Want to eat with me anyway?"

I can't really see Hayden's face, but I can sense his hesitation. He wants to lie back down and go to sleep again. He wants to bury his head under some pillows and block out the rest of the world. Which like, I get, but the dude's gotta eat, right?

"Come on." I give him a playful shake. "Please?"

It takes him another moment or two, but he eventually gives me a tentative nod.

Hayden lets me lead the way as we shuffle out to the kitchen, then hangs back when I open the fridge to see what our options are.

"I think there's some cheese in the deli drawer," Hayden's voice is groggy and rough, and even though I know he's hurting, the low, rumbly sound sends warmth spreading through me.

I pull open the deli drawer to find several types of cheese that I've never heard of. I pull them all out, along with the grapes I spot in the fruit drawer.

"Crackers are over there." He points to a cupboard.

I'm not a cook. I don't trust myself to boil water. But I know how to wash grapes and cut up cheese. I make a pretty impressive plate, enough for both of us, while Hayden watches with his arms wrapped around his middle.

My mind races for something to fill the heavy silence with, but something tells me Hayden doesn't want to talk.

So I bite my lip and let the silence stretch. It's okay not to talk. Sometimes all we need is to be with someone, to be present, to let them know they're not alone.

I hold up the plate and selfishly nod toward the window. It's so stuffy in here with all the sadness and hurt and despair. "Want to sit outside?"

Hayden hesitates again before nodding. We climb out and squish in side-by-side on the steps. I dive into the cheese and crackers and after a few nudges, Hayden nibbles on some too.

Outside is still pretty hot and muggy despite being the middle of the night. The heat hasn't cleared even though the sun's gone down. Over the tops of the buildings around us, the sky glows with light from the city. The sounds of cars and sirens in the distance are a constant, unending soundtrack.

When the plate is empty, I set it aside and sling an arm around Hayden's shoulders to haul him to me. He doesn't resist, letting me slot him into my side. "You don't have to talk about it," I say, whisper-quiet. "But I'm here to listen if you want to."

He doesn't say anything for a long time. And that's cool. I said he didn't have to. But when he does, it's in the tiniest, most heart-wrenching voice. "I don't know what's wrong with me."

I have so many questions. Like, does he have any suspicions? How long has this been going on for? What does it feel like when he has one of these episodes? Why doesn't he want his friends to know?

"It's been getting worse."

My heart breaks and I swallow down a grunt of pain.

"There's this voice." He speaks slowly, with long

pauses between each sentence. "In my head. It says things. I know they're not true, but… they feel true."

"What kinds of things?" I'm not sure I actually want to know. They can't be anything good. But I think he needs to say them out loud. So they're not bouncing around inside his head, growing louder and louder with each ricochet. So someone else can hear them, witness them, and tell him he's not crazy.

"Bad things. About me."

"Mmhmm." I try to keep my breathing even. Slow and steady. Calming.

"It says… I'm a loser."

My deep inhale is involuntary, an indignant reaction to the utterly unfounded statement.

"That I'm pathetic. Worthless. Unlovable." His voice cracks and he buries his face into the crook of my neck.

I hold him there, fingers carding through his hair as his shoulders shake from silent sobs.

"Why?" he wails quietly. "Why is this happening to me? Why won't it stop?"

"I don't know, babe. I don't know." I sniffle as tears fill my eyes. I wish there was something I could do, something that would take away his pain.

"I just want it to go away."

"We'll figure something out. We'll get you help," I promise him. Mom went to see a therapist before she started getting better. She was even on medication for a bit. I'm not an expert, but that feels like a good first step: find a professional who knows more than we do.

"Please. Please." Hayden clings to me, fisting my shirt in his hands like he's afraid I'll disappear on him.

"I'm here. I'm not leaving. You're not alone. I've got

you." Tears spill down my cheeks, but I don't bother wiping them away. I want to cry them. I want to feel them wet my face. I can't imagine how many tears Hayden's shed in all of this. It's the least I can do to cry a few with him.

We eventually make our way back inside. Hayden's kind of comatose, eyes unfocused and a little unsteady on his feet. He goes where I direct him, shuffling along slowly as if he's walking through water.

Instead of taking him back to his room, I lead him to the bathroom. We've both slept and cried and sweated in our street clothes and we could both use a shower before climbing back into bed.

I crank on the water and help him undress. He goes in first and I strip quickly to follow him. The shower isn't really big enough for two grown men and we have to bear hug each other to keep from falling over.

Despite the seriousness and heaviness of the past several hours, my body can't help but react to a naked Hayden in my arms. Hard muscles. Wet skin. My dick stirs and I try my best to keep my hips away from him.

I help him soap down, running my hands over his broad shoulders that narrow to a slim waist. A rounded ass I'd love to sink my teeth into. Thick thighs and muscled calves.

I turn him around. Golden blond hairs dust the tops of his toes and his calves. His quads flex under my touch. Then I'm face to face with his cock, completely soft but still impressively huge. I'm gentle as I make sure to get all the little crevices, lifting his balls to get between his legs. He sighs as I work, leaning against the wall.

Through the mist of the shower, I glance up at this man

standing before me. His eyes are closed. His brows are furrowed. Every few seconds, his face muscles twitch like he's flinching from some unseen attack.

Protectiveness like I've never felt before rises up in me.

As the baby of the family, I'm usually the one who gets coddled and protected, even when I don't want to be. But now, with Hayden, I want to be the protector. I want to take care of him and keep him safe. I want to be the person he can turn to, no matter what, the person who will always be there for him, no matter how bad things get.

I soap up his stomach, then his chest. His eyes blink lazily open when I reach his shoulders and quickly wash each arm. He watches me through clumped lashes, lips hooded over his brilliant green eyes. Lip rosy and swollen from where he's been chewing on them.

I brush his wet hair away from his face and he turns into my hand like a touch-starved puppy. Eyes drifting shut again, he doesn't resist when I pull him into my arms. Bare chest against bare chest. Stomach against stomach. My semi is nestled against his hip, but I don't care if he notices anymore. All that matters is that he knows I'm here for him. That he can always count on me.

CHAPTER
NINETEEN

HAYDEN

"Denny!"

Heavy footsteps echo through the apartment and I groan. I've never understood how Rhys can be such a loud walker when he's literally half my size.

"Denny!"

What does he want? Why is he waking me up? Doesn't he know how early it is?

"Denny?"

Next to me, someone moves, sitting bolt upright and dragging some of the covers with him. Cold air from the air conditioning rushes into the warm cocoon I've been nestled in. I whine and squirm, trying to burrow back into the warmth.

"Uh, this isn't... we didn't..."

Santino. My brain finally registers what's going on. We're in bed together—but not my bed. In his bed, in his room. We're both naked, save for our underwear. Because we didn't bother putting clothes on again after our late-night shower. And because I liked the feeling of his skin against mine, with nothing between us, nothing separating us.

But now it's morning and I guess Rhys has just found us in bed together?

"Denny! Wake up!"

"Dude—chill. He had a late night, okay?"

"Yeah, I'm sure you both did."

"What the hell is that supposed to mean?"

"Okay, let's all take a breath." That's Sebastian. What's Sebastian doing here? "Why don't you guys get dressed?"

"But Sebby—"

"Come on, Rhys. Do you really want to talk to them while they're lying naked in bed?"

Rhys lets out a frustrated sound, then stomps out toward the living room. "I can't believe they're in *my* bed."

For some reason, that's the thing that wakes me all the way up. *His* bed. Rhys's bed. That he left here when he moved out.

I roll over and open my eyes blearily. Santino is sitting up, covers pooled in his lap. I can see the crease of his ass from this angle. The long, elegant curve of his back. The deep valley of his spine.

He turns and lies back down next to me, pulling the covers up to my chest.

"I thought we were supposed to get dressed," I mumble, rubbing my eyes.

Santino gives me his lopsided smile. "They barged in here unannounced. They can wait a few minutes for us to wake up."

I sigh. I'm awake. Unfortunately. I'd much rather be

asleep and unconscious, all wrapped up in the safety of Santino's arms. "What are they doing here?"

Santino's shoulder rises and falls in a half-shrug. "I don't know. But Rhys is definitely upset."

Which is never a good sign. Especially not when you're on the receiving end of his ire. I don't know what he could be upset with me about though. We haven't spoken in a couple days and he's not the type to sit on something if it's bothering him. If I did something or said something that pissed him off, he would've told me already.

Sebastian, on the other hand... I groan and slap a hand over my face. Fuck. He's been trying to talk to me for days now and I've been avoiding him at every turn. He probably called Rhys to see if he knew anything. Then they both decided to show up for a what—an intervention?

Santino's gentle fingers wrap around my wrist and carefully tug my hand away from my face. "Hey, you don't have to talk to them if you don't want to. But..." He tilts his head and his brows draw together in concern. "It might not be a bad idea. They're your friends. They care about you. They want to help."

Panic and fear seize me. No, I can't let them know. Not now after I've spent so many months lying to them. They'll be hurt and upset. They won't understand why I didn't want to tell them. They'll think it's their fault. That they did something wrong. When it's not their fault at all. It's mine. Everything is my fault. I'm the one to blame.

The ache grows, gradual but steady, until it feels like an anvil sitting on my chest. I sit up, wincing as I force my lungs to expand.

This is it. This is when your friends find out just what kind of piece of shit human you are. They're here to break up with you. They're here to tell you never to contact them again.

No. Stop. Go away. I slam the heels of my hands against my temples as if that will make the voice shut up.

"Hayden?" Santino wraps himself around me and presses kisses to my shoulder. "What is it? Is it the voice?"

I nod as shame fills me. God, I can't believe I told him about that yesterday. He must think I'm a fucking freak.

Yeah, he totally does.

"Whatever it's saying, babe, you know it's not true, right? You're not a loser. You're not worthless."

What the hell does he know? He just met you. He hasn't seen how depraved you are on the inside.

"Hey, babe." Santino rearranges us so we're facing each other, then pulls my hands away from my head so he can cup both of my cheeks. "Listen to me. You can't fight this on your own. You *shouldn't have to* fight it on your own. Let us help you. Let your friends help you."

No, but... god, I want that so much. I want to stop fighting. I want to give up. I want to throw my hands up in the air and let this be someone else's problem. And yet, I don't. I can't. I don't understand. My friends are amazing. I know they want to help. Why is it so hard for me to let them?

You know what would really help? If you actually gave up. Just walk straight into the ocean. Sure, they might miss you for a bit. They'll even have a nice funeral. But they'll go on with their lives. They'll be fine. And eventually, it'll be like you never existed in the first place.

The pain is searing. Right in the middle of my chest. Like I've been stabbed straight through my heart. I squeeze my eyes shut against the pain. I struggle to breathe. I lie back down, curled up in a little ball.

I just want it to end. Please, just let this end.

"Hayden? Hayden. Hey, talk to me. What's happening? What's going on?" Santino puts his face right in front of mine. Forehead to forehead. Nose to nose. "Babe, please. Talk to me."

You can't tell him. What's the point? You're useless. Hopeless. There's nothing they can do to help you. You're beyond saving.

"I can't stop it." I sound like I'm dying. I feel like I'm dying. I kind of want to. Dying means not having to go through any of this anymore.

"Stop what? The voice? What is it saying?"

"It… it…"

You won't actually say it out loud. You don't have the balls. Haven't you been humiliated enough? Why let him know how truly perverted you are?

"It says I should…"

Don't dooo it. Don't dooo it.

"Should what, babe? What should you do?"

I swallow past the lump in my throat. My lungs burn. My chest burns. My stomach twists up in knots. "Die." I just barely manage to croak the single word.

Santino doesn't respond. Not immediately. Maybe he didn't hear me. Maybe he did and he thinks I'm a lunatic. Maybe he thinks I'm insane and needs to be locked up for my own good.

But then he hauls me to him, cradles me in his arms, head tucked under his chin. "No. Just no. You hear me? No." He holds me so tight, rocking me side to side. His legs hook around mine, locking behind my knees. It's like he's afraid I'll run off. Like he can physically stop me from doing something stupid.

I cling to him. I don't want to die. Not really. I just want this to stop. Please, somebody make it stop.

"No. You can't. I won't let that happen. I just found you. I can't lose you. Do you understand? We'll get you help. We'll get you help and you'll get better and I'll be here the entire way so you're not alone. You never have to be alone."

The words tumble past Santino's lips in a jumble, so fast I'm not even sure he's talking to me anymore. But I feel every syllable he utters like a tether drawing me in, securing me, keeping me anchored. I let his words wash over me, soothing and calming, until the bone-deep hurt starts to ease.

I'm not sure how long we lie there, all tangled up in each other. It's long enough that I think Rhys and Sebastian must have left. There's no way Rhys would wait around without knocking on the door every five minutes.

But when we finally manage to dress and drag ourselves out of bed, they're still there. Sitting in the living room. Rhys is on his phone. Sebastian's on his laptop. Waiting as if they have all the time in the world.

Embarrassment rushes through me. I wish they'd gotten impatient and left. Then I wouldn't have to face them. Then I could avoid this conversation a little longer.

They both glance up at me from their spots on the couch with equal parts concern and hope. God, I'm such an asshole. I'm so fucking selfish. I've made things so much worse than they needed to be. If I'd been honest from the start, we could've dealt with it and moved on. But no, I had to pretend I was a tough guy who could handle things on his own. And where's that gotten me? My friends are wasting their day away, sitting in my living room, waiting for me to get my shit together.

"Do you guys, um, want something to drink?" I ask, not knowing what else to say.

"Oh my god, Denny, just sit the fuck down." Rhys slaps his hand on the spot next to him.

Except it's only big enough for one person and I don't want to let go of Santino's hand. Rhys must read my hesitation on my face because he rolls his eyes and moves so there's enough room for both of us.

"You go sit. I'll get drinks." Santino gives me a nudge toward the couch.

It takes me a split second too long to let him go.

"You want to tell us what the hell is going on?" Rhys asks when I sit down. "And don't say you're fine, because we know you're not fucking fine."

"Rhys," Sebastian scolds.

"What? It's true." Rhys is curled up with his knees tucked against his chest, arms wrapped around his shins. He's got a glower on his face that could rival Noel's and his chin is stuck out in an epic pout. But he's on the verge of crying with his eyes filling with tears.

Guilt makes my embarrassment worse. Rhys is crying because of me. Because I lied to him and hid the truth for so long.

"I'm sorry," I say, shaking my head. "I don't know what's wrong with me."

"I knew I shouldn't have moved out." Rhys wipes angrily at his cheeks. "I knew something was wrong. I should've stayed."

"No!" The word comes out a little too forcefully. "No,

you deserve to be with Angel. I didn't want to get in the way of that."

"But not at your expense!" Rhys shifts so he's kneeling on the couch cushions, ready for a fight.

I shrink into myself, slouching down so he looms above me. I know he's not trying to be mean. I know he's only yelling because he's worried and scared. And I'm responsible. If I'd said something sooner, none of this would've happened. If I had told him the first dozen times he asked if something was wrong, we wouldn't be here right now.

Santino comes back with an armful of LaCroix. He sets them down on the coffee table without bothering to hand them out. The second his ass hits the couch, he's got his arm around my shoulders and I lean into the comfort of his body.

Rhys's eyes narrow and he glares at Santino, who just holds me tighter. "Are you two fucking?"

Sebastian groans and drops his head into his hands. "Oh my god, Rhys."

"What? It's a legitimate question. Just because they filmed a scene together doesn't mean he gets to take advantage of Denny."

"You don't know what the fuck you're talking about, bro," Santino spits back at Rhys. "I'm the only one who's here. I'm the one who noticed he was hurting and did something about it. What the fuck have you done?"

Rhys blanches and more tears escape his lashes. "How dare you. How fucking dare you? You've been here for what? A couple weeks? And you'll be leaving soon too. I'm Denny's best friend. I'll still be here when you're long gone."

"Some best friend you are."

"Okay!" Sebastian jumps to his feet, hands held out to stop them both from continuing. "That's enough. You two arguing over who cares more about Hayden isn't actually helping."

Santino harrumphs and Rhys's chin lifts an inch. God, I'm such a terrible person. I'm an awful friend. All I did was make two perfectly nice people argue with each other over something so stupid. What does it matter who cares more about me? I don't deserve it either way. They have better things to do with their lives.

Sebastian moves the cans of LaCroix out of the way and sits down on the coffee table in front of me. He pins me with that look he has. The one he uses when he's in charge and on a mission. No one says no to Sebastian when he's like this. "This didn't start when Rhys moved out, did it?"

I hesitate, aghast that I'm actually going to admit to it. But I shake my head, feeling like a schoolboy getting scolded by the principal.

"It's been months already." Sebastian tilts his head in thought. "Maybe a year?"

I nod.

"Can you tell us what this is all about?"

CHAPTER
TWENTY

SANTINO

Hayden is shaking. Like full-on trembling. I hold him tighter and rub my hand up and down his arm to help ground him.

Sebastian's right. I shouldn't have shouted at Rhys. It was a stupid argument to begin with, but more importantly, it wasn't going to help Hayden any. If anything, it only made him feel worse than he already did. I should've known better.

But honestly, what the fuck. I get Rhys is worried about his friend, but he doesn't have to be a bitch about it. I'm only trying to help someone we both care about. Jesus.

"I feel bad," Hayden says, voice small, eyes downcast. He's all huddled in on himself. "Heavy. Dark. Scared. Angry. Sad." He presses his hand to the middle of his chest. "It hurts. Here."

"Hurts how?" Sebastian asks.

"Like… something's clawing at me from the inside."

On the other side of Hayden, Rhys sniffles. He tilts his

head back like that's going to stop the steady stream of tears rolling down his cheeks.

"Is it all the time? Or does it come and go?" Sebastian prompts.

"Comes and goes," Hayden answers. "But it's never really gone. Not really. It's always there."

I think of the voice. The one whispering all those ugly, awful things to Hayden. I don't know if it's like, a metaphorical voice, or if he's actually hearing things that aren't there. I mean, either way, it's bad. But if it's always there, always whispering, sometimes shouting… Jesus, that would drive anyone insane.

"I think—" I cut myself off when Sebastian flicks his gaze to me. It's sharp and calculating, like his brain is running at a hundred miles an hour. I gulp and push forward. "I think he needs to see someone. Like a therapist."

Hayden flinches, but he doesn't say no.

"There's nothing wrong with seeing a therapist," Sebastian continues. "I have a therapist."

Rhys nods in agreement.

"My mom…" I pause, uncertain if I should be comparing Hayden to my mom. They're different people, going through different things. But if it can help… "She had depression after my grandmother died. She started seeing a therapist and learned a bunch of techniques to manage her moods. She still sees a therapist now, even though it's been years."

Sebastian nods as if I've made a good point. "I think a therapist is a good idea. I can call mine and see if she's taking new clients. She knows what we do for a living and she's cool with it, for what that's worth."

Hayden's still unsure.

"I can go with you, if you want," I offer.

"I can too," Rhys jumps in and I have to bite back a snarky comment about too little, too late.

"You don't have to," Hayden says, though it's not clear who exactly he's talking to. "I mean, yeah, I'll go see someone, but you guys don't have to come with me." His voice trails off, the last few words coming out in a mumble.

Like hell I'm not going with him. As if I'd let him face that on his own.

Over Hayden's head, I catch Rhys's gaze. We share a knowing look and I recognize the stubborn determination in his eyes. We're thinking the same thing. Hayden's not getting rid of us so easily.

"Good. Cool." Sebastian reaches for his laptop. "I'll have something set up and send you the info. In the meantime, I can find someone else to help with the cameras and we can reschedule your shoots."

Hayden's head snaps up, his breath caught in his chest. He opens his mouth, but nothing comes out. He looks conflicted, like he doesn't know if he should agree to Sebastian's suggestion. We watch him expectantly, waiting for him to put words to whatever's running through that beautiful head of his.

"I, um, I can still work. If you still want me."

"If I still want you?" Sebastian repeats the weird phrase, head cocked in confusion.

"If you want to find someone better."

A look of remorse comes over Sebastian's face and for a second, I can see the soft-hearted, compassionate friend underneath the hardnosed, solution-focused strategist.

He puts a hand on Hayden's knee and leans in to stare

Hayden in the eye. "There is no one better. You're the best."

"I just don't want to get in everyone's way." Hayden is so quiet we all have to lean in to hear him.

"You're not in our way. Trust me, I'd tell you if you were." Sebastian doesn't sound comforting anymore. He sounds like a director who doesn't take shit from anyone. "We wouldn't have gotten this far on the documentary if it hadn't been for your help."

Hayden sniffles, squeezing his eyes shut. "You don't have to say that."

Sebastian's brows slam together in a scowl. "I'm *not* just saying that. It's the truth. I know it's hard for you to believe right now, but I wouldn't lie about something like that."

"Seriously. Sebastian doesn't joke around about work," Rhys adds.

Hayden chews on his lip and I can tell the lie is still ringing loud in his head. I give him a squeeze, hoping he can feel how much I care for him.

It was only a couple weeks ago, but I can't quite remember what my life was like before Hayden was in it. San Francisco feels so far away, not just like, distance-wise, but time-wise too. It feels like a lifetime ago.

Not much has changed in the past couple weeks, and yet *everything's* changed. I don't feel like the same person who got off the plane at JFK. That person was lost and directionless, hoping to find some meaning in his life in this new city. And I'm not saying I've got everything figured out now, but it feels like things are happening. I'm moving forward. My life is taking on a shape that I like, that I want more of.

And so much of that is because of Hayden. Because he's made me feel comfortable out here where I didn't know anyone. He's given me a home away from home. He's given me something to look forward to when I wake up in the mornings. He's given me an opportunity to do something with my life that never would've been possible if I was still back on the West Coast.

I owe Hayden so much. Yeah, we've only known each other for a short while. And yeah, he's been going through a lot of shit the whole time. But if this is what he can do in the middle of all that, I can't imagine how fucking awesome he'd be when he's at a hundred percent.

"Okay, how's this?" Sebastian says, making an executive decision. "We keep everything the same for now. For both the documentary and your second video. But you'll say something if you're not feeling up to it, got it? If you're feeling like shit or you need a break, you have to tell us. No more pretending you're fine when you're not."

Hayden nods, still looking a little wary. "Okay."

Satisfied, Sebastian starts gathering his things. "Cool, I've got to go, but I'll see you guys tomorrow for the tux fitting scene."

"I don't have anywhere to be." Rhys jumps to his feet and reaches his hands above his head to stretch side to side. "Want to go get lunch?"

Hayden hesitates before answering. "I'm not really hungry."

Disappointment flashes across Rhys's face. "Oh, uh, how about we go for a walk? Hang out at the park?"

Hayden drops his gaze. "I don't know…"

"What about the library? You love the library."

Hayden takes a couple breaths before answering. "Actually, I'm kind of tired."

Rhys looks like he's going to keep arguing with Hayden when Sebastian puts a hand on his shoulder. A silent message passes between them. Rhys pouts, chin lifting, but he lets it go. "Fine, but this weekend. I expect to see you at The Bronzed Rail," he says, pointing a stern finger at Hayden. "Got it?"

Hayden tries for a smile, but it looks more like a grimace. "I'll try."

I see Rhys and Sebastian out and we pause by the front door, lowering our voices so Hayden can't overhear us.

"Let us know how he does, okay?" Sebastian instructs. "And if anything happens, give us a call and we'll be right over."

"For sure." I clap his outstretched hand and lean in for a shoulder hug. When we pull back, Rhys has his arms crossed over his chest, watching me with one raised eyebrow.

"You didn't answer my question earlier. Are you guys fucking?"

"Jesus Christ, Rhys," Sebastian mutters.

I cross my arms to match his and lean against the doorframe. "What if we are?"

Rhys's gaze is shrewd as we stare each other down. "You seem like a nice guy," he finally says after a few tense seconds. "But if you hurt him, I'll hunt you down and end you."

I don't fight the smile that spreads across my face. I have absolutely no intention of hurting Hayden. I would never forgive myself if I did. Hayden needs to be protected at all costs, and there's nothing else on earth I want to do more.

Sebastian and Rhys head down the stairs and I close the door after them. When I get back to the living room, Hayden is exactly where I left him. Arms wrapped around himself, slouched all the way down on the couch.

"Do you want to eat something?" I ask because I totally get Hayden not wanting to go out, but he's still got to eat.

He shakes his head. "No, I'm not hungry." Moving slowly, he pushes himself to his feet. "I think I'll take a nap."

I follow him to his room where he crawls into bed and pulls the covers up to his chin. "Want me to stay with you?"

He doesn't meet my gaze, insecurity wafting off him. "You don't have to if you don't want to."

So it's going to be like that, huh? I scramble to climb into bed with him. "I always want to stay with you."

He glances up at me, like he's trying to see if I'm serious. Newsflash, pretty boy, I'm dead serious. A look of relief washes over his face and he snuggles into my side.

Truth is, I'm not the least bit tired and I'd normally go out of my mind if I was forced to lie in bed, staring up at the ceiling with nothing to do. But this time, I don't mind. Because Hayden is here and he needs me to be with him. And I can't think of another place I'd rather be.

He dozes off at some point, so I guess he really was tired. Carefully, I slip from the bed and sort through a pile of books sitting on the floor. There's an autobiography of some Japanese dude, a book about the brain, a bunch of other stuff, and a detective mystery book. I pick the last one and settle back into bed, sitting next to Hayden as he sleeps.

The book is set in Venice, about an Italian detective who solves murders. I'm just starting chapter two when Hayden wakes up. He blinks blearily at me and his brows furrow with confusion when he sees the book.

"What are you doing?"

"Reading," I answer.

"But I thought you weren't into reading."

I shrug. "But you're into reading, so I want to see what the hype is about."

He doesn't respond, like he's not sure how to process the statement.

"Want me to read to you?" I ask on a whim.

"Really?" He sounds skeptical. Well, I'll show him.

I clear my throat and start reading, waving my hand in the air and channeling my best Mario Brothers impression. I barely get a sentence in before Hayden bursts out laughing.

"What are you doing?" he asks.

"What? You don't like my Italian accent?" I say, still trying to sound like Mario.

Hayden's laughing so hard, he can't even talk. He shakes his head and covers his face with his hand. I laugh too, feeling like a fucking hero.

I can make Hayden laugh. Even at his lowest and darkest, I can still make him laugh, bright and loud and unreserved. If that's not a superpower, I don't know what is.

CHAPTER
TWENTY-ONE

HAYDEN

I *really* did not want to go to the tuxedo fitting shoot. But I also *really* didn't want to be left at home by myself either. What I *really* wanted was to stay in bed with Santino the whole day.

Like what we did yesterday after Rhys and Sebastian left. I drifted in and out of sleep, trying my best to ignore the voice and the heaviness whenever it tried to consume me. Santino was next to me the entire time, holding me from behind or sitting up next to me, reading a book.

That was so fucking adorable. The silly accent he put on, waving his hand in the air like he was some sort of Italian chef. It made me laugh—like actual, real laughter that I felt right down in my belly—for the first time in a really long time. It was such a relief, a bit of lightness that kept me from sinking too far into the darkness again.

Even so, I didn't want to get out of bed this morning.

I feel like I'm moving through thirty feet of water. Everything is slow and sluggish. Sounds are muted. Light is diluted. It takes me several seconds to process what other people are saying and then several more seconds to figure out a response. I feel so tired.

It doesn't help that everyone's acting weird. They're all like, "Heeeyyy… are you okay? Are you sure? Do you need anything? Let me know if you need anything. Do you need to take a break? Don't push yourself too hard. Self-care is important."

I never know what to say. If I'm honest and say that I feel like shit, that I'd rather be curled up in bed and unconscious, then they'll insist I go home. But I don't want to go home to an empty apartment. So I lie and say I'm fine, then feel guilty because I told Sebastian I wouldn't pretend anymore.

I know my friends mean well. I know they care. But all the special treatment only makes me feel like more of a burden than I already am. They're going so far out of their way to make sure I'm being taken care of. I swear it'd be easier for everyone if I just left so they could get on with things without constantly worrying about me.

They'd totally be better off without you holding them back.

My chest pangs at the thought, but I push it away. I can't dwell on it. I'll start spiraling if I do.

Santino's the only one who's treating me like a normal human being. He teases me and jokes around with me. He's not asking if I need to take a break every five minutes or offering to bring me endless bottles of water.

He's got this really subtle way of checking in on me. Just a hand to my waist or back or arm and then he waits for me to meet his gaze. He cocks a questioning eyebrow and if I'm okay, I nod. If I'm not, I won't, and he always seems to know exactly what I need without me telling him. A silly comment that brings a smile to my face. Helping himself to a seat so I don't feel too conspicuous when I sit down next to him.

He's my lifeline, the one thing keeping me from floating away and drowning. The only source of air that keeps me from suffocating.

"Places!" Sebastian calls out. We've already been at the tailor for a couple hours, shooting Noel's and Sebastian's fittings and now we're switching to Bellamy and Santino.

Sebastian wanted the group split into two so it would look like two separate fittings. Kind of like how a bride and groom aren't supposed to see each other's outfits before the wedding.

Noel's outfit wasn't even really a tux. He had on this black corset with a burgundy-colored lace overlay and wide-legged pants. As his best man, Sebastian wore a simpler black suit. Now Bellamy and Santino are hiding behind the thick curtains of the changing stalls, waiting for their big reveal.

"Roll camera!"

I hit the record button on the camera I'm holding, then give Sebastian a thumbs up.

"Action!"

Bellamy and Santino shout a couple lines that Sebastian's scripted for them, then the dark purple crushed velvet curtains are pushed back and they step out.

I'm watching the scene through the camera's viewscreen, making sure the framing and focus are good. But the second Santino comes into the frame, I forget about the camera entirely.

He looks so good.

His suit hugs his body like a glove. The color is

supposedly called champagne, but the fabric looks like it's been shot through with gold thread. It picks up on the golden specks in his eyes, making them sparkle and glow. The white shirt underneath is open at the collar, exposing Santino's throat, his collarbones, the top of his chest, and a hint of chest hair. There's a silk burgundy handkerchief tucked into the breast pocket of his jacket.

The pants are almost indecently tight, showing off his thick thighs and muscled calves, the hem hitting right at his ankles. On his feet are burgundy leather sneakers, polished to a sheen.

My dick's been in a coma since we filmed our scene, even with the skin-on-skin contact when we cuddle, even while naked and wet in the shower. At most, there's been a little heat in my stomach, spreading warmth through my body. Now, though, my breath catches in my chest and parts of my brain that have been dormant for months spark back to life.

Santino is a very attractive man. He steps up onto the platform in front of the three-sided mirror and the tailor tugs on the jacket and the pants to test their fit. The spotlight above him washes away any imperfections, leaving him glowing and exquisite.

I can't tear my eyes away from him. I don't even know what Bellamy's wearing, and honestly, I don't care.

I catch Santino's gaze through the reflection in the mirror. He adjusts the gold cuff links on the French cuffs and smirks at me like he knows exactly what's going through my mind.

I gulp and drop my chin to my chest. I shouldn't be perving on him—not in the middle of a shoot when I'm supposed to be focused on the cameras. Certainly not when I'm mentally ill and unstable.

He probably thinks I'm gross. Compromised. Crazy. He doesn't want a total nutcase ogling him. What a violation.

You're a sick pervert.

I wince at the voice as my skin crawls with the feeling of dirt and filth.

That's why he's leaving.

I gasp silently. I don't actually know if he's leaving. He hasn't said. I've just ignored the fact that there's a clock ticking on our time together. But the voice is right—if he's staying, why hasn't he told me? We're getting close to finishing the documentary. Why leave it up in the air? Maybe he hasn't decided yet. Or maybe he has, but he doesn't want to tell me in case I freak out on him.

Because you're a freak.

I don't want him to go. I don't know what I'll do if he leaves. He's the one thing keeping me tethered to this side of sanity and who knows how far I'll spiral if he's not here to stop it. The darkness will consume me. The voice will break my mind. No one will be able to help me then. Not my friends. Not the professionals. No one.

Who says they can help you now?

How did I ever live without Santino by my side? Falling asleep beside me. Waking up next to me. Holding me when my world is coming apart. He's become a necessary, essential part of my existence and if I don't have him, there's no point in existing anymore either.

Just put yourself out of your misery already.

My heart is in my throat as I try to keep my hands from shaking. I stare at the little markings on the dials and buttons of the camera, not blinking until my vision blurs and my eyes sting with dryness. Fear grips my chest so tight, it feels like someone has cut it open and my organs are falling out.

I try to swallow around the panic tearing through me. We're still in the middle of a take. I can't drop everything and run. Sebastian will realize he's made a mistake letting me come back. He'll send me home and I'll never hear from anyone ever again.

I keep my head down, waiting for Sebastian to yell, "Cut!" The second he does, I set the camera down and bolt for the bathroom.

You're such a loser. A failure. A deadbeat.

They're all waiting to get rid of you.

They're going to pawn you off to a shrink and wash their hands of you.

You're a burden they never asked for.

You're a waste of space, a deadbeat.

You have nothing to live for.

You're better off dead.

I flip the deadbolt on the door and sag against it. I can't breathe. My vision goes black around the edges. I push the heels of my hands into my eyes. I try to scream, but no sound comes out. Just emptiness. Nothingness. An echoing cavern of silence.

I'm tired. Just so tired.

So give up.

Tired of fighting. Tired of trying. Tired of staying strong and pushing through. Tired of hoping things will get better when they never do.

Just give up.

I'm afraid it'll get worse. That I'm a lost cause. That there's no cure, and even if there is, it won't work on me.

Give up.

I want to. I want to give up and end it. So I'll stop hurting, stop being in pain. The darkness and the voice can't get to me when I'm dead. Everyone will be relieved. It will solve all our problems.

"Hayden?" Santino raps his knuckles on the other side of the door. "You in there?"

I jump, relief and shame swirling inside me. He came for me. He noticed I was missing and came searching for me. Again. Because I keep fucking up. Because I keep needing to be saved.

"Hayden? Are you okay?"

I stifle a sob. I'm not okay. I need help. But how do I ask for help I don't deserve?

CHAPTER
TWENTY-TWO

SANTINO

"Hayden? Babe? Can you let me in?" I try to keep my voice steady and calm, even though I want to pound on the door and demand he open the damn thing.

Hayden had been doing okay for most of the day. I mean, not great, not by a long shot, but he'd been managing. He was present and engaged, not disconnecting from the group and drifting off on his own.

But that all changed in a second. I have no idea what happened and I'm not even sure how I knew. One moment, I was getting good vibes from him, and the next, I wasn't.

He wouldn't make eye contact with anyone. His body language was all tense and jerky. He was *this close* to chewing a hole through his bottom lip.

But we were in the middle of a take and I didn't want to interrupt everything. It would've drawn too much attention when he'd already been bristling over everyone treating him with kid gloves.

Then he ran away and locked himself in the bathroom.

What the fuck, Hayden. Let me the fuck inside.

"Please, babe? I just want to make sure you're okay."

Silence. Nothing. Fuck this. I'll just ask the store manager for the goddamn key.

The lock flips. I grab the doorknob and twist before he can lock it again. The door slides open easily and I slip inside.

Hayden is crouched on the floor, back against a wall, hands gripping fistfuls of hair. The backward baseball cap he was wearing is lying upside down on the floor. He's taking these loud inhales and exhales like he's hyperventilating.

Oh fuck. He's having another episode. Attack. Whatever the fuck it's called.

I shut the door behind me and lock it again before moving to him. I try to pull him into my arms, but he flinches away. "Hayden? Babe?"

He shakes his head. The movement looks painful for some reason. "I can't," he says in a strained, choked voice.

What the fuck is that supposed to mean? "You can't what?"

"I can't. I just can't." He shoots to his feet and stalks to the other side of the bathroom.

It's one of those fancy places with real hand towels rolled on a plate next to the sink. There's a wing-backed armchair in the corner. And instead of piss, the room smells flowery.

Hayden bangs his head not-so-lightly against the wall when he reaches it. His knuckles are white from how hard he's ripping at his hair.

Christ. I think this is the worst I've ever seen him. Worse than the park. Worse than cake-tasting day.

Maybe he shouldn't have come today. Maybe this was too much for him. But there's no way I would've left him at home by himself either. Who knows what would've happened if he was all alone while the rest of us were here.

I should've stayed home with him. Yeah, that's what I should've done. I should've told Sebastian we needed to reschedule and stayed home with Hayden until he felt better or until we could get him in to see a therapist. This is my fault. It's my fault he's spiraling now.

God fucking damnit. I wish there was something I could do. Like a magic pill or secret spell or *something*. *Anything*. It's excruciating to see Hayden like this. I didn't know it was possible to hurt for someone this badly. To feel like his suffering is my suffering. To want to bear his pain so he doesn't have to.

I approach him slowly, afraid of touching him in case he flinches again. I stop behind him, just an inch away, and carefully lean forward to rest my cheek against his shoulder. He tenses for a moment, holding himself so still. Like he doesn't know if he should accept my touch or shrug me off.

Come on, babe, don't push me away. Let me help you.

The tension eases from his body slowly. His breaths come in ragged ins and outs. My hands drift up to settle on his hips and I press my front against his back. After several long moments, he relaxes into my embrace.

We stand there as minutes tick by. I don't know what to say. I'm not sure anything I could say would make any difference. There's an entire battle playing out inside Hayden's mind and I have no idea how to help him win.

"I'm sorry," he finally says. His voice cracks with emotion.

I slide my hands from his hips around to clasp in front of his stomach. "About what?"

He shakes his head, forehead still resting on the wall. "Everything."

I want to say that he has nothing to be sorry for, that none of this is his fault. But would it matter? Would he believe me?

"We're getting you help," I promise, pouring all the tenderness and affection I feel for this man into my words, hoping it'll be enough. "You're going to get better."

"What if it doesn't work? What if I don't get better?"

I squeeze him around the middle. "It will work. You will get better. I'll make sure of it. If Sebastian's therapist isn't a good fit, then we'll find someone else. We won't stop until we find the right person."

Hayden takes a couple more labored breaths before continuing. "I'm just so tired."

"Want me to take you home? You can take a nap and get some rest. I can order something for dinner."

He shakes his head again. "I don't want to fight anymore. It's too hard. I can't do it."

He's not talking about being sleepy. He's talking about something that scares me to my very core.

"I just want to give up. Stop trying. What's the use anyway? I'm never going to get out of this."

Fear grips me, icy cold in my veins. I turn him around and he doesn't resist. He lands with an *oomph*, back against the wall, shoulders slumped, chin resting on his chest like his head is too heavy for his neck to hold up.

I bracket both sides of his face and tilt it up so he has

no choice but to look at me. The normally brilliant green of his eyes looks muddy and dull. His eyes are bloodshot and his cheeks are tear-stained. He looks like he's given up. Like he's done fighting. Like he's going to do whatever that goddamn voice in his head tells him to do.

"Babe, look at me. You can't give up. You can't stop fighting. I know it's hard. I know it feels impossible, but you can do it. I know you can. You don't have to do it on your own. You've got me. You've got all your friends. We're getting you help. You just have to hang in there a little bit longer."

He squeezes his eyes shut as a few more tears slip free of his lashes. "I don't know how much longer I can take this."

The anguish in his voice makes my own eyes sting with tears. I hate feeling so helpless. I hate that I can't whisk him away from all his demons and hide him somewhere they'll never find him.

I touch my forehead to his. "Just a little bit longer," I whisper into the small space between us.

A tortured sound escapes him. It tears through me, leaving me raw and fragile. I've never felt this way about anyone else before. Like I can only breathe if he breathes. Like my heart can only beat when his beats. Like my very existence hinges on Hayden's well-being.

I'm pretty sure I'm in love with him. I don't know what else this feeling could be. Maybe I just feel important and needed in a way I've never been before. Maybe I'm taking advantage of the guy and inserting myself into his life when he's at his most vulnerable. But I don't think it's either of those. Because deep in my heart of hearts, I truly believe that no matter how we could've met, we would've been drawn to each other. No matter what either of us is going through, we would've found comfort and solace in each other's souls. Isn't that what love is?

A soft knock sounds at the door. "Guys, everything okay in there?" It's Sebastian.

I lean back just enough to give Hayden a questioning look. Does he need more time? Is he ready to get the hell out of here?

He nods, just a small motion.

"Yeah, we're good," I call back to Sebastian.

Hayden goes to the sink and splashes some water on his face. I grab his hat from the floor and help him reposition it on his head.

"Ready?"

His one shoulder rises and falls, the movement so dejected I can't stand it. Without thinking, I lift my chin, push onto my toes and plant a quick kiss on the corner of his mouth. He blinks in surprise, like he doesn't understand why I would want to kiss him. What I can't understand is why I haven't been kissing him more. I should've been kissing him non-stop since our scene. I should've been showing him how much I want him, how much I would hurt if he wasn't here.

Hayden's hands come to my waist and he closes the distance between us. I sigh into the kiss as tingles spread across my cheeks and my scalp, then down my arms. I press myself against him, heat pooling in my groin.

I love this man. That's it. I've decided. With every cell in my body, with every breath in my lungs. I love his vulnerability and his beauty in the midst of his brokenness. I love how he nerds out over books. I love how he likes cooking from scratch. I love his quiet brightness, how much he shines even when he never seeks the spotlight.

When we break the kiss, there's still so much sadness in his eyes, so much defeat in the line of his mouth. Worry eats away at me as I run my fingers over his forehead, cheeks, jaw, trying to erase that look from his face. He can't give up. He has so much to live for. He needs to keep fighting.

Hayden reaches up and takes my hands by the wrists. One at a time, he plants kisses on my palms.

"Hayden." My voice breaks when I say his name. I don't want to lose him. Not when I've just found him. We haven't had enough time together.

A knock at the door again. "You guys coming out any time soon?" Sebastian calls.

Hayden drops his chin to his chest with an air of resignation that I don't like. As he takes a step toward the door, I grab his hand and intertwine our fingers. Clutching it tightly, I press myself against his arm, wrapping my other hand around his bicep and holding it to my chest. I'm not letting go of him. I don't care what he says or what happens when we walk outside. I'm not ever letting him go.

Hayden opens the door and Sebastian gives us both quick, assessing looks.

"Everything alright?"

Neither of us responds. I'm not alright and Hayden definitely isn't either. We stare at Sebastian in silence and I guess that's enough of an answer for him.

Out in the dressing room, everything's already packed up and stacked in neat piles. Bellamy and Noel are standing together, gazing into each other's eyes, as if no one else exists in the whole wide world. The love emanating from them is thick and sickeningly sweet.

I know the moment Hayden clocks them because he stiffens, his hand tightening in mine. I mean, yeah, Bellamy and Noel are like, obnoxiously in love with each other. But the way Hayden turns sharply away feels like more than just annoyance with their public display of affection. It's more like he's disgusted or offended. He heads straight for the store's main entrance and by the time we get there, he's shaking, breathing hard, wound up with tension.

"Hey, bro," I call to Sebastian. "I'm taking Hayden home."

"Cool. Thanks," Sebastian calls back.

The summer heat hits us as we step out onto the sidewalk, but it doesn't help with Hayden's shaking. If anything, his breathing gets more labored with the heavy, humid air.

I'm quick to find a cab that will take us home and when we slide into the backseat, Hayden slumps low, wrapping his arms around his middle. I loop my arm around his shoulders and pull him to me. He resists for a moment, like he doesn't want the comfort I'm offering, but then he melts into my side.

I press a kiss to the top of his head. You're not getting rid of me that easily, babe. If you can't fight anymore, then Imma fight for you.

CHAPTER
TWENTY-THREE

HAYDEN

He only kissed you because he felt bad for you. It was a pity kiss.

You'll never have what Noel and Bellamy have. What Rhys and Angel have. What Sebastian and Christian have.

Why would Santino want you? Why would he want a loser with a defective dick?

The voice is loud in my ear the entire way home, dismantling and destroying the spark of joy I felt when Santino kissed me. I'm not allowed to have good things. I don't deserve to have good things—and Santino is the very best thing I've ever come across in my life.

Santino won't let go of me. Not in the car. Not as he tries to unlock the door with one hand. Not when we get inside and stop in the middle of the living room.

I'm torn between wanting to burrow myself deeper into him and shoving him away. If I can't have him, it would be better to lose him now before I get even more attached than I already am, right? It would hurt less if I choose to distance myself rather than have him ripped from my hands.

But I'm weak. I'm a coward. I'm not brave enough to let him go. And yet, I know that if I hold on too tightly, he'll slip through my fingers anyway. Because that's how the world works. The more I want something, the more likely I'll lose it.

Like he did in the bathroom at the tailor shop, Santino runs his fingers over my face. My eyes flutter closed at the gentle, reverent touch. Why is he doing this? Why is he being so perfect? Why is he making it so difficult for me to step away from him?

He steps in close and presses his body against mine. Warmth spreads from my front through the rest of my body, soothing, calming, irresistible. It disassembles my resolve one piece at a time until I'm nothing more than sensations, desires, want.

When his lips touch mine, I give in to my selfishness and take whatever he's offering. All of it. For as long as it's available.

My hands float up to his waist as his lips part for me. Our tongues dance and his warmth infuses all the nooks and crannies hidden deep inside me, filling me up until I'm overflowing. It soothes all the cuts and bruises I've sustained over the past several months and the relief brings bittersweet tears to my eyes.

I pour everything I feel into the kiss. All of my gratitude and appreciation. All of my affection and care. Santino saw me when no one else did. He offered me comfort and safety without being asked. He is the light in my darkness, the lifeline keeping me from drowning.

Warmth pools in my groin and my dick stirs, but

doesn't harden. I'm turned on, but my body still doesn't want to cooperate.

He drops his head back with a whimper as I lick my way down his neck, chasing that spicy cinnamon flavor. He arches against me and his bulging erection presses against my hip. Feeling the evidence of his arousal gives me a degree of satisfaction. At least I know I can make him feel good. At least I know I can bring him pleasure.

Santino takes my hand and leads me to his room where we silently undress. We're not rushed. There's no reason to hurry. Time stretches out before us and I want to savor and memorize every single second.

He's already hard when he pushes his underwear down. As he straightens, he steps into the afternoon sun filtering in through the window. It lights him up from behind, making him glow like an angel sent from heaven. The air shimmers around him and he shines.

He takes my hand again and we climb onto the bed together, lying down side by side. Our heads are on one pillow, noses touching. Our arms and legs are all tangled up together. His skin is scalding hot against mine and I revel in the heat.

We kiss. Make out. Slow and lazy. Tasting every corner of the other's mouth. Until we're both breathless and boneless and quivering with desire.

Santino slips his hand between our bodies. It slides down, fingers exploring until they wrap around my semi. I grasp his wrist, knowing what he wants to do and also knowing it won't work. This is as hard as I've been able to get on my own in a while. And I've only been able to get this far because of Santino.

"You don't have to," I murmur against his lips.

"I want to try," he murmurs back. "But only if you're okay with it."

I don't know if I'm okay with it. I just don't want him to be disappointed when it doesn't work. But he wants to try and I'll never say no to Santino.

He pushes me onto my back and like he did during our video, he starts licking and kissing his way down my body. It feels good. It feels great. My dick stirs, valiantly trying to get hard, but it doesn't.

I hiss when Santino takes me into his mouth. The heat and wetness are incredible and I want so very much for my dick to cooperate. But no matter how wonderful it feels, my cock stays stubbornly soft.

I run my fingers through his thick, lush hair, loving how silky it feels threading through my fingers. He moans when I rake my blunt nails across his scalp. The vibrations send a shudder of pleasure through me. This would be perfect if only…

Eventually, I tug on his shoulder to get his attention. His face is wet with spit, his lips red from our kisses and his very thorough blowjob.

"I'm sorry," he says, lying down next to me again.

"Don't be sorry. That felt really good." I kiss his mouth, his chin, his cheeks.

"Yeah?" he asks, voice laced with concern.

"Yeah, it felt great. Exactly how it's supposed to feel. Everything except… you know."

He looks chagrined, like he might want to keep trying. But it's my turn to play.

I push him onto his back and take a second to admire the sight before me. Dusky nipples topped with hard pebbles. Scattering of dark hair across his chest. A treasure trail that cuts down the middle of his flat stomach. A beautiful cock lying on his hip, already wet with pre-cum.

Gorgeous. Stunning.

I lower myself to worship him the way he worshiped me, leaving wet trails all over his body. I spend long minutes torturing each nipple until Santino's squirming and shouting profanities loud enough for the neighbors to hear.

"Fuck, Hayden. Fuck. Christ, that feels good. Ah! Yes! Fuck!"

He nearly flies off the bed when I finally get to his cock. I tease it with the tip of my tongue, flicking that sensitive spot right under the head. I dip into his slit to taste more of his slightly bitter pre-cum. I mouth at the base of his dick, close to the spot that connects to his balls.

He smells so good. The cinnamon scent is stronger down here, darker and muskier. I breathe it in, letting it fill my senses and block out every other thought, every other voice.

Santino spreads his legs as my attention shifts toward his balls and I rearrange myself between them. My tongue bathes the loose skin of his scrotum before I take a testicle into my mouth.

"Oh fuck. Oh god, your mouth is so hot. Goddammit." He keeps lifting his head to watch me, then dropping it back onto the pillow and throwing his arm over his eyes. And every time he does that, a tiny bubble tickles my stomach. He's so cute. So funny and adorable.

I move on to his taint. Smooth skin interrupted by one thick seam that I lick along, nibble on. Santino's voice rises an octave as I lave my tongue over that area, then press on it with my thumb.

He automatically lifts his legs when he senses me moving lower. To his hole. That hallowed entrance to his body. The muscle twitches like it's winking at me. Like it's begging me to lick it, stretch it, fill it. I wish I could. I wish I could sink myself so deep into Santino that I don't know where I end and he begins.

At the back of my mind, the voice starts to whisper. Just incoherent pspsps that I can't make out. I shut it down before they coalesce, diving back into Santino's body instead.

Using just the very tip of my tongue, I tease the wrinkled skin around his hole. The muscle clenches and releases at the barely there contact. Clasping the backs of his knees, Santino lifts his hips farther off the bed. "Please, Hayden. Please. Fuck me. Please."

The whispers get a little louder, but I push them away.

I fill my palms with the two globes of Santino's ass and hold him in place. Then I seal my lips around his hole and spear my tongue at the tight opening. Again and again. Unrelenting. Until he relaxes enough to let me inside.

His flavor explodes on my tongue. Dark and spicy and entirely intoxicating. I shove my tongue in as far as it'll go, searching for more. And when I can't seem to find anymore, I add a finger to the mix.

Wet with my spit, my index finger sinks slowly into Santino's body. I watch that spot where it disappears, where I can't see it anymore because it's inside Santino. I twist the finger, then curl it and listen as Santino howls.

His cursing and begging have devolved into babbling and I can't help the smile that tugs on my lips. It feels weird in my cheeks, the muscles unaccustomed to bunching in that way. I haven't really, truly smiled in so long, my face has forgotten how.

I add a second finger, alternating my fingers with my tongue. Santino can't hold still under me. His squirming is quickly escalating into thrashing. More bubbles tickle my stomach.

Adding a third finger stretches him nice and wide and Santino moans his approval.

"Yes, fuck yes. Just like that. That's perfect."

I work my fingers around, twisting and curling them until I find that bundle of nerves hidden inside him. When I press down on it, Santino almost levitates off the bed.

"Fuck! Oh fuck. Holy fucking Christ. Do that again," he demands.

A smile breaks across my face. I'm more than happy to oblige.

CHAPTER
TWENTY-FOUR

SANTINO

He's killing me. Hayden is killing me and I won't regret a single moment of it.

I don't think I've ever had my prostate played with. I would've remembered if I had. Because this is like mainlining cocaine and heroin and meth all at the same time. It's fucking euphoric.

My fingers dig painfully into the backs of my knees, not just to hold my legs up, but also to keep myself from coming too soon. I'm already inching so close to the edge, I need to do everything I can to stave it off.

Hayden's got three fingers in me. Which isn't quite as thick as his cock at full mast, but it's pretty damn close. And every time he pushes at my prostate, fireworks go off behind my eyes.

He licks a path across my taint, his tongue wiggling back and forth over the seam running down the middle, then pops my balls one at a time into his mouth for a quick suck. When he finally gets to my dick, I'm almost scared of how it'll feel.

His tongue swirls around the angry, purple head, licking up pre-cum leaking from my slit. Then he gradually feeds my cock into his mouth. So hot. So wet. The tight suction has me shaking uncontrollably.

I hit the back of his throat, but that doesn't stop him. He swallows and I slide right down. His nose is flush against my pelvis. His fingers are tapping away at my prostate. He swallows in time with the taps and the dual sensation is driving me out of my mind. No one's ever done anything like this to me before. He's ruined me for anyone else.

Hayden starts up a rhythm between his fingers and his mouth. Bobbing and thrusting and swallowing and tapping. It's a non-stop onslaught of pleasure pulsing through my body that completely scrambles my brain.

I hear someone screaming. I think that someone is me.

Just when I think I can't take anymore, Hayden rubs his thumb on my taint a few times and presses. The pressure on my prostate from another angle sends a different kind of pleasure coursing through me. Now he's coming at me from three directions and it's too much.

He thrusts his three fingers as far into my ass as they'll go, pressing on my prostate from the inside. His thumb pushes from the outside. He swallows my dick down like his throat is giving me a massage. Altogether, all at the same time, it sends me flying over the edge.

My entire body goes taut as I explode in Hayden's mouth. My vision goes white. My ears ring. Every cell lights up as pleasure rushes at me like a tidal wave.

There's no way to escape it. There's nowhere to hide. It crushes me under its intensity and I'm fucking ded.

I black out.

I'm not sure how long I'm out for, but when my brain decides to start working again, I find Hayden lying half on top of me. His face is pressed against my neck and his short, fast breaths are hot against my skin. He's tense and rigid and not in a good way.

"Babe?" I brush my fingers through his hair, trying to get a better look at his face.

He clings to me tighter, burrows even deeper.

"Babe, what's wrong?" If he's having another one of those attacks, I'm going to feel like the biggest jackass in the entire world. Here I am, getting my rocks off so hard I passed out while Hayden's struggling through a mental health episode.

"Is it the voice?" I ask, my heart sinking as he gives a few jerky nods. Guilt sits like a rock in my stomach, wiping away every last trace of pleasure still lingering in my system. I start second-guessing everything.

I shouldn't have kissed Hayden at the tailor shop. I shouldn't have kissed him when we got home. I shouldn't have pushed him to have sex. I should've stopped when he couldn't get it up. I shouldn't have let him go down on me.

"Fuck, I'm sorry," I clutch him to me, pressing kisses everywhere I can reach. Our sweat cools and I reach for the blanket to keep us warm.

My guilt morphs into anger at the unfairness of it all. Why does the darkness always seem to strike right when he's feeling good? Like it wants to give him a taste of happiness before stealing it away again. What kind of sadistic shit is that?

Why is this happening to Hayden at all? He did nothing to deserve this. He was just living his happy life, spreading joy wherever he went. He's a good person. Why did the depression pick him?

But then, there's never any logic to this type of thing. No matter how much evidence or proof there is, no matter how unreasonable the thoughts are, it's hard to argue against feelings that intense. The shit Mom used to say when she was at her worst made absolutely no sense. Even now, sometimes she'll get stuck in these loops where her fear overrides all common sense. Like being afraid she'll lose me forever…

I push the thought away. Hayden's shaking. He tries to smother the sound of his crying, but a sob or a hiccup manages to get through every once in a while. He keeps muttering, "I'm sorry. I'm so sorry," but I don't know what he could possibly be sorry for.

So I whisper back every encouraging thing I can think of. "You're good, babe. You're fine. There's nothing to be sorry for. Everything's going to be alright."

Staring up at the ceiling, I hold Hayden until his breathing gradually evens out and he falls asleep. Carefully, so I don't wake him, I ease myself out from under his lax weight.

My phone is in my shorts pocket, abandoned on the floor. I dig it out and tap a quick message to Sebastian.

SANTINO

Yo, where we at with the therapy appointment for Hayden?

SEBASTIAN

I'm working on it. Why? Did something
happen?

I mean, yeah, I had maybe the best orgasm of my life
and then Hayden fell apart on me while we were both still
naked and sweaty. That's probably TMI.

SANTINO

Just the usual. I don't know how much
longer he'll be able to go on like this.

SEBASTIAN

I'll follow up with the therapist's office, but
it might be a week or two.

A week or two? That's too long. Who knows how much
worse Hayden will get by then? And there's that constant
niggle of worry at the back of my mind—what if he takes
matters into his own hands? I can't say it out loud or even
type it in a text message. It makes it too real. But Sebastian
doesn't need me to spell it out.

SEBASTIAN

Unless you think he's going to hurt
himself?

The other option is the emergency room
and asking for a 72 hr hold.

My stomach drops as I realize what Sebastian's
saying.

SANTINO

You mean, like the psych ward? Like
straitjackets and padded walls?

SEBASTIAN

No straitjackets or padded walls. They just keep an eye on him to make sure he doesn't hurt himself.

I shake my head even though Sebastian can't see it.

SANTINO

No, we don't need that. I can keep an eye on him. I won't let him out of my sight for the next two weeks.

The three dots at the bottom of the screen bounce, then stop, then bounce again before Sebastian's message comes through.

SEBASTIAN

Your flight is next Wednesday.

My what? Oh. My flight back to San Francisco. Because, hey, I don't actually live in New York. Because I was only supposed to be here temporarily.

I guess I forgot to tell Sebastian I'm not going back. I don't know if there's room for me in The Camboy Network. Or if Sebastian even likes me enough to offer me a place. But it doesn't matter. If I'm going to be unemployed, getting by on odd jobs, I can do that just as easily here as I can in San Francisco. And New York has Hayden. San Francisco does not. In the end, it's not a hard decision at all.

SANTINO

Can you cancel the flight?

SEBASTIAN

Cancel? Not reschedule?

No, just cancel it. I think I'll stick around
for a while longer.

A split second after Sebastian's message comes through, my phone starts vibrating. A picture of Mom fills the screen and dread fills me. How am I going to tell her I'm moving to New York? How am I going to explain I'm *already in* New York?

My thumb hovers over the red Decline button to make her Future Santino's problem. But is there any point in putting this off? I've already made my decision. Nothing she says will change it. Might as well get it over with now.

With a quick glance toward Hayden to make sure he's still asleep, I swipe to accept the call with one hand and grab my discarded underwear with the other.

"Hello?" I say as I slip out of the room and close the door behind me. I hold the phone with my shoulder as I hop into my underwear.

"Tino, where are you?"

Uh… shit. Maybe I should've put her off until I came up with a good way to break the news to her. "Um, at a friend's? Why?"

"Louisa's in San Francisco today and I gave her some frozen meals to drop off for you. When will you be home?"

I scrunch my face together and stifle a groan. "Um, yeah, about that. I won't be home today."

"You're not? Why not? Where are you?"

I take a deep breath as my stomach clenches with nervousness. Here goes nothing. "I'm in New York."

The only sound that comes through the line is a commercial for toilet paper from the TV Mom always has on in the background. She's silent for so long, I hope I didn't, I don't know, give her a stroke or something.

"Hello? Mom?"

"You're where?" she asks and it's not because she didn't hear me the first time.

"New York," I say, quieter this time, voice going up at the end like it's a question.

"Why?" she demands.

"Um… for a job?" I slap a hand over my face and drop down on the couch.

"What kind of job?"

"Uh…" My mind blanks as I scramble for something plausible to say. Because I sure as hell can't tell my mother I'm doing porn. "Remember my old roommate, Bellamy? He's an actor and he's working on this, uh, documentary. And they asked me to be in it."

"Why would they ask *you* to be in it? You're not an actor."

She… has a good point. "Uh, well, it's a documentary, right? So they wanted people who actually know Bellamy." Which is totally and completely true.

Mom is silent for another second and I hold my breath. I feel like I'm waiting for the planet to explode.

"When are you coming home?"

I don't bother covering up my groan this time. "Yeah, about that. I'm, um, not."

"Not what?"

"I'm not coming home." I really want to tell her about Hayden. About how wonderful he is. About the ways he reminds me of her. About how much I love him. But I've already dropped one bombshell on her on this call and I'm not sure she'll survive two.

"Santino Antonio Baldoni, you get on a plane right this minute and come home. You hear me? Right now. On the next flight. I'm sending Dad to the airport and if you're not there, so help me god, I will go to New York myself and drag you home."

I hold my phone away from my ear as Mom shouts. Disappointment courses through me, though I don't know why. I knew this was how she'd react. Hoping otherwise was always going to end in a letdown. She'll never get it. She'll never understand.

"When did you even go to New York? How long have you been there? Have you been lying to me the whole time? I cannot believe you. Of all the selfish, irresponsible, naive things to do. Why do you always have to take such unnecessary risks? Why can't you just come home?"

My heart rate is shooting through the roof as my body starts to shake with anger. Why did she think I would lie to her? Because I knew she'd overreact! She'd get overprotective and jump to the worst-case scenario.

Her voice gets higher and louder the longer she keeps going. I can hear her getting worked up, her thoughts spinning around and around, amplifying and growing each time. A part of me feels bad—I hate causing her distress. But a bigger part of me wants to shout right back at her.

"Why are you always leaving me? Am I not a good mother? Do you not love me?"

My simmering anger completely boils over and I shoot to my feet. "Oh my god, Mom! Stop it! I'm not trying to leave you! I'm just trying to live my own life!"

"Why can't you live your life here? You want to be an actor? Fine. Be an actor here!"

"Because!" I snap my mouth shut and squeeze my eyes closed, willing my temper to behave. Getting into a shouting match with her won't make the situation any better. "Mom, please. Let me explain."

"Explain what? What is there to explain? You're leaving me. It's as simple as that."

"I'm not leaving you, Mom." I swallow around the emotions suddenly lodged in my throat. Lots of anger still, but also frustration and sadness. "I'm just trying to do something meaningful with my life, something that makes me happy. Don't you want that? Don't you want me to be happy?"

"You need to be on the other side of the country to be happy?" she snaps.

"Yes! I do!"

"You're not making any sense right now. I don't understand what you're talking about." Her voice is wobbly, like she's about to burst into tears. Guilt threads its way through my anger, but not enough to shake my resolve. I can't live my life on my mom's terms. I have to do what I need to do.

"I know you don't understand. I don't expect you to. I just…" I take a steadying breath and resign myself to this new reality with my mom. "I just wanted you to know. I'm staying in New York."

"No. No, absolutely not. I let you move to San Francisco and that is far enough. I'm not letting you move out there. I forbid it."

I'm pretty sure she's crying now, but it doesn't matter. She can forbid me all she wants, but she can't stop me. I'm a grown man. I can do what I want. "I'm sorry, Mom."

"No. No. Just wait till I tell your father about this. He'll be furious. You'll see."

"I've gotta go, Mom. I'll talk to you later."

"No! Don't you hang up on me, Tino! I'm not done talking to you!"

"Goodbye, Mom."

"This isn't over! I—"

Bracing myself, I end the call. Silence echoes loud in the living room. The only thing louder is the frantic beating of my heart. I never wanted to upset her. I never wanted things to spiral out of control like that. But what choice did I have?

"You're not leaving?"

I spin around to find Hayden standing in the doorway. His hair is a mess and his eyes are still droopy from sleep. I want to drag him back to bed, lose myself in him, and forget that the rest of the world exists.

And then I realize, he's just heard every word I said.

CHAPTER
TWENTY-FIVE

HAYDEN

He's not leaving. That's what he said on the phone to his mom. He's staying in New York.

Santino's grin is wide and lopsided. "Uh, yeah, I told Sebastian to cancel my flight. So I guess that means…" He lifts both hands, then lets them drop to his thighs. "You're stuck with me." His grin fades as a touch of uncertainty bleeds into his expression. "Is that okay?" he asks more quietly.

My eyes prickle with tears and I don't know why. This is what I wanted, what I hoped for. So why am I crying over getting something I want?

Santino closes the distance between us with two steps. "Hey, hey." He cups my cheeks and wipes at the stray tears with his thumbs. "What's wrong? Do you not want me to stay? I can move out if you want your own space—"

"No!" The single word bursts from somewhere in the middle of my chest. So loud Santino blinks a few times at its force. "I mean, no. I don't want you to move out. I want you to stay."

His grin comes back, goofy and full of joy. Just seeing it soothes the constant pain eating away at my insides and I find myself smiling back at him.

"You're wonderful, you know that?" Santino's words grate on my skin like rough sandpaper.

I shake my head. I'm not wonderful. I'm fucked up and defective. Selfish and manipulative. A burden. A nuisance. I make life harder for all my friends. If he stays with me, I'll make life unbearable for Santino too. I'm a mess and he should run as far away as he possibly can.

"Yes, you are." Santino nods. "I don't care what that fucking voice is saying in your head. You're the most wonderful person I've ever met."

I'm still shaking my head and tears are trailing down my cheeks as I fall into Santino, letting him pull me tightly against him. My arms wrap around his waist. My face is buried in the crook of his neck. He whispers kind words that peel off layer after layer of skin.

"You are so smart. I don't know anyone else who reads as much as you do."

But I haven't read a book in weeks.

"You're so talented in the kitchen. You cook better than my mom. Better than the chefs at the restaurant."

I'm cooking less than half as much as I used to.

"You're incredibly selfless. You put all your friends before yourself. Even when you shouldn't."

That's not true. I'm selfish. I've been using him. If I was selfless, I should be pushing him away so he doesn't waste his time with me."

"You're really fucking hot. Like one of those Greek gods. Which one is the really hot one?"

"Adonis," I mumble into his neck.

"Yeah, that guy. You're Adonis."

Except my dick won't get hard unless I take drugs.

"Want me to keep going?"

I shake my head, but Santino doesn't listen.

"Not only are you hot, but you're adorable too. Like a puppy. Your heart is so pure and all you want is to be happy and full of joy. You're incredibly responsible and reliable. Sebastian always turns to you first whenever he needs help. You're so supportive of your friends, always hyping them up to other people."

The tears flow as Santino's words strip me bare. I'm raw and exposed with no defenses left to protect me. I want to be all the things Santino's described. I used to be all those things. But I don't know if I'll ever be able to find my way back to that version of myself. Old Hayden might not exist anymore. He might be lost forever.

Santino guides me to the couch and helps me sit down. "Hold on, just one sec." He rushes to the bedroom and comes running back with all the blankets in his arms. "I didn't want us to get cold," he explains as he lays the blankets over me.

We cuddle on the couch until my tears slow and stop. I'm exhausted, but I don't want to sleep. I feel like I've been sleeping for days and it's only making me more tired. I rest my head on Santino's shoulder. He tilts his head to rest it against mine. Together, we stare across the living room at nothing.

"Is everything okay with your mom?" I ask, remembering his phone call.

Santino heaves a sigh. "No, everything is super not okay. She thinks I don't love her and that's why I'm moving so far away from her. But..." He pauses and nuzzles the top of my head. When he speaks again, his voice is laced with remorse rather than anger. "She's probably just scared. Both my sisters live within ten minutes of my parents. They've never had a kid who up and left and my mom doesn't know how to handle it."

"Will she get over it?" Because my family couldn't care less who stayed or who left and they certainly wouldn't get upset over it.

"I hope so. I should text my sisters and tell them what happened. They can check in on her in case she has a relapse."

"A relapse?" That doesn't sound good. A thread of guilt tightens around me at the possibility that I've caused Santino's mom to succumb to her depression again.

"It's not really a relapse. That's just what we call it. It's more like she gets stuck inside her own head and she can't snap out of it to see reason."

His description lands with painful accuracy. "Like me."

Santino pauses for a beat before speaking again. "Is that what it feels like for you?"

I don't know exactly how it feels, except it hurts. I've never quite been able to put it into words. "Kind of."

Santino presses a kiss to the top of my head. "We'll find a way to get you out. I promise."

I want to believe him. But I'm afraid that's a promise he won't be able to keep.

———

"Sebby said he got you that appointment with his therapist?" Rhys asks from under his big floppy hat.

We're sitting on a picnic blanket in the middle of the park. Noel is on the other side of Rhys. Angel and Christian are at the barbecue, grilling up sausages and hamburgers. Bellamy, Sebastian, and Santino are throwing around a frisbee. Normally, I'd be up there with them, helping with the food or running after the frisbee. Normally, I would be smiling and laughing and having a good time. But I don't feel like it today.

I didn't even feel like coming to the picnic at all. But I didn't want to be at home when all of my friends were out having fun. Maybe that's not a good reason for coming, but it got me here.

Old Hayden loved picnics. He loved being in the park with the sun shining and the grass freshly cut. He loved seeing all the people of the city out and about, living their lives. I still like those things too, I guess. They just don't hold the same appeal they used to. They don't fill me with a sense of freedom and joy anymore.

"Yeah," I say absentmindedly to Rhys while my gaze drifts to Santino, who jumps for the frisbee. He grazes it with his fingertips, but doesn't manage to get his hand around it.

It's been a couple days since that call with his mom. He's been on the phone a few more times with his sisters. His mom is still upset and angry, though he says she hasn't fallen into depression again. That's good, I guess. But it doesn't lessen the guilt I feel for my part in the whole thing. If I wasn't keeping Santino for myself, his mom and the rest of his family wouldn't be going through all that.

Everything bad that happens is your fault.

"Do you want me to go with you?" Rhys continues.

In the distance, Santino laughs as Bellamy stumbles and crashes on the grass. He holds out his hand and helps Bellamy to his feet, giving him a clap on the shoulder before they take up their places again.

"Um, no, it's okay. Santino's coming with me."

Rhys cocks his head in confusion. "I thought he was going home before then."

"Didn't you hear?" Noel jumps in, sounding smug. "The dude canceled his flight."

Rhys furrows his brow. "He did?"

"Our little Hayden whipped out his magic dick and now the guy can't get enough."

Rhys gives Noel the middle finger while casting him a dirty look. "Don't be an asshole, asshole."

"What?" Noel laughs with a self-satisfied smirk. "I've seen his dong. It's the size of a fucking horse. Who wouldn't fall for that thing?"

My chin drops to my chest and I twist a blade of grass until it rips between my fingers. My dick isn't magic. My dick doesn't even work.

Why the fuck would Santino want to stick around for a cripple?

"Oh, shut up already. Nobody asked you." Rhys slaps Noel on the arm, but Noel shrugs it off. "Don't listen to him, Denny. He doesn't know what he's talking about."

I try to breathe through the vise tightening around my chest. Noel doesn't know about my deformity. He's just being an asshole for the sake of it. He wouldn't make that joke if he knew what was wrong.

He would laugh in your face. He would be disgusted.

I rip another clump of grass from the ground.

"Food's ready!" Angel calls out, bringing over a big covered platter from the barbecue.

I glance up just in time to watch Santino wind up and fling his arm out, sending the plastic disc flying through the air, aimed directly at Sebastian. Sebastian catches it easily, spins around, and tosses it toward Bellamy. Bellamy dives for it, snatching it right before it touches the ground. Hopping to his feet, he jogs back to us with Santino and Sebastian trailing behind him.

Santino heads straight for me, plopping down on the ground next to me.

"Oh my god, I'm starving," he says, eyeing the food hungrily.

The sausages are piled in a pyramid on the plate, each toasted with just a little char and glistening with grease. The hamburger patties are stacked into neat towers. I can smell the cooked meat. But it doesn't smell good to me. It doesn't smell like anything.

My appetite's taken a nose dive in the past week and even though Santino's been really good about reminding me to eat, I haven't been able to swallow down much. I'm just not hungry. It's starting to show. I look a tad gaunt in the mirror and my clothes are hanging a little too much off my frame.

I reach for the stack of plates and grab two for me and Santino. I feel like I'm moving through water as I fill the plates with Greek salad, handfuls of berries, and small mountains of chips. Then I make up a sausage on a hot dog bun for Santino and a hamburger for me.

I won't be able to finish all this, and actually, I feel a little nauseous just looking at it. But I force myself to pick at the plate. I force myself to chew and swallow even though every bite tastes like ash.

Santino casts me an approving smile right before he takes a huge bite out of his sausage. A mix of ketchup and mustard oozes out the corner of his mouth and his tongue darts out to lick it up.

"Mmm, this is so good," he moans around a mouthful of food. His eyes are closed as he chews, like this is the best meal he's ever had in his life.

A yearning grows inside me at the sight of him. At how easily he's able to enjoy the simple things. I want to be like that too. I want to shake off this heaviness weighing me down. I want to laugh with my friends while sitting in a park, having lunch on a beautiful summer day. I don't want to feel this empty, hollowness anymore. I don't want to hear the voice in my head all the time.

Santino's eyes flutter open and he catches me watching. "What? Do I have something on my face?" He wipes his mouth with the back of his hand.

The move is so innocent, so unselfconscious, it makes me smile. Just a small one. I've been trying to do that more often. Just to make sure my cheeks don't forget what it feels like. I shake my head. "No, you're perfect."

Santino pauses for a moment. Did I mean perfect as in he doesn't have food on his face? Or did I mean perfect because he is actually perfect in every conceivable way? I don't know what I meant when the words slipped off my tongue, but now I'm leaning toward the latter.

CHAPTER
TWENTY-SIX

SANTINO

Hayden and I were supposed to film our second video together, but Sebastian ended up rescheduling it. He didn't say why, but I'm pretty sure he wanted to wait until Hayden was able to get in and see that therapist of his first. And since I'm not going back to San Francisco just yet, there's no rush.

So instead, we're filming the bachelor party scenes for the documentary—in Atlantic City.

Noel's pretty pissed about it, actually. He wanted to go to Miami or Cabo or something like that. But Sebastian vetoed those ideas, saying they were too far away and we're on a strict timeline and budget.

I don't know what Noel's complaining about. Atlantic City looks pretty cool to me. We're at this really nice resort that's right on the water. The room Hayden and I are sharing has a super dope view of the ocean. Sebastian's got a whole itinerary planned for us—hanging out by the pool, couples massages for Noel and Bellamy in the spa, fancy dinner at the hotel's rooftop restaurant, then partying at a gay strip club.

"Miami would be so much nicer. It's not *that* far away," Noel grumbles as he pouts on his lounge chair. We've taken over a whole row of them by the outdoor pool.

"Oh my god, will you please shut up!" Rhys exclaims as he rubs sunscreen on Angel's back.

"I'm just saying," Noel continues. "I don't mind paying for it. It's my bachelor party, isn't it? Shouldn't I get to go where I want?"

Sitting on the chair next to him, Bellamy reaches over and pats Noel on the shoulder. "There, there, honey. We can go to Miami some other time. It's not like you've never been before."

"That's not the point." Noel glares at him and manages to pout even harder.

I have zero interest in getting involved with that argument. Instead, my gaze settles on Hayden, who's setting up the GoPros so he can hand them out to everyone.

He's wearing baggy shorts and a baggy t-shirt that hang off his body more than they should. The baseball cap he's wearing is pulled low over his eyes. He's been pretty quiet during the trip so far, only really talking when someone asks him a question. He doesn't make eye contact with anyone and always hangs back at the edge of the group.

Honestly? He looks miserable. But I don't know. Maybe that's the best we can hope for, considering. I mean, I hate thinking that, but at least he hasn't had one of those episodes where he spirals out of control and breaks down in tears. That's good, right? He's moving slower than he normally would, like every task is way more difficult than it should be, but it could be so much worse.

I can tell he's trying, forcing a smile when he needs to, pretending he's having a good time. This is Noel and Bellamy's bachelor party and we're supposed to be having fun and celebrating. He doesn't want to steal attention away from his friends or ruin the trip for everyone.

If anybody asked me, I'd say Noel was doing a better job of ruining the mood than Hayden. But no one asked me, so whatever.

We spend the next hour or so at the pool. Rhys and Noel stay on the lounge chairs and bicker, while Bellamy, Angel, Christian, and I play keep-up with a beach ball in the water. We've each got GoPros strapped to our wrists and Sebastian and Hayden circle around us on the deck with their cameras.

It's fun. I have a good time. Mostly. It's hard to truly enjoy myself when I'm worried about Hayden. I don't want to be overbearing, though. He'll just feel more like a burden if I hover too much. So I keep an eye on him and try to check in without being too obvious.

On the deck, Sebastian checks the time, then calls it. "We're good here. Noel and Bellamy need to get to their massage appointment. The rest of you can chill until dinner."

Hayden grabs an armful of towels and hands them out as we climb from the pool. I put my hand on the last one, but I don't take it until he meets my gaze.

I don't ask if he's okay. I can already tell he's not. He holds himself like he's bracing for impact, tension radiating off his body. He's chewing a hole through his bottom lip. His eyes have a slightly vacant look in them, like he's not a hundred percent here.

I need to get him back to our room so he can rest.

I help him gather all the GoPros and stuff them into the equipment cases. Then the second Sebastian gives us the okay, I take Hayden's hand and drag him toward the elevators.

When we get to our room, Hayden stumbles toward the bed and collapses. He curls up on his side, a pillow hugged to his chest. His breaths are coming hard and fast, like he can't quite get enough oxygen in his lungs.

Gently, I reach for the one sandal that's still dangling off his foot and set it on the floor where the other one fell off. Then I pull at the duvet so I can fold one half over his body. He sighs as I tuck the thick covers around him, turning him into a burrito.

"Sorry," he murmurs as his breathing slows to something closer to normal.

Sitting next to him, I slide his hat off and run my fingers through his matted curls. His eyes drift shut as I pet him.

My heart aches for him. So much it feels like my chest might crack open. I wish there was more I could do. I wish we didn't have to wait so long to see the therapist. It's so hard to see him suffering like this. And if it's this hard for me to watch him, I can't imagine how much harder it is for him to actually live through it.

Leaning down, I plant a kiss on his head. "I'm gonna shower, 'kay? I'll be real quick."

He nods silently and I rush into the bathroom to take the fastest shower in my life.

Hayden is in the exact same position when I come back

out and I climb onto the bed with him, curling myself around his back. He snuggles down into me with a sigh. Gradually, the tension melts away and I think he falls asleep.

But he hasn't. "What about your apartment?" he asks after an extended silence.

I don't understand what he means at first. My apartment is his apartment… unless he wants me to get my own place in New York? My stomach sinks for a moment at the thought of Hayden not wanting to live with me. Then it clicks. "You mean my apartment in San Francisco?"

He nods. "And all your stuff."

I haven't really given it much thought, but what really is there to think about? "I'll give up the apartment. There's a new guy in Bellamy's old room, so he can take over the lease. And I don't have that much stuff. Most of the furniture belongs to the landlord."

He falls silent again for a few minutes. "What about your family?"

He means my mom. Guilt sits like a rock around my neck every time I think about her. I haven't spoken to her since that day. My sisters say she just needs time, that she'll come around. I hope she will, but I'm not optimistic.

"Will you miss them?"

"Yeah, I will." And I'm sure they'll miss me too. But people live away from their families all the time. It doesn't mean they don't love each other or anything like that.

"What will you miss most?"

A pang of nostalgia hits me. As much as I gripe about them sometimes, I really do love hanging out with them. My cousins were some of my best friends growing up. My nieces and nephews are hilarious. I'm glad I'm from a tight-knit family. I just wish I had a little more breathing room.

A smile tugs on my lips as memories pop into my head. "Oh man, our family get-togethers are legendary. My parents have this industrial-sized barbecue and my dad really likes to do pulled pork and beef brisket."

Hayden shifts, turning on his back so he can peer at me through his blond lashes. "Is that why you love meat so much?"

I laugh out loud. "Yeah, it probably is."

Hayden's lips curl into a smile and for the first time since we left New York, it actually looks genuine. His eyes crinkle a bit at the edges and the greens of his irises are a touch brighter.

"What else?"

It doesn't take much thinking. "My mom's potato salad is to die for. I swear to god she puts crack in it or something, it's so good. And my sister Paola is like, a master baker. She does cakes, pastries, pies—basically anything that goes in an oven."

My stomach gurgles loudly. Hayden and I stare at each other for a split second before both bursting out in laughter.

He ducks his chin, nearly disappearing into the duvet he's wrapped up in. The laughter clears out some of the heavy darkness weighing him down and suddenly, he looks a little lighter, a little more alert.

Hayden's laughter might be my favorite thing about him. I love how it sounds, low and rumbly, like a warm hug I want to wrap around myself. I love how it snaps him out of his spirals. I love how it lifts him up and makes him shine so brightly.

"You're hungry?" he asks.

I shrug. "Meh. I can wait till dinner. Are *you* hungry?"

Hayden shakes his head. I'm not surprised. He's never hungry these days. He doesn't eat much of the food I put in front of him. I know he's trying, but he's still losing weight.

We lay in bed together until it's time to go to dinner. Dressing in silence, we move around each other in the bedroom and bathroom like we've been doing this dance together our whole lives. The little touches on the waist as we pass each other. When we catch each other's gaze in the mirror. The way he hands me the deodorant right when I need it, without me asking.

It's so simple. So normal. So domestic. But it fills me up with this deep, rich happiness I've never felt before. Like this is where I was always meant to be. Like this is where I belong. With Hayden. Sharing a life with him.

I want to tell him I love him. So badly sometimes I can physically feel the words on my tongue. So badly my chest feels tight with all the love just waiting to pour out. I don't know if it's the right time yet. I'm not sure how he'll take it when he's still struggling so much. I want to wait until we get a diagnosis for him, until we have a plan of treatment in place and we're not wandering blindly in the dark.

Until then, I'll show him I love him with every word and every touch. With every moment of silence I spend holding him and every silly joke I crack to tease a smile out of him.

At the door of our hotel room, we pause.

"Ready?" I ask Hayden.

He's chewing on his bottom lip. I reach up and tug it out from between his teeth with my thumb. Leaning in, I plant a kiss on the poor, abused lip.

I love you. I think in my head as loudly as I possibly can. Maybe he'll hear it somehow. Maybe he'll feel it. Maybe my love can help heal some of the brokenness he carries around inside.

CHAPTER
TWENTY-SEVEN

HAYDEN

I didn't really want to go to dinner. What I wanted was to stay in the hotel room with Santino and listen to him talk more about his family. But Sebastian needed me to work the cameras and I couldn't say no. And besides, everyone else would be there.

The hotel restaurant is nice. Everyone's all dressed up. The food is really fancy. Everything looks great on the viewscreen of the camera I'm using, and honestly, concentrating on that might be the only thing getting me through the night. If I'm too preoccupied with making sure the footage is decent, then my brain can't go rogue and spiral out of control. If I stay focused on the task at hand, there's not enough room in my head for the voice to intrude.

The other thing helping me get through the night is Santino. He keeps glancing over at me when he should be paying attention to the scene. He casts small smiles in my direction, like we're sharing little secrets just between the two of us. I might have more footage of Santino than anyone else, but I don't care.

Sebastian stands from the table and waves me over. "Can you get a shot of Bellamy from this angle?" He shows me what he wants with his arm as a guide.

I line up the shot, then let Sebastian check it on the viewscreen.

"Perfect." He slips back in his chair. "Action."

At the end of the table, Bellamy stands and clinks the back of a knife against his champagne glass. A hush falls over the group. Gazing lovingly at Noel, Bellamy launches into the script Sebastian wrote for him.

He talks about how he and Noel are such an unlikely couple and how he was just as surprised as everyone else when their rivalry turned into love. He talks about how well they complement each other and how they help each other become better people. He talks about how he can't imagine his life without Noel in it.

If I hadn't already known Sebastian scripted the speech for him, I would've thought Bellamy was speaking off the cuff. The love shining in his eyes is so potent. The emotion in his voice is so visceral. There's no way anyone can watch his speech and not think he and Noel are crazy in love.

A pang of longing hits me in the chest. I want what they have—so much it feels like a hunger gnawing at my insides. At the same time, a powerful, toxic anger simmers, threatening to boil over. I'm not even sure what I'm angry at, just that there's this ball of ugliness lodged in my stomach that hates everything it sees. And over everything is this filthy, disgusting blanket of sadness and self-pity.

Why did this happen to me? What did I do to deserve this? Is this karma or something? Am I really such a bad person?

Out of the corner of my eye, I see Santino watching me. I don't know if he can read the thoughts running through my mind. Or maybe he sees how my shoulders are hiked up to my ears, how my hands are shaking, how I'm struggling to breathe.

It takes everything I have to keep the damn camera in focus and pointed at Bellamy until he lifts the champagne glass for a toast. The second Sebastian yells cut, my arms fall to my sides and I almost drop the camera on the ground.

Santino's next to me in a flash, taking the camera from my hands and safely depositing it on the table.

"Sorry, I..." I run my fingers through my hair. I don't even know what I'm apologizing for anymore. For ruining the shot? For not being able to complete such a simple task? For distracting him from the scene? For being a giant pain in the ass who needs his hand held every fucking second of every fucking day?

God, what is wrong with me? Why am I like this?

The darkness rolls in on menacing, thundering clouds. It swirls around my head, obscuring my vision and blocking out sounds. I latch onto Santino, afraid if I let go, I'll collapse on the floor in a useless heap of limbs.

"I'm here. I've got you." Santino pulls me close and I stumble in the direction he guides me.

When he pushes me into a chair, I'm holding on to him so tightly, I nearly pull him down with me. Cradling my head against his stomach, he cards his fingers through my hair and rocks me side to side.

A hand settles on my arm. It's not Santino's hand—it's smaller, delicate, but strong. I'd recognize that hand anywhere. Rhys pulls me away from Santino and launches himself at me, grabbing me in a bear hug that shouldn't be possible for someone so small.

Humiliation follows close on the heels of my surprise. Oh my god, I forgot he was here—that *everyone* is here. And everyone is currently witnessing my breakdown.

But as Rhys holds me in that tight hug, my body slowly remembers what it's like to be held by him. I melt into his embrace. I've missed this. I've missed the times we spent cuddling on the couch together for movie nights. I miss how generous he is with his affection and his fierce loyalty. I've missed my best friend.

My eyes sting with unshed tears.

"I love you, you know," Rhys murmurs in my ear. "No matter what happens. I always will."

I try to blink back the tears when he lets me go. But then Sebastian appears out of nowhere to take his place. His hug is just as tight as Rhys's. "I'm so sorry, dude. We should've done better. We will do better."

I squeeze my eyes shut, but stray droplets escape my lashes. Embarrassment crashes through me at the attention I'm getting, attention I'm stealing away from Noel and Bellamy. This is *their* bachelor party. They should be the focus—not me. My friends shouldn't be making such a fuss about me. I'm not worth it.

When Sebastian steps back, I'm shocked to find Noel waiting his turn. I don't remember the last time Noel and I hugged—if we ever have. But he pulls me in for something quick and solid. "Don't be a smartass and try to do everything yourself. You're not that good at it and I've got a shit ton of money to throw at every problem."

Despite myself, a laugh bubbles up inside me. Trust Noel to find the most insulting way to be encouraging. He gives me a stinging slap on the back, then suddenly, I'm tugged to my feet and enveloped in a group hug with Rhys, Sebastian, and Noel pressing in on all sides.

Something inside me breaks and the tears come pouring down my cheeks. I can't hold back the sobs any longer. I've been carrying this secret around for so long, trying to hide it from my friends, trying not to burden them with it.

My friends are all so cool in their own ways and I've always felt I should stay in the background so they can have the spotlight. But then I feel invisible, like they never see me, and it hurts.

That's not their fault, though, is it? It's mine. I should've said something when things started to get bad. I shouldn't have avoided their questions or tried to run away. I should've trusted my friends to care about me, that they want to help.

Bellamy, Angel, and Christian step up behind their partners, forming a second circle around us. They all press in tighter, squeezing me until it's a little difficult to breathe. I don't mind. I feel like I've barely breathed in months and being in the middle of this group hug is filling me up with something more important than oxygen.

The group shifts and suddenly Santino is there. I latch onto him, drawing him into the middle of the circle. I want to get better so badly. For Santino. For my friends. For myself. I don't want to be this broken, damaged person anymore. I want to be happy and healthy and whole.

But what if I don't get better? What if I can't? What if the doctor can't help me and I stay broken forever? What if I get worse?

Will I lose my friends? Will I lose Santino?

All the pain I've carried around this past year comes tumbling out in great, heaving sobs. Fear and anger, my waning strength and bone-deep fatigue. I let it all go and admit defeat. I can't fight the darkness anymore. Not on my own. I need help.

I cling to Santino, burying my face in the crook of his neck. He holds me as other hands rub my back and arms, as fingers card through my hair.

I don't have to fight the darkness on my own anymore. I never should've tried to begin with.

When my tears finally slow, it's not because there's no reason to cry anymore. It's because I've run out of tears. I'm wrung out and raw. It feels like the ugly mess I've kept inside all these months has been siphoned out of my body, leaving me staggering and off-kilter.

"I'm so sorry," I croak when the sobs fade.

"Denny! You have nothing to be sorry for." Rhys grips my arm and turns me toward him. His eyes flash with determination and a fierceness I've always admired. "*We're* the ones who should be sorry. We never should've let you drift so far away. But that's not happening again. We're going to take such good care of you, you're going to get sick of us." Rhys's words sting like blood rushing back into a limb that's gone numb.

"But I don't—" The words get caught in my throat. I'm about to say I don't want to be a burden, but voicing it out loud feels so stupid and pathetic.

"Nope, you have no choice." Rhys crosses his arms

over his chest and lifts his chin. "You're stuck with us whether you like it or not."

"Yup." Sebastian gives me a "sorry, not sorry, dude" smile.

And when Noel doesn't say anything, Rhys jabs him in the side with an elbow. "Ow, what the fuck? Yeah, Jesus, of course I'm going to help. I'm not an asshole."

The entire group falls silent as we turn as one to stare at Noel.

From behind him, Bellamy leans in to rest his chin on Noel's shoulder. "Babe, you've got a good heart, but you are one thousand percent an asshole."

Noel smirks, all smug and arrogant.

"So, um, now I have to be the asshole because we need to get to the club." Sebastian winces as he speaks. "But you and Santino don't have to go."

My brain is still a little slow from the meltdown and it takes me a second to figure out what Sebastian is saying.

"Yeah? You sure?" Santino perks up like this is what he's been hoping for.

"Yeah, totally. We'll... figure it out."

"Wait, what? No, I don't... I can still... camera stuff." I can't quite put together complete sentences yet, but they seem to know what I mean.

Sebastian shakes his head. "Don't worry about it. We can shoot the scene in stages. Christian and I will work the cameras first. Then we'll film our portion after and I'll edit it all together so it looks like everything's happening at the same time. It'll be fine."

Except I can hear the slight tension in his voice and the tightness in his expression. It probably would be fine, but Sebastian doesn't like last-minute changes like this. I'm supposed to work the cameras while the other guys are in the scene. That's the plan.

Even though I know he's looking out for me and making sure I don't push myself too hard, a small part of me still feels like Sebastian's trying to get rid of me. Like he thinks the shoot will go more smoothly without me there to fuck things up.

I'm torn. Going back to the hotel room and cuddling with Santino sounds really nice right now. But I also don't want to make extra work for Sebastian. I don't want to make things harder for him, but I also don't want to be left behind. I want to do the things all my friends are doing. I don't want to miss out.

"No, I'm okay. I can do it," I say, my voice sounding stronger than I feel.

Sebastian gives me an assessing look, then his gaze flicks to Santino.

Santino looks skeptical, but he shrugs. "If he says he's okay…"

Sebastian hesitates for several long moments before he relents. "Fine, but you'll let me know if you change your mind."

I nod eagerly, hoping I haven't just made a liar of myself.

"Alright, then let's go."

CHAPTER
TWENTY-EIGHT

SANTINO

I don't know if this is a good idea. Hayden just had a very emotional breakdown and now he wants to keep working for several more hours? He really should be drinking a shit ton of water and lying down to get some rest.

But he was adamant about going to the club, and like, I kind of get it. He doesn't want to miss anything. He doesn't want to be left behind when everyone else is there. But still.

I stick close to his side as we head over and get set up. It's a gay strip club and Sebastian's made arrangements with management for the shoot. We've taken over the VIP mezzanine level overlooking the club's main stage. A series of glass-fronted, glass-floored mini-balconies line the glass railing, jutting out over the space below. Across the back are semicircular booths with padded leather benches.

Okay, confession time. I'm actually really excited for this shoot. It's going to be... different. From anything we've done for the documentary so far. And apparently, from anything The Camboy Network's ever done before. Up to this point, the documentary has been very safe for work, but that's about to change tonight.

If it'd been up to me, I would've dragged Hayden back to our room. But I would've been pretty sad to miss this.

"Everyone knows what they're doing?" Sebastian checks in before we start.

The club sold special tickets to tonight's show and the audience is already gathered on the floor below. There's an electric hum in the air that dances across my skin. We've set up cameras around the VIP area and Hayden's armed with one in his hands.

"Bouncers are stationed at the stairs to keep people out and there's no one else here but us. If you need a break or want to stop altogether, just give Hayden a signal. This is the first time we've done anything like this, so we're all kind of figuring it out as we go. Questions?"

I glance around this group of guys I'm quickly coming to see as my friends. They're all so different from one another and yet, when they come together, it feels like a real family.

Gratitude wells up inside me. I was pretty lost and desperate when I left San Francisco all those weeks ago. And in such a short time, I've found a place where I feel like I belong, I've found friends who are entirely committed to one another, and I've found a wonderful guy I've totally fallen in love with.

Hayden's got a furrow in his brow and his bottom lip is caught between his teeth. He looks serious and deter-mined, like he's about to launch himself into battle. I'm really proud of him for fighting when things have been difficult, for not giving up even when he's wrung out.

"Alright, let's get started." Sebastian claps once and rubs his hands together.

The group disperses. Bellamy and Noel take up their spot in one of the mini-balconies, in full view of the audience below. Rhys and Angel take one end of the middle booth—not as prominent as the balcony, but still plenty visible. Sebastian and Christian take the other end of the booth.

Hayden hits record on his camera.

Sebastian gives the signal for lights and music, then he calls out, "Action."

I don't know where to look.

On the balcony, Noel grabs Bellamy by the front of his shirt and yanks him forward like they're about to get into a fist fight. At the booth, Angel sits back on the padded bench while Rhys gives him a lap dance. Sebastian climbs into Christian's lap and they snuggle down together like there's no one else in the entire club.

Colored lights flash and spin around the space. The music is a thumping, driving beat that reverberates through the air. My stomach flutters in excitement and anticipation.

The guys are all over each other, hands groping, bodies rubbing, mouths coming together in messy kisses. I mean, I've seen all their videos before, but it's something else to see it happen live, in front of my face. The chemistry each couple has on screen is about a thousand times more potent in real life. To the point where it feels like the air is saturated with fucking pheromones or something.

I'm heating up, even though I haven't done anything

but sit here and watch. My groin tightens and my dick stirs in my pants.

Hayden is focused on Bellamy and Noel at the moment, getting a close-up shot of them kissing. Noel is shoving his tongue down Bellamy's throat like he's trying to choke him with it.

After a few minutes, Hayden switches over to Rhys and Angel. Rhys has one leg propped up on Angel's shoulder, his legs spread in a standing split. His feet are clad in dangerous-looking heels and Angel's rubbing his face against the shoe.

Sebastian and Christian are by far the most tame of the group. They're just making out with sweet little kisses, hands gently petting each other over their clothes.

I can't help wondering what Hayden and I would look like if we were out there together. If Hayden didn't have to be behind the camera, what would we be doing? Kissing sweetly like Sebastian and Christian? Attacking each other like Bellamy and Noel? Rubbing up against each other like Rhys and Angel? Or would we do something completely different? Something that's uniquely us?

Hayden's pointing his camera at Sebastian and Christian, but he lifts his gaze to me like he can hear what I'm thinking. Even with the flashing lights of the club, I can tell there's something heated in his eyes. Is he affected by what he's seeing too? Is he wishing we were together in front of the camera rather than behind it?

I'm palming myself through my pants before I even realize my hand has moved. Hayden's eyes narrow when he sees me, his gaze dropping to my crotch. I slouch down a little and spread my legs a bit wider. His throat works and my dick hardens against my palm.

Bellamy's got Noel's button-down shirt open and the two sides pushed apart. He licks at Noel like he's a fucking popsicle stick while he flicks and twists the bar piercing through Noel's nipple. Noel grips the top of the railing like he's hanging on for dear life.

Rhys is straddling Angel's lap now, back to chest. With his knees spread wide, his miniskirt is hiked up around his hips, revealing a lacy G-string. Angel drags a hand up Rhys's inner thigh as Rhys squirms. When he reaches Rhys's crotch and wraps his hand around Rhys's bulge, Rhys arches up, his hips jutting forward into Angel's touch.

Sebastian is also straddling Christian's lap, but they're facing each other, mouths glued together. Christian's hands are on Sebastian's ass, squeezing and kneading like he can't wait to get his dick in there.

Hayden's on his knees in front of Rhys, camera pointed at his crotch. Angel has pushed the lace panties to the side and Rhys is fucking his cock into Angel's meaty fist.

Holy shit. I squeeze my dick as it strains against my pants. They're really doing this. They're actually going to fuck.

I mean, I knew this. Sebastian explained it all in excruciating detail. But it's one thing to know the plan, and it's something else entirely to see it happen. And it. Is. Happening.

I have my pants undone and my hand shoved in my underwear before I can think twice. Hayden swings his camera toward me and a shudder of pure pleasure rushes through me.

I'm not supposed to be in this scene. I discussed it with Sebastian. Since my videos with Hayden haven't been released yet, he wanted to save me for another time. This scene is supposed to be about the already established couples in The Camboy Network. But Hayden doesn't seem to care and neither do I.

I grab the hem of my shirt and tug it up high enough to stuff it in my mouth. Hayden's camera focuses on my face, but I look past the lens at the man behind it. At the mop of blond curls that need a trim. The darkened eyes trained on me. The bottom lip that's bruised and swollen from all his chewing.

I drag my hand down my front, flicking at my nipples and Hayden follows its progress with the camera. When I reach my cock, I pull at the waistband of my briefs and tuck them under my balls. The release sends another surge of pleasure through me. I'm stroking myself and Hayden's recording it all on the camera.

I'm in public, in front of dozens and dozens of people who can see everything I'm doing. I'm exposing myself, pleasuring myself, not only for someone somewhere who might watch the recording someday. But for a live audience I can almost reach out and touch.

My gaze flicks to the crowd gathered below us. Eyes are glued to the show on the balcony. Hands are roaming. Clothes have been thrown to the floor. The scent of sex fills the air, mixing with the ever-present smell of sweat and alcohol.

Noel's bent over the railing now, his pants and underwear shoved down to his thighs. Bellamy's kneeling behind him, face buried between his ass cheeks.

Jesus fucking Christ. He's eating out Noel's ass like we didn't just come from dinner, adding fingers in there while Noel swears up a storm.

Angel's taken his shirt off, revealing a chest full of hair, and Rhys is on his knees on the floor, inhaling Angel's cock.

Sebastian's still straddling Christian's lap, but his pants have disappeared somehow and Christian's fingering his ass while they keep making out.

Hayden's shoulders rise and fall as his breathing speeds up and he keeps licking his lips like he's thirsty. When I glance down at his pants, though, there's no tent, no bulge. That douses my desire somewhat, but when I meet his gaze, the hunger I see there has it roaring back a hundredfold. I want to put on a show for Hayden. I want him to see what he does to me.

Pressure builds in my groin as my hand flies over my cock. I massage my balls with the other, pulling and twisting just enough for the pain to add to the pleasure. Oh god, I'm going to come. Fucking hell, I'm going to come. I squeeze my eyes shut and ease back on my jerking off to drag this out.

"Motherfucker!"

My eyes fly open to find Bellamy ramming his cock into Noel's ass. Noel's spewing every profanity under the sun as if he doesn't actually want Bellamy to destroy his hole.

His curses mix with the high-pitched cries coming from Rhys. His feet are planted wide on the floor as he squats over Angel's lap, fucking himself down on Angel's cock.

And on the other side of the booth, Sebastian and Christian gaze lovingly into each other's eyes as Sebastian rocks back and forth on Christian's dick implanted in his ass.

"Fuck!" The word is muffled from the hem of my shirt

I still have in my mouth. I watch my new friends fucking in front of me. I watch strangers watch my friends. I watch Hayden with his camera, capturing it all. This is crazy. This is insane. It's the hottest fucking thing I've ever seen in my entire fucking life.

"Fuck!" I cry out again as my balls pull up and my groin tightens.

Hayden swings the camera in my direction. He's got the camera pointed at me, but he's not looking at the viewscreen. His gaze darts from my face to my dick and back like he can't decide what he wants to look at.

I can't hold it back anymore. Not when Hayden's looking at me like he wants to devour me and rip me limb from limb. Not when he looks like he wants to crawl up inside me and never leave.

"Fuck!" I scream as I jerk myself through wave after wave of cum flying out of my slit. It lands on my stomach and chest, so much that some slides off my sides and pools in my belly button. I don't stop until my dick gets too sensitive and it's too painful to keep going.

My head falls back on the padded booth and I shudder with aftershocks of the orgasm. When I have enough strength to open my eyes again, Hayden's still there behind his camera.

I can't help but wish he was in front of it with me.

CHAPTER
TWENTY-NINE

HAYDEN

We won't be releasing the videos of me and Santino until after the documentary comes out, but I already know Santino will be a star.

He's a natural. The way he looks at the camera, like he can see the person on the other side. It feels like he's reaching through the screen and bringing you right into the action.

Plus, he's really fucking hot with his shirt caught in his mouth and his body on display. He touches himself with so much confidence, completely unapologetic, as he brings himself pleasure. It's almost hotter to watch him than to get in on the action.

He comes all over himself and his shirt falls out of his mouth as he goes lax. He drags his fingers lazily through the cum on his stomach and I desperately want to lick it off his skin.

Technically, I'm not even supposed to be filming him. But how could I not when he looks like that?

Still in his post-orgasmic bliss, he blinks up at me with those long, dark lashes. My knees go a little weak and my stomach tightens with desire. I need to get back to filming the other guys, but I don't care. I can't turn away now.

Lowering the camera, I set one knee on the bench next to Santino and bend down to capture his lips with mine.

He moans into the kiss, hand coming up to thread through my hair and hold me in place. A shudder runs through me when I lick into his mouth and his tongue touches mine.

His other hand trails down my front, scratching lightly at my stomach, then ventures lower to cup my stubbornly soft dick. It feels really good to have his hand on me, even though I'm not getting hard. A groan reverberates from my chest as tendrils of pleasure curl through me. God, I wish I wasn't broken. I wish I was normal like everyone else.

Exhaustion from the long day is catching up with me. The adrenaline boost I got when we arrived at the club is wearing off. I'm so tired. Physically. Emotionally. I just want to lie down and wrap myself around Santino.

But there's still work to do. Sebastian's depending on me to get the footage he needs. I insisted on coming when he wanted to send me away. I can't let him down and make him regret trusting me.

Reluctantly, I pull away from Santino. But not before I rest my forehead against his for a moment to catch my breath.

I don't know what I'd do without Santino. I definitely wouldn't have made it this far. Either I would've gone completely mad, or I would've killed myself. Santino's the one who's kept me here and kept me sane.

Bellamy's speech comes back to me. All that stuff about being complementary, about making each other better. I want that so badly. I want that with Santino.

But does he want that with me? I'm too scared to hope for it. I'm too scared to ask if that's why he's doing so much to take care of me. What if he's just being nice but doesn't actually have feelings for me? What if he's trying to pay me back for giving him a place to stay?

I can't quite tell the difference between what's real and what's not real anymore. The darkness is so confusing and it makes me second-guess everything. What did he mean when he said I'm wonderful? Does he want to stay in New York to work with Sebastian or to be with me? What if I ask and it turns out this whole thing has been one-sided? Then the voice would be right.

"Babe." Santino's hands bracket my face as he studies me with concern. "You're shaking."

I didn't even notice. "I'm fine," I say, grabbing the camera I dropped on the bench.

"Do you want to call it quits?" Santino stands with me as I straighten, stuffing himself back into his pants.

I need to finish the job. I need to prove I'm not totally incompetent. "No, I'm fine."

Santino doesn't believe me. And he doesn't look impressed.

"Please," I beg him to understand.

It takes him a moment, but then he nods and I spin back toward the guys.

Bellamy's pounding into Noel so hard, I'm surprised the glass doesn't shatter and send them tumbling down to the floor below.

Angel's got his hands behind Rhys's knees, holding his

legs up, spread wide in the air. Rhys is suspended against Angel's chest as Angel fucks up into him.

Sebastian and Christian have changed positions. Sebastian is now kneeling sideways with one knee on the bench and the other leg extended, foot on the floor. Christian is behind him, gripping him by the hips and pulling him back to meet each thrust.

It's all very hot and sexy and everything, but it does nothing for me now. Now, I just want to get through the rest of this shoot in one piece.

Rhys comes first, hands free. Cum shoots from his cock as it bounces on his stomach. Angel lifts him off his cock and gently places him down on the bench. Then he grabs his dick and jerks off onto Rhys's stomach. He mixes their cum together with his fingers before leaning down to lick it all up.

Christian and Sebastian are next. Christian roars as he slams himself into Sebastian's ass and comes inside him. He carefully pulls out and then dives in to suck the cum out of Sebastian's body. Meanwhile, Sebastian reaches between his legs, crying out as he jerks himself off with Christian's tongue in his hole.

Finally, it's Noel and Bellamy. They're standing side by side now, each holding the other person's dick. They're both facing the audience, separated by a pane of glass. Noel comes first, his cum landing on the glass and dripping down in streaks. Bellamy isn't far behind, adding to the cum painting that's clearly visible to the audience below.

A weird silence hangs in the air, louder than the music being pumped through the speakers. Noel and Bellamy stagger back to the booth, where they collapse in a heap of limbs. The other guys are all limp and half-conscious. I glance down at the audience gathered on the first floor. I kind of forgot they were there.

When Rhys performs at The Bronzed Rail, the audience is always loud and rowdy, impossible to ignore. But here, I barely heard a sound coming from them. The reason becomes obvious as I scan the crowd. There are maybe a dozen dicks out in the open and almost everyone's got that dazed, post-orgasm expression on their face.

I feel more than hear Santino come up behind me. He takes the camera from my hands and sets it down, then drags me in for a hug. I wrap my arms around his waist and sink into the comfort he offers. The shoot is over. I got the job done.

It takes much too long for Sebastian to recover. By then, Santino and I are almost finished taking down all the cameras and packing them up. He takes one look at me as he tucks himself back into his pants and nods toward the stairs. "You guys can take off."

Santino and I don't wait for him to change his mind. Santino grabs my hand and marches me back to our room.

"Want to take a shower?" Santino asks when the door snicks shut.

I nod, heading directly to the bathroom. While I strip, Santino turns the water on and steam starts billowing out and filling the room. The water is hot when I step under the spray and I sigh with relief. My eyes drift shut while I sway on my feet. I could probably fall asleep like this.

Then Santino steps in and an entirely different kind of heat spreads through me. This shower is much bigger than the one we have at home, so we don't have to be plastered to each other. We still are, though, coming together so my front is flush with his.

We stand there, letting the water sluice over us. It washes away not only the dirt and grime of the day, but also some of the residue left over from all the emotional ups and downs. I didn't expect my friends to rally around me like that. The voice almost had me convinced they hated my guts.

Santino pulls back an inch to look at me and I manage to curl my lips into something resembling a smile. He cocks one eyebrow to tease me over the poor attempt. Something shifts inside me, like a pair of glasses that help me see... perhaps not better, but differently. Like maybe there is a way out of this hole I've dug for myself. Maybe I'm allowed to hope for something good.

Santino pumps body wash into his palm and starts running his hands all over me. Over my chest and stomach. My sides and hips. He bends down, skipping my dick to do one leg, then the other. I turn when he nudges me and he slathers soap all over my back.

Then he hugs me from behind, his lips grazing the nape of my neck. His hands roam over my stomach and my chest before finally venturing between my legs.

I'm a little chubby from all the pampering Santino's poured out on me. But even as he takes me in hand, I know I can't get fully hard.

Turning my face into the shower spray, I let Santino play with my cock and balls. I focus on the physical sensation of his touch while my mind provides memories of him jerking off at the club earlier. Gentle pleasure builds slowly in my limbs and in my stomach, so gradual it's easy to miss. But eventually, I'm breathing hard, my blood is flowing, and if my dick was still functional, I'd be ready to sink into Santino's hot, tight body.

I try not to let it get to me. It's okay if I can't get hard. I can still feel pleasure. I can still give Santino pleasure. But I want more. I want it all.

Pulling Santino's hands away from my cock, I turn in his arms. "I, um, I brought the pills." It feels safer to say it in here, with the water insulating us from the outside world.

Santino's expression is concerned and sympathetic. "You want to take them?"

I nod.

"You don't have to do it for me, you know. I like a little wet noodle." He pushes his hips forward to rub his hard-on against my soft one.

I groan at his joke. It's not very funny and I'm not even sure what it means. But it's silly enough to pull me a little more out of the darkness and into reality. "No, I want to."

Santino grins that lopsided grin of his. "I'll never say no to getting fucked by you."

I cringe at the cheese, but Santino lets out a laugh that echoes around the bathroom. It's bright and shiny and I think... I think I'm in love with him.

I'm not sure when it happened. I don't think there was any specific moment. But somewhere between him seeing me at The Bronzed Rail that first night and the last time he helped me shower, I think I fell in love with him.

But he doesn't love you back. He'll never love you back.

I gulp as the voice tries to take control of my thoughts. It's true I don't know whether Santino loves me. He could even care about me without actually loving me. It would be really easy to succumb to the voice and let it grind me down to nothing. Or I can ignore it and enjoy whatever's left of the night.

I turn the water off and reach for the towels.

If Santino doesn't love me, then at least I'll have tonight. For the next few hours, I can pretend we're hopelessly in love and eager to spend the rest of our lives together. I'll deal with whatever heartbreak my fantasy will bring me tomorrow.

I didn't actually intend to bring the ED pills with me this weekend. I just grabbed the same duffle bag I normally use for shoots and it was already in there. But now, it kind of feels like it was meant to be. I pop one pill dry and turn to find Santino waiting for me next to the bed.

He holds out his hand for me and when I take it, he guides me to sit down. Rubbing his hands up and down my thighs, he drops to his knees and peers at me through his lashes. My breath catches at the desire I see in his eyes. Desire for me. Want for me. Lust for me.

Leaning down to kiss him, I pour everything I feel into that kiss: gratitude, tenderness, affection, love. I kiss him like my very life depends on it. Like I'm suffocating and he's the only source of oxygen in the world.

Santino breaks the kiss and we inhale and exhale together as we catch our breaths. Then he trails his fingers lightly up and down my dick. It's still only chubby, but his soft touch sends tingles up to my stomach and down my legs.

Lifting my cock out of the way, he leans forward to kiss my balls, his face pressed right in between my legs. He catches one between his lips and sucks it into his hot, wet mouth.

I let out a low groan, eyes fixed on Santino. I can't look away. I want to see everything he does and commit it to memory. I want to record every second of this so I can pull it out and rewatch it in my mind again and again.

He makes appreciative little moans as he sucks on my balls, the same ones he makes when he's eating something delicious. His pupils are blown wide and yet his eyes are super focused on his task. He licks all around, bathing my balls with his spit, then returning to my cock and doing the same.

When he takes me into his mouth, I gasp. So hot. So wet. My erection roars to life so fast I get a little light-headed. Santino grins like he won the fucking lottery. He tries to take me all the way in, but when I hit the back of his throat, he gags. The wet, slurpy sound sends shivers up my spine.

What he can't get into his mouth, Santino covers with his hand. And when he pulls off to catch his breath, a strand of saliva stretches from the tip of my dick to his lips. He blinks at me with a pleased, satisfied smile, his hand still lazily working my shaft.

I pull him to me. I need him closer. I need his body pressed against mine. I need zero space between us.

He lies down on me, his bare chest on mine, and the simple intimacy of the touch has my entire body shuddering with pleasure. His lips are wet and messy and I kiss them greedily. I thrust my tongue into his mouth and drink down every moan he lets out.

I clutch him to me, writhing under him. My nipples are tight and sensitive and electricity zings through me when they brush against his soft chest hair. I slide my hands down his muscled back to his round ass, filling my palms with them. The pitch of Santino's moans changes with every squeeze and tug and knead.

"Fuck, I need you inside me, babe. Like right fucking now." He pushes away to grab a bottle of lube from his suitcase.

I hold out my hand for it. "Let me."

Santino smirks at me, heat in his eyes, and when he hands it over, he gives me a kiss that scorches me down to the soles of my feet.

He jumps on the bed, positioning himself right in the middle on his hands and knees.

I take a second to marvel at the sight of him. The taper of his waist and the curve of his spine. The fullness of his ass and the two little dimples right above them.

Santino peers over his shoulder when I take too long, pinning me with a look hot enough to burn. "Hurry up, babe, I want you inside me."

I pump the lube out on my fingers and carefully drag them over his hole. The skin around it is a shade darker than the rest of him and I rub circles around the wrinkled opening.

Santino lets out a satisfied moan and drops his head to the bed. He widens his knees and tilts his ass up to give me better access.

I can feel him bearing down on me when I press one finger inside, then his muscles clench tight around me.

"Fuck, yes, more."

I slowly work my finger all the way in until my knuckles are flush against his ass, then I slowly pull it out. It goes in easier when I push in again, carefully fucking him with my finger. When Santino starts squirming impatiently, I add a second finger, twisting them around as I push in and pull out. I curl them inside him, petting his inner walls until I find the spot I'm looking for.

I rub my fingers against the bundle of nerves and Santino's ass clamps down impossibly tight. He throws his head back, spine arched, body taut as I increase the pressure.

"Fuck, babe. That feels so good."

Reaching around him, I palm his cock. Hard and leaking, even though he's already come once at the club. It's the perfect size for my hand and I press my face into Santino's back, savoring just how well we fit together. Like maybe we were made for each other. Like maybe we were meant to be.

"I swear to fucking god, babe, you better put that dick inside me right fucking now."

I don't know what it is, but something about Santino's words mixes with my bruised emotions and something bursts inside me. It's joy and happiness and more than a little bit of delirium. Laughter comes pouring out of me, brighter than it has in a long time.

"Are you serious, dude? I'm fucking dying over here and you're laughing? Christ." Santino's words have no heat behind them and he's smiling wide as he reaches for me. "Get over here and fuck me already."

He drags me over his body so my front fits against his back. I reach between us and guide myself to his hole. There's hardly any resistance and we both groan as I sink all the way in.

CHAPTER
THIRTY

SANTINO

I don't think I've ever laughed in the middle of sex before. Those two things don't feel like they should exist in the same space. But with Hayden, it feels like the most natural thing in the world. With Hayden, it feels like what sex should be—fun, carefree, joyous.

I hang my head forward as he bottoms out, his thick cock stretching me wide. His whole body curls around mine, from knees to shoulders, and his face is pressed against my neck. I'm entirely engulfed in Hayden, surrounded on the outside and filled on the inside, and it feels so fucking good.

I mean, physically, yeah, it's fucking amazing. But it's more than just the physical. It's the tenderness in his touch, the way he's so soft and gentle with me. Like I'm something precious to him. Like he wants to imprint every moment onto his memory.

For the past couple weeks, I've usually been the big spoon to his little spoon. I like being the big spoon. I like holding him close and giving him the comfort and protection he needs.

But being the little spoon is pretty damn awesome too. With his bigger body, he makes me feel so small and fragile. Like I don't have to find my way through this huge, intimidating world all by myself. Like we're in this thing together.

His arms wrap around me and I sigh contentedly. "Fuck, yesss," I say with a chuckle. "Oh my god, this is perfect."

Hayden pulls out halfway and thrusts back in almost lazily, like it's an afterthought. And something about the casual, unrushed movement makes my heart fill with so much peace my limbs grow weak. I fall onto the bed, Hayden's weight pinning me to the mattress.

I grab a pillow to prop my head up and spread my legs a little wider so he has better access. Turning my head, I give him a blissed-out smile. Hayden smiles back and we both descend into giggles.

The laughing changes the angle of Hayden's cock inside me and I clamp down around him. A shiver of pleasure runs through me as he hits parts of me that feel like they've never been touched before.

"Oh, Jesus, fuuuck." I groan through the laughter. "I think I can come like this."

"Yeah?" Hayden asks, snapping his hips forward. "Like this?"

My body lights up with a kind of pleasure I didn't know was possible with sex. It's bubbly and fizzy, like I'm going to disintegrate into a thousand tiny explosions. "Fuck! Christ! Yes, like that. Goddammit."

Hayden pants in my ear. His hips slap against my ass.

We're both making these silly laughing-moaning sounds, like we can decide whether this is the funniest or sexiest thing to ever happen.

With each thrust, Hayden shoves us closer and closer to the headboard until my head butts right up against it.

"Ahh!" I cry out, even though it doesn't really hurt.

"Oh, sorry!" Hayden reaches a hand up to cushion my skull.

"Don't you dare stop. Keep fucking me, dam,it."

Peals of laughter escape from Hayden as he tries to keep up his rhythm and protect my head at the same time.

"Forget my head! Just fuck me!"

"I don't want you to get hurt!"

"I don't care about a few bruises on my head! I'm going to die if you don't make me come!"

"Oh my god." Hayden's laughing so hard, it almost sounds like he's crying. "Stop. I can't keep going if you say stuff like that."

"Hurry up and make me come and I'll stop!" To be honest, I don't even care about coming anymore. All I care about is the sound of Hayden's laughter filling my ears. All I want is to make it last as long as I possibly can. If that means saying the dumbest things while his cock is in my ass, then that's a small price to pay.

Hayden growls with a note of determination and he props himself up on both hands. This angle gives him more leverage and his hips start flying. His cock pounds away at my prostate so hard it wipes every thought from my mind and expels all the air from my lungs.

I don't have any more silly, ridiculous words for him. All I can do is gasp as Hayden makes it his mission to destroy my hole. It doesn't take long. The orgasm rushes at me like a tidal wave—fast and huge and unavoidable.

"Oh fuck, oh fuck!" I scream into the pillow as my dick pulses where it's caught between my stomach and the bed. Wet heat spreads across my stomach as Hayden fucks me right through the high.

It feels like it lasts forever and Hayden's hips don't miss a single beat. He's still going strong as the high eases and everything grows sensitive.

"Come on, babe, give it to me," I say, my words slurred. "Give me your cum."

Hayden bursts out in another round of giggles that transform into cries as he comes in my ass.

"Yeah, that's it. Fill me up. Paint my insides."

"Stop, oh my god, stop." Hayden buries his face in the crook of my neck as his body shakes with the aftershocks of his orgasm combined with unrelenting laughter.

Who knew it was possible to laugh while coming? I sure as hell didn't. But now that I know, that's the only way I want to fuck for the rest of my life.

———

Hayden seems to get better over the next several days. We head back to New York, hole up at home for a bit, hang out at The Bronzed Rail with the guys one night.

Everything feels good. Everything feels right. Like if I don't rock the boat and just keep coasting like this, nothing will ever go wrong again. That doesn't happen, of course.

The darkness rears its ugly head again on the morning of Hayden's appointment with the therapist. It's not really that surprising. Hell, I'd be nervous as fuck too if I were him. We've been waiting for this day for a long time. There's so much riding on this going well.

Hayden's awake when I open my eyes in the morning. I'm barely conscious and I can already feel the tension radiating off him. He tries to put on a brave face, tries to smile as we get ready to leave, but he can't hide how anxious he is.

I can see the darkness descending on him the closer we get to the therapist's office. I squeeze his hand, but he doesn't squeeze back. He doesn't even look at me. His gaze stays kind of empty, like he's looking at something that's not actually there.

I guide him through the crowded sidewalks and into the gray medical building. He goes where I lead him, walks when I walk, stops when I stop. I don't know if I've ever seen him like this before. Like he's catatonic or something. It's way scarier than when he cries uncontrollably and can't stop.

We're sitting in the therapist's waiting room and I'm debating whether I should say something encouraging. Like, it's going to be okay. Or you're going to be fine. But I don't think it'll make any difference, and honestly, it feels a little fake. Like nice-sounding words that don't really mean anything.

So I just hold his hand, trying not to let on how worried I am. His hand is limp in mine. His complexion is kind of gray. He's not even chewing on his lip, which isn't a good sign.

I jump when the door to the therapist's office opens. Hayden barely reacts.

A tall middle-aged woman with dark hair streaked through with gray stands in the doorway. "Harry?"

Slowly, Hayden turns to look up at her, blinking like he can't understand her.

I look back and forth between them. Who's Harry? Does she mean Hayden?

"Harry Smith?" she asks again.

Hayden inhales like he's coming out of a fugue state and his hand tightens around mine. "Oh. Yeah, that's me."

"I'm Dr. Tina. Come on in." She steps aside, gesturing into her office.

But Hayden doesn't budge. His whole body is tense now, like he's bracing for impact. The grip he has on my hand is so tight, it actually hurts a little.

"Hey, babe." I nudge him until he turns to meet my gaze. There's legit fear in his eyes, like afraid-for-his-life level of fear, and my heart breaks for him. I cup his cheek, rubbing my thumb over his cheekbone. "I'll be right here the whole time. I'll be sitting in this very chair when you come back out. I'm not going anywhere, okay?"

Hayden's throat works and I know he's trying to swallow down his panic. His lip is caught between his teeth again and there's a wild look in his eyes. I can tell he wants me to go in with him. I mean, I kind of want to go in with him too. But that's not how these things work. I'll always be with him, no matter how rough things get. But there are some things he needs to do by himself.

I stand, pulling Hayden with me. Then I give him a long, hard hug. "I know this is difficult. I believe in you. You can do this."

Reluctantly, I step back from the hug and gently guide Hayden toward the door.

The therapist meets my gaze over Hayden's shoulder. Her expression is neutral and polite, but I get the feeling she sees more than she lets on. That's good, right? We want a therapist who's perceptive, right?

The door closes with a soft snick and I drop back into my chair. An hour. The appointment is one hour long, then we'll know what to do next.

I pull my phone out and send a message to Sebastian.

SANTINO

He's with the therapist now.

SEBASTIAN

Good. How was he this morning?

Not good. Like, empty stares and shit.

Fuck.

Yeah.

Dr. Tina will help him. She's the best in the field.

Thank you, btw. You didn't have to do any of this, but we're all really glad you're here.

I stare at his message, not sure how to respond. I mean, I appreciate the thank you, obviously. But Sebastian makes it sound like I'm doing them a favor—which I absolutely am not. I'm doing this for entirely selfish reasons. Because *I* want Hayden to get better. Because *I* want to be with him. Because *I* want him to feel good about being himself.

Don't they get that? Haven't they noticed how much I care about him? How much he means to me?

SANTINO

You don't need to thank me.

I hesitate with my thumbs hovering above the keyboard, not sure if I should type the next message. Should I tell Sebastian I love Hayden? Before I've even told Hayden himself? I glance at the closed door as if it will tell me what to do.

My gut says he loves me just as much as I love him. Maybe he doesn't realize it yet because he's a little preoccupied with, you know, being depressed. But he'll get better and when he does, he'll see that what we have is special. It isn't an accident or a fluke. We are two people made for each other, made to be together.

SANTINO

I love him.

SEBASTIAN

Yeah, I figured.

Welcome to the squad.

A smile breaks out across my face and for the first time in a long time, I finally feel like I'm home.

HAYDEN

Dr. Tina's office looks like… an office. I don't know what I was expecting. Like, maybe an examination table with a bunch of weird instruments laid out on a stainless-steel tray. Like she's going to strap me down and start cutting me open to figure out what's wrong with my head.

But it's nothing like that. There's a desk in one corner with a computer and a few file folders on it. Then a sitting area by the window. One couch and two armchairs. A low coffee table in between. The walls are a warm cream, decorated with pictures of colorful landscapes, and a bunch of plants are scattered around the room.

"Grab a seat." Dr. Tina gestures toward the sitting area. "Whichever one you want."

Where should I sit? Which spot is the right one? Will she judge me if I pick the wrong seat? Is this some kind of test?

I sneak a glance at her, but she's just standing off to the

side, patiently waiting for me to choose. She gives me an encouraging smile, but doesn't rush me.

Crap. I just have to pick one, don't I? I inch toward the couch, sneaking another glance at Dr. Tina, but she gives nothing away. When I slowly sit down, she takes the armchair opposite me.

I perch on the edge of the couch, not sure if I'm allowed to sit back. Will she think I'm unprofessional if I lounge on the couch? That I'm not taking this seriously enough? That I don't actually want to be here?

I mean, I'm not sure I do want to be here. At least, that's what the voice keeps shouting in my mind. That this is a waste of everyone's time. That the therapist won't help me because I can't be helped. That I'm hopeless. Useless. Worthless.

"So, Harry. What brings you here?" Dr. Tina has her legs crossed comfortably in the armchair, hands clasped casually in her lap. She doesn't have a notebook with her, nothing to write down the shit I say or do. She looks like she's just having a chat with any random person.

"I go by Hayden." I don't know why those are the first words to come out of my mouth. I didn't even consciously think to say them. They just slipped out.

But Dr. Tina doesn't even bat an eye. "Okay. Hayden."

Where do I start? How do I explain what's been happening to me over the past year? This person is a complete stranger and I'm supposed to open up and tell her my deepest, darkest secrets?

I want so much for this to work. I want her to cure me of this awful thing that's taken up residence inside me—whether it's depression or something else. I *need* to get better so I can be the man Santino deserves. But none of that will happen if I can't find the words to tell her what's wrong.

The panic that started in the waiting room grows, making my heart race and my throat close up. What if I can't do this? What if I can't explain my problem and so she can't give me a solution? It'll be my own fault. I'll have wasted everyone's time. Santino will be so disappointed.

"I… um… I don't really know how to start?" I say, begging her to throw me a lifeline.

"Why don't you tell me about yourself?" Dr. Tina responds, which isn't super helpful, but it's something I can work with.

"I'm, uh, a performer?" I pause, watching for her reaction, letting out a breath when she nods in understanding. "I like my job. I work with my best friends. We're like a family. I have a good life."

So why the fuck are you here, dumbass.

"But sometimes… it doesn't feel that way." I wring my hands in my lap, hating how pathetic I sound. "Sometimes, it feels like…"

Across from me, Dr. Tina doesn't say anything. She doesn't try to finish my sentence for me. She doesn't smile encouragingly or frown in confusion. Her face is impossibly neutral and I have no idea what she's thinking.

"Like everything sucks." Guilt winds through me at the admission. My life is *good*. I have nothing to complain about. There isn't a single thing I would change. So why am I throwing myself a giant pity party all the time? Why do I let these feelings get the better of me? Why do I indulge them?

I curl in on myself, wrapping my arms around my

middle as the weight of the darkness falls heavily on my shoulders. The horrible ache spreads across my chest.

This was a stupid idea. I shouldn't have come here. There are so many people who have it worse off than I do. Dr. Tina should be helping them, not wasting her time sitting here with me.

"I'm sorry." A sob tries to bubble up my throat, but I swallow it down and press my hand across my mouth. I focus on breathing through my nose so I don't break down in tears.

A beat passes in silence before Dr. Tina speaks. "What are you sorry for?"

Everything. All of it. For being such a burden. For being so difficult.

I don't trust myself to speak without falling apart, so I just shake my head. God, I wish Santino was in here with me. I wish he was right next to me, holding my hand, wrapping his arms around me, squeezing me tight. It would be easier if he was here. Everything feels easier with him.

Dr. Tina doesn't rush me, doesn't repeat the question, doesn't even try to comfort me. She just sits patiently, waiting for the whirlwind of thoughts and emotions to blow through my mind.

And amazingly, after a few minutes—maybe the longest fucking minutes in my life—the panic stops trying to choke me. It doesn't go away, not completely, but it recedes just enough that I can actually think semi-coherent thoughts.

"I… get these… I don't know what to call them. Episodes, I guess? It feels like something's trying to suffocate me. It's hard to breathe. My chest hurts. Everything's dull and muted and heavy, like I'm moving underwater."

At some point, I scooted back on the couch and I'm bent over at the waist, arms folded between my chest and my knees. I stare at this spot on the carpet where there's a swirl in the design.

Dr. Tina is still silent.

"Sometimes, I cry," I continue, throat tight as unruly emotions ricochet around inside me. "Sometimes, I get these really bad thoughts."

"What kind of thoughts?" Dr. Tina jumps in unexpectedly. She's been so quiet this whole time, a part of me wondered if she was actually paying attention.

I sneak a glance up at her. She's studying me, like she's not only listening to what I'm saying, but what I'm not saying too.

"Um, bad ones," I say, hoping she won't make me actually voice them out loud. "Like, about myself."

"About hurting yourself?"

Tears spring to my eyes so fast I don't have time to react. They pour down my cheeks like a waterfall being unleashed. Like my chest cracked open and all the shit that's been bottled up inside me comes rushing out.

I feel like I'm being carried over the edge and then free-falling for god knows how many feet. There's nothing I can do to stop it, nothing I can grab ahold of to save myself. I'm going to crash into the rocks below and it's going to hurt. But in the middle of the chaos, there's this weird sense of freedom, of peace.

Someone knows now. Someone who might be able to do something about it. Someone who might be able to help me.

The sound of something sliding across the coffee table has me blinking my eyes open. Dr. Tina's pushed the box of tissues in my direction. I grab handfuls and try to stem the flood coming out of my eyes.

"Have you done anything to hurt yourself?" she asks once I've sort of gotten control over myself.

It takes me a second to understand what she's suggesting and horror fills me when I do. I shake my head vehemently. "No, I haven't. I'm not—" *Suicidal*. The word gets caught in my throat.

"Have you made plans to hurt yourself?"

I shake my head again. "No!" I can't believe I'm having this conversation. I can't believe she's asking me these things.

Is this who I am now? Someone who might hurt himself? Who's on some sort of watch list and needs to be monitored? Oh god, that's bad. Like, really bad. I mean, I knew things were bad, obviously. But this is like, next-level bad.

"No, I—they're just thoughts. I don't know where they come from. It's like there's this other person or thing or something planting them in my head. They're not my own. They're not me." How do I explain this so she gets it? How do I make her understand that this isn't who I am?

"I used to be a really happy person." I sniffle every few words, the tears still dripping down my cheeks. "Like, positive and optimistic. 'Cause like, I have a good life. But this thing… it makes me so negative and angry all the time. For no reason. I feel so… bitter and resentful. I hate feeling this way. I want to be happy again."

"When did it start?" That's the first question Dr. Tina asks that feels like she's guiding me toward an answer.

And for some reason, it gives me hope. Like she's trying to get to the source of the problem.

I try to remember the first time I felt the darkness. "Over a year ago. I think? It's all kind of hazy now."

"What was happening in your life around that time?"

Guilt trickles in to mix with my earlier horror as I think back to last summer. "My best friend started seeing a guy. But it's not his fault!" I rush to add. "I'm not upset they're together or anything like that. I'm really happy for them."

"How did your life change when they started seeing each other?" Dr. Tina asks as if she already knows what I'm going to say.

I don't want to say it, though. Because it makes me ungrateful and selfish. It turns me into a bad person who doesn't care about his friends.

But Dr. Tina still sits there, watching and waiting. The question hangs in the air between us like a noose gradually tightening around my neck until I answer it.

"I… got left behind." Fresh tears spring to my eyes. Not quite the waterfall, but a steady stream I keep having to wipe away. "He didn't do it on purpose. And it's like, normal he wants to spend more time with Angel. I get that. I don't have a problem with that. It's just… then I'm all alone."

"How did that make you feel?"

I furrow my brow in confusion. Isn't it obvious? Haven't I already said it? It makes me feel like shit. The darkness, the pit, the voice. That's how I feel! I feel… "Sad," I croak as I swallow back a sob. "I'm really sad."

I drop my chin to my chest, pressing new tissues into my eyes. A small mountain of used ones is growing by my side. "I miss all my friends so much. I mean, they're not like, gone or anything. But it's not the same. We're not the same as we used to be. And they've all moved on. But I'm still here."

The guilt is overwhelming. I'm such a bad person. What kind of asshole gets sad when he sees his friends finding love? What kind of douchebag blames his problems on his friends being happy? That's so fucked up. I'm so fucked up.

"Grieving is normal when you go through a loss."

Dr. Tina's comment doesn't make sense. I haven't really lost anything. I mean, I'm still friends with Rhys and the guys. We still see each other, talk to each other, hang out together. We just spent an entire weekend in Atlantic City. What does grieving have to do with anything?

When she sees my confusion, she continues. "Any kind of change includes a component of loss. Your best friend is now in a romantic relationship with someone else. So you've lost some of the time you would've spent with him. You've lost some of his attention. It's okay to grieve that loss."

Is that what's been happening? I've been grieving? It can't be that simple, can it? This doesn't feel like grief.

"I'm not saying what you're experiencing is only grief. But it might be a contributing factor."

"So…" I blink as my tears finally dry. "If it's not just grief, then what else is it?"

CHAPTER
THIRTY-TWO

SANTINO

Sebastian keeps me company the whole time Hayden's in his appointment. This guy is like, a genius. His brain operates at five times the speed of a normal human. He texts me ideas for the second scene I'm supposed to do with Hayden. Then ideas for maybe a third. Then how we can promote the entire series. And on and on and on.

By the time Dr. Tina's door opens, my head is spinning with everything Sebastian wants me to do. Don't get me wrong. It's a lot. But that's a good thing. It means I have a place here. It means I belong.

Hayden practically stumbles out of Dr. Tina's office. His cheeks are splotchy. The tip of his nose is red. His eyes are all puffy and swollen. He's been crying, obviously. And it looks like it was a hard cry.

I shoot to my feet, rushing to steady him before he tumbles to the floor. Glancing past him, I don't see Dr. Tina following him out. Is that a good sign? A bad one?

"What happened? Are you okay?" I ask, brushing my fingers over his face and through his hair.

Hayden takes a deep breath and sighs. "I… think so?"

He looks dazed and lost. Like he's just gotten off a rollercoaster and can't tell which way is up. I want to grill him and ask him all the questions. What did you talk about? What did she say? What's going to happen now? But Hayden can barely keep his eyes open. I need to get him home.

We hail a rideshare downstairs and Hayden immediately slouches down to rest his head on my shoulder. I think he's asleep before the car even pulls away from the curb. I pull my phone out.

SANTINO

Hayden's out. I'm taking him home.

SEBASTIAN

How is he?

Wiped.

I'll check in a bit later.

Hayden doesn't stir the entire ride home and I feel terrible waking him up when we arrive. His steps are heavy as we climb the stairs and the second we're in the apartment, he heads directly to his room.

Hayden flops on the bed, eyes already closed. He makes a soft sound at the back of his throat and reaches out one hand to me. As if he knows I'm here. As if he knows I will always take his hand when he reaches for me.

I toe off my shoes and climb into bed with him. He

curls himself around me and in less than three seconds, his breathing evens out, slow and steady.

I study his face as he sleeps, the light fan of his lashes across his cheeks, the curl of his bottom lip where it connects to his chin, the angle of his nose. I wish I could say he was more peaceful when asleep, but he flinches every once in a while, like maybe he's fighting off demons even in the dream world.

Mom used to get tired like this after her therapy appointments too. As if rather than spending the hour talking, she was put through a boot camp instead. It'll get easier for Hayden over time, but at least we've taken the first step.

———

I don't remember falling asleep, but it feels like hours later when my brain pushes me toward consciousness again. My vision is blurry when I open them and it takes me a moment to notice Hayden is awake beside me. His head is on the pillow next to mine. His face only inches away. And he's watching me with such tenderness in his gaze.

"Hey." My voice is groggy. "What time is it? How long was I out for?" I reach up to rub the heels of my hands in my eyes.

"Not long."

I drop my hands back down and turn onto my side so we're facing each other. His eyes are still puffy and red, but he looks way more alert and present than he did this morning.

"How are you feeling?" I ask, hoping with every cell in my body he's doing better than before.

He lifts a shoulder in a shrug and his lips quirk up in one corner. "I'm okay."

Okay is good. I'll take an okay.

"What did Dr. Tina say?"

"She wants to see me again. Every week. She said I'm probably grieving. And I probably have depression."

That's pretty much what we were expecting, so I'm not surprised. But it's good to have my theory confirmed by a professional. "And… how do you feel about that?"

Hayden's half-smile grows. "You sound just like Dr. Tina."

I cringe. "Sorry. You don't have to answer that."

Hayden nestles in closer so our noses almost touch. "It's okay. I want to tell you. I just… I'm not sure how to feel about it. Like, there's treatment for depression, right? So that's good. But like, how the hell did I get depression?"

I chuckle. "You make it sound like a contagious disease."

Hayden gets a wry look on his face. "Sometimes it feels like it."

We share a look, an unspoken understanding passing between us. There's still a long way to go and a lot of work needs to be done before Hayden gets back to the person he used to be. But we're doing something about it. And we'll do it together.

"You want to order something for dinner?" I ask, running through some of the places we've ordered from in the past few days.

"Actually…" Hayden's eyes go all wide and puppy-dog. "Do you want to help me cook?"

I don't even need to think about it. I'll never say no to Hayden's cooking. "Hell, yeah, I do." I jump from the bed, all traces of sleepiness gone.

Hayden follows a little more slowly. "What do you feel like eating?"

"Anything. Literally. If you make it, I'll eat it."

He laughs out loud, the sound filling the apartment as we head to the kitchen. I smile at the way it bounces off the walls and makes the place feel so much brighter. That must be how the apartment felt before Hayden's mental health took a turn for the worse. And that's the way it'll be again soon.

"How about seafood linguine?" Hayden asks, going through the cupboards and freezer.

"You can make seafood linguine?" I exclaim.

He gives me a look that's half-sheepish and half-amused. Like, of course he can make seafood linguine. Why am I even surprised?

"That sounds amazing, babe," I insert myself between him and the fridge to give him a long, lingering kiss. We stop only when the fridge starts beeping at us to shut the door.

Watching Hayden work in the kitchen might be one of my new favorite hobbies. Every movement is so sure. The way he holds the knife when chopping up the garlic and onions. How he swishes the butter around in the pan. It's like he's a rock star and the kitchen is his instrument. I'm so mesmerized by watching him, I don't even realize he's finished until he holds up two plates of steaming pasta.

"Can you grab us some cutlery?" Hayden asks as he brings the plates to the small table by the wall.

We've never actually used it before. Usually, we'll just eat on the couch with something random playing on the TV. But Hayden sets the two plates down, then goes digging through another cupboard. He comes out with an armful of stuff—placemats, fancy cloth napkins, candles.

"Wow," I murmur under my breath as Hayden decks out the table.

He slides the placemats under the plates and folds the napkins into neat triangles. He lights the candles, then turns off a couple overhead lights.

"Um, do you want some wine?" Hayden asks, almost nervously, wringing his hands.

I'm not a huge wine person, but if that's what Hayden wants to drink, then I'm game. "Yeah, sure!"

Hayden grabs a bottle from the fridge. It's been in there since I first got here, but it's still new and sealed. Which makes me wonder if having wine for dinner was something he did on the regular before he started feeling unwell.

He pops the bottle, pours the wine into two fancy wine glasses and sets them next to each plate. Then he stands behind one chair and holds it out for me. My insides melt at this unexpected, yet incredibly romantic gesture. I thought we were just having dinner, but Hayden's turned it into a *dinner*.

I let him push my chair in for me, then wait for him to take the other seat. I reach my hand out and he slots his fingers in between my own. Our palms press together.

"This is amazing, babe," I say, gazing directly into Hayden's eyes.

They reflect the flickering flames from the candles as he

gazes right back at me. "I want to… do something, you know? Like, not just lie around feeling sorry for myself."

I cock an eyebrow at his self-deprecating comment, but Hayden continues before I can object.

"I know, I know. But like, I'm so tired of being tired. I don't want to lose any more time to this depression thing. I want to live." His voice gets thick and a little unsteady as he speaks.

"I get it. Just, like, don't push yourself too hard, alright?" I don't want him to crash because he tried to take on too much too quickly.

He nods with a shy smile that makes my heart swell with so much love, it feels like my chest is going to burst. "I hope you like the pasta."

I stab my fork into the noodles and twirl it around to pick up one giant mouthful. The groan when it hits my tongue is completely involuntary. "Oh my god, this is the best thing I've ever tasted in my life."

Hayden chuckles. "You always say that."

"It's true, though! This is *so* good. I can't think of a single thing that tastes better right now." I skewer a shrimp and pop it in my mouth. "Mmm, so good."

A couple moments pass in silence as we're both occupied with eating before Hayden speaks up again. "So…"

"Mmhmm?" I hum with my mouth still full.

"Dr. Tina mentioned something during my appointment."

I swallow and set my fork down on my plate, refocusing my attention from the creamy, saucy linguine to Hayden. "Yeah?"

"She said… sometimes people with depression go on

medication." Hayden's gaze is locked onto his plate where he's pushing around a scallop.

I nod. "Yeah, Mom did that for a bit." It didn't magically cure her, but it helped manage her moods better. "Does Dr. Tina think *you* should go on medication?"

Hayden gives me a one-shouldered shrug. "Maybe. She said she needs to see me a few more times before suggesting it. But she wanted me to know it could be an option."

"What do you think about it?"

Hayden drops his fork and reaches for his glass of wine. He takes a few big gulps before answering. "I don't know."

He stares at nothing for a few beats and I can see the wheels turning in his mind.

"I'm not against it, I guess, if it'll help. It's just… it's weird, admitting I have this thing, this illness. Like, I'm not physically sick, but I am up here." He taps his temple with one finger.

Mental health really is a weird thing. There's no X-ray or scan you can do to diagnose it. It's not something you cut out or zap or wrap up in bandages, but it hurts just as much as any physical illness. It's this invisible thing and yet it's so real.

Suddenly, Hayden cringes and shakes his head. "Anyway, sorry. You probably don't want to hear this." He picks up his fork and nudges at the food on his plate.

"Hey." I reach across the small table and grasp his hand to still it. "I do want to hear this. I want to hear everything. Every thought that runs through that beautiful head of yours. Every lie the voice might try to convince you of. I want to hear it all. You don't have to do this alone, remember? I'm here. I want to help." *I love you.*

I want to tell him. Hell, I want to shout it from the rooftops so everyone in the whole damn city knows. But Hayden's already been through the wringer today and I don't want to put more stuff on him now.

Soon. I'll tell him soon. I just have to find the right time.

HAYDEN

I went to my second appointment with Dr. Tina yesterday and I only cried for about half the time I was in her office. I count that as a win.

Santino went with me again, but then, we're never really apart anymore. We sleep together, eat together, and shower together on most days. Santino managed to drag me out to the park for an afternoon. And we went grocery shopping so I could make him fish tacos and guacamole. But other than that, we've spent a lot of time in the apartment, cocooned in blankets on the bed or on the couch. We take turns reading to each other. Sometimes we play video games. We've generally been taking it pretty easy. I don't have the energy for much more.

I kind of feel bad about it. Santino should be out enjoying the summer and exploring the city, not stuck inside with me every day. Bellamy's offered to show him around a few times, but he keeps saying no. I get a little rush of relief whenever he does. Because I'm selfish and needy and I want him to stay with me for snuggles and naps. I'm a horrible person.

At least, that's what the voice has been telling me nonstop for days. I'm taking advantage of Santino. I'm hogging all his time and attention. If I really loved him, I'd let him go live his life rather than drag him deeper into my mess.

The thing is, wrapping myself around Santino and getting lost in him is the only way to make the voice shut up. So I feel bad for wanting Santino to stay home with me —but I don't feel *that* bad.

To be honest, I can't remember what life looked like before he moved in anymore. I can't imagine waking up without him next to me, or not being able to reach out and touch him, or not having the warm scent of cinnamon in my nose. Being apart from him for even a few minutes feels like too much sometimes.

Rhys stopped by one day to check in on me and when Santino went to the bathroom, Rhys jokingly asked why I didn't go in with him. Except, I don't think he was really joking. He said something about not becoming too dependent on Santino and getting too attached, but I'm way past worrying about that now. It's too late. I'm already dependent on him. I'm already attached.

And now, we're shooting our second scene. Sebastian wanted to put it off for another week or two to give me more time to settle into therapy. As if a couple more sessions with Dr. Tina is going to cure me of this depression. I mean, that'd be fan-fucking-tastic if it does, but I'm getting the sense this will be a very drawn-out process.

And I don't want to hold the schedule back any more than I already have.

So we're at this penthouse apartment Noel found for us that has a private outdoor terrace with a pool and a hot tub. In between the lounge chairs are plants and trees that provide a bit of privacy from the surrounding buildings and there's a fully stocked bar at the far end. It feels like we're at some tropical resort rather than in the middle of New York City.

But the most exciting part about being here is Santino's reaction when we first walked in. He looked like he'd just walked into a buffet with all his favorite foods. His jaw hit the ground and his eyes went as big as saucers. Every room was cooler than the last. The terrace was the coolest out of everything. He couldn't wait to strip down and jump in the water.

And now he's practically bouncing off the walls as we wait for Sebastian and Christian to finish setting up. I'm sitting on a couch, watching Santino examine every single thing in the room—the picture frame on the wall, the coasters on the coffee table, the cast iron pokers next to the fireplace, the vase of fake flowers on the mantel. He can't sit still and I would probably find it adorable if I wasn't trying to fight off the empty ache in my chest.

I know it's not real, as in there's nothing physically wrong with me. There isn't some alien clawing at my insides trying to escape from my body. It's just the depression—my brain registering phantom signals my body hasn't sent.

It's fine. I'm okay. Everything's going to be alright.

You keep saying that, but...

Santino plops down on the couch next to me and immediately leans against my side. "This place is sooo cool," he says for maybe the eightieth time.

"Yeah, it is." I curl myself toward him, seeking the comfort of his weight, his warmth.

Santino turns his head, takes one glance at me, and lifts his arm so he can rest it across my shoulders. He plants a kiss on my temple. "How are you feeling?"

"Okay, I guess."

We both know I'm lying.

"You're sure you want to do this today, babe? We can still cancel it, you know. I don't care what Sebastian says. You come first." Santino's voice has a hint of defensiveness, like he's ready to fight anyone forcing me into something I don't want to do—including if that someone was me.

But I shake my head. I don't want to cancel. I'd just have to do this some other day and there's no guarantee things will be any better then. I might not be great right now. But I could be so much worse.

"No, I don't want to cancel. I want to do this."

"Positive?" Santino's brow is furrowed in mock sternness.

"Yeah, positive." I sigh as Santino tugs me a little closer to him and I melt into his body. The ache in my chest eases enough for me to take a few deep breaths. Everything's always better when I'm in Santino's arms.

"We're ready for you guys!" Sebastian calls through the sliding glass doors.

Santino jumps to his feet and we hold hands as he leads us out to the terrace. The sun is bright and the sky is blue without a single cloud in sight. A decent breeze blows across the terrace, cooling the hot, summer air.

As Sebastian walks us through the scene, Christian quietly taps me on the arm.

"Do you need…?" he gives me a meaningful look.

I gulp as embarrassment heats my stomach and I shake my head discreetly. "I already took one."

Christian nods and gratitude fills me at his simple question and simple acceptance. Like my dick not working isn't a big deal. Like it might be normal.

Sebastian finishes showing us where he wants me and Santino positioned and where he'll be with the camera. Then it's time to start.

We head back inside so Sebastian can film us coming out. I'm first, shrugging out of the bathrobe I'm wearing and tossing it across a lounge chair. Underneath, I've got on a Speedo that's a size—or two—too small. It's barely covering my dick and definitely riding up my ass crack.

I pretend to stretch as Sebastian moves around me with his camera. When he gives me the signal, I jump into the pool, making sure I do that head toss thing when I surface. Water sprays in an arc over my head, catching the sunlight and casting rainbows everywhere.

It looks really cool. The water is super refreshing. And despite the darkness doing its best to sink its claws into me, I can feel its grasp slipping. I'm going to be okay. Everything's going to be fine.

I push off the wall and swim a few laps back and forth.

It's weird. Sometimes, when the darkness has me in its grip, it feels like I'm underwater—I can't breathe, everything's dull and muted, I'm sluggish when I try to move.

But now that I'm actually in water, it feels nothing like that.

It feels nice moving my arms and legs in a way I'm not used to. They slice through the water quickly and easily. I can hear the sound of my steady heartbeat, the rhythm of my breaths, the splashes I make when I swim. The swirling blue patterns on the bottom of the pool are clear and bright, and I can feel the warmth of the sun on my back.

My hand touches the wall and I reemerge to find Santino crouched down on the deck in front of me. He's also wearing nothing but a too-small Speedo. Sebastian's off to the side with his camera pointed at us. Christian's behind me in the water with a GoPro.

I smile up at Santino, squinting a bit at the sun in my eyes. "Hey."

He smiles back and it honestly feels like joy exploding inside me, chasing away every dark and evil thing. Love spreads through my body, finding all the cracks and crevices and filling them up. I love him. For all the things he's done for me. For the way he makes me feel. For just being who he is—patient, selfless, devoted, caring.

"How's the water?" Santino asks.

"Come in and find out." I lift a hand and flick some water at him.

He flinches and jerks away for a moment and when he turns back, he's got a mischievous, playful look in his eyes. He stands and takes a couple steps backward. Then runs and cannonballs into the pool.

I get a face full of water as it sprays everywhere. Waves slosh over the sides of the pool. I've just managed to wipe the water from my eyes when Santino splashes me again. He laughs while swimming away and I give chase.

We play, squirting water from between our palms, kicking water in each other's faces. Eventually, we graduate to wrestling, dragging and pushing each other under the surface. It doesn't feel like we're shooting a video. I kind of forget Sebastian and Christian have cameras trained on us. It feels like we're hanging out at the pool. It feels like we're having fun.

When we're both breathless and tired from swimming and treading water and attacking each other, we end up in the shallow end. Santino latches onto me—legs around my waist, arms around my neck. I hold him close, loving the heat of his body against the coolness of the water.

He brushes my hair off my face, wipes the water drops from my skin. The sunshine makes his eyes look more golden than brown and there's a tenderness in his smile that makes my heart skip a beat. He's so beautiful—on the outside and the inside. His soul is so good and precious and pure.

You don't deserve him. How dare you think you're good enough for him.

No. I'm not going there. I'm not giving the voice any room in my head for its lies. Deserving has nothing to do with anything. Santino chose to be here. He chose to stay. He can leave whenever he wants and I need to trust he knows how to make decisions for himself.

He draws the tip of one finger down between my eyes, along the bridge of my nose. Then he gives me a cute little boop. I catch the finger with my lips, sucking it into my mouth.

Santino gasps as I swirl my tongue around the tip of

his finger and I can feel his dick growing where it's pressed against my stomach. I scrape my teeth lightly over the pad of the finger and he lets out a small whimper.

Santino tugs on his hand and I release him. He grasps me by the chin to hold me in place as he leans in for a kiss. It's hot and hungry, like we're two starved men presented with a gourmet spread. His tongue lashes against mine. Our teeth clash together. He bites down on my bottom lip hard enough to send shivers through my body.

I glide us through the water as Santino slides his fingers through my hair. He grabs a fistful and pulls my head back so he can lick and kiss at my jaw, my neck, my collarbone.

"Stairs!" Sebastian calls out and I reach backward to catch us before we crash.

I sit on a step, Santino in my lap, and lean back. Water laps around my hips as Santino licks and kisses across my chest. He sucks one nipple into his mouth, nibbling on the tender flesh, flicking it with his tongue.

Pleasure winds through me, touching every part of my tired and broken body. It breathes new life into me, like a promise of better days ahead. My groin tightens and my cock starts to fill, straining against the tight fabric of the Speedo.

Santino finishes with one nipple, then switches to the other. The first pebbles hard when exposed to the air again and the gentle wind feels biting against my sensitive skin.

I watch with half-lidded eyes as Santino feasts on my body. Once in a while, he'll cast a heated look up at me and every time he does, my heart swells a little more in my chest. He's so beautiful, it takes my breath away. I love him so much, it scares me.

I've been hesitant about telling him because I don't really trust myself. I mean, I know I love him. But there's still this tiny niggling doubt that makes me pause. What if I only think I love him because he's been so kind to me? What if the depression has tricked me into it somehow? I haven't wanted to say anything until I'm sure. Like *sure* sure. But I don't know when that day will come—if it will ever come—and I don't want to wait any more. I want to tell him and I want to know if he loves me back.

CHAPTER
THIRTY-FOUR

SANTINO

Hayden's body is delicious. Even with the chlorinated pool water, the salty, musky taste of his skin explodes on my tongue and makes my dick achingly hard.

I lick along the deep slanting valley at his hips—first one, then the other—and rub my face against his thick cock.

Hayden lets out a low groan as I mouth at it, coaxing it to life. I love doing this, watching his dick harden gradually. Seeing this most intimate part of his body grow through the various stages of arousal. Knowing I'm the one responsible for making him feel good.

His cock stretches the already too-tight Speedo and I carefully lift the scrap of fabric away. I drag my lips across the spongy head, swirl my tongue around it and dip into the slit. A drop of pre-cum lands on my tongue and I moan at how good it tastes. I suck on it like a lollipop, letting the tip slip out of my mouth between pursed lips, then taking it back in again. My hand is wrapped around the base, giving it short, tight strokes.

It takes a few minutes to get him to full mast and when I finally do, I lay his dick on his stomach and take a minute to enjoy the view. His cock is beautiful, especially when displayed out in the open like this, lit by the brightness of the sun. The mushroom head glistens from the water and my spit. The veins running up and down his length are plump and juicy. His balls are two perfect orbs nestled right underneath.

My gaze wanders to the V cut into his hips, the eight-pack of abs on his stomach, the roundness of his pecs, the bulge of his arms. He's skinnier than when I first met him, but still incredibly gorgeous.

His elbows are braced on the step behind him. Water laps at his hips, pools in his belly button and in the dip at his sternum. The sun makes his blond hair look like spun gold. The greens of his eyes sparkle as he watches me like I am his whole world.

Kneeling between his legs, I'm suddenly overwhelmed by emotions. Hayden really is like a Greek god, beautiful yet tortured, blessed and cursed at the same time. I love him so much. Every single part of him—even the parts I don't know yet and the parts he's too afraid to reveal. I love him because he's the best human being I've ever met. And I love him because he deserves to be loved.

I take his cock in my hand and guide it to my mouth. More pre-cum spills on my tongue as I seal my lips around the head and suck. A strangled sound escapes Hayden. His eyes are glued to me. His jaw hangs open and his entire body is taut, like he's afraid he'll spoil the moment if he moves.

I slide his cock deeper into my mouth until it hits the back of my throat. My jaw is stretched wide. Spit pours out between my lips. I try to swallow around the engorged bulb at the end of his cock. Whatever I can't fit into my mouth, I stroke with my hands.

His hips come off the step, then pull back like he doesn't want to choke me. Water sloshes against my face, gets in my eyes and in my mouth. I don't care. I stay focused on Hayden's cock, sucking and stroking every inch I can reach.

I lose myself to the blowjob, dropping into a trance where nothing else exists but this delicious cock in my mouth. I don't hear Sebastian calling cut or repeating my name a few times. I don't stop until Hayden physically pushes me away with a hand on my shoulder.

I come up panting and dizzy. My knees sting from kneeling on the hard pool tile. My jaw aches from being stretched for so long. I push back from the steps and sink under the water for a second. When I stand up again, Hayden's sprawled on the stairs, limp and loose.

I wade back to him as he pushes himself upright on the stairs. There's a peacefulness in his expression I don't see very often. Like maybe he's free of the darkness, if only for a little while.

We smile at each other as if we're sharing a secret no one else knows. As if it's me and him against the world.

"Alright, you guys switch positions," Sebastian directs. "Santino, Speedos off."

Under the water, I hook my thumbs in the piece of fabric barely covering my junk and push it down my legs. I lift it up out of the water and fling it at Hayden. It hits him square in the chest. He jumps at the squelching impact, stunned for a split second, then he bursts out in laughter.

Out of the corner of my eye, I notice Sebastian bringing his camera up and pointing it in our direction again.

Hayden takes the swimsuit and tosses it on the step, then reaches for me. He hauls me into his arms, naked chest to naked chest. Our mouths clash in a wet, messy kiss.

"You're amazing, you know that?" Hayden says when we break the kiss, the smile on his face is the most gorgeous thing I've ever seen.

"You're pretty amazing yourself, babe."

He spins us around suddenly and I let out a yelp that dissolves into giggles. The giggles melt into moans when he turns me so my back is against his front and he starts nibbling my ear. His thick cock pokes me in the ass and I can't wait to get the damn thing inside me.

I kneel on the step again, leaning forward so I can brace my elbows on the pool deck. The water comes to the top of my thighs, leaving my ass and hole totally exposed.

Hayden's hands land on my ass, two hot brands searing my skin. He kneads them like he's making a loaf of bread, then pulls them apart to lick a stripe up my taint and over my hole. A shiver runs up my spine and I push my ass back into his face.

"Oh fuck, yes, please."

He licks and stabs at my hole with his tongue, eating my ass out and humming like he's enjoying every goddamn bite.

Between my legs, my dick is burning up. If I tilt my hips forward, it dips into the water and the cold shock makes all my senses go haywire. I can't tell if I'm too hot or too cold. I can't tell if I want to go deeper into the water or climb out of the pool. All I know is I need more of Hayden—today, tomorrow, forever.

I'm about to beg Hayden to fuck me when Christian beats me to it.

"Hayden, catch." He tosses Hayden the lube.

Hayden doesn't waste a second before squirting the lube directly on my hole. Lube is normally pretty cold at first, but today, it's been sitting in the sun for a while. Warm liquid hits my hole and I let out a shriek of surprise. And when Hayden pushes it into me, it almost feels like he's pouring hot water into my ass.

"Oh my god, fuck." I can't hold still. My body is so confused over what it's feeling and what it wants. "Holy fuck. Jesus Christ."

Behind me, I can feel more than hear Hayden's giggles. Memories of that day last week when we couldn't stop laughing while we fucked spring to my mind and giggles bubble up inside me too.

"God, babe, stop torturing me and fuck me already," I call out.

Hayden slaps me on the ass in response. "I'm getting there. Don't rush me."

I laugh at how he talks back at me, so confident and sure of himself. Behind his camera, Sebastian's eyebrows are up at his hairline and he looks like he's trying not to laugh along with us. I hope the fans on the other side of the camera lens will feel the same way. I hope they'll see the love and joy Hayden and I share and want to laugh out loud too.

I let out a long, drawn-out moan when I finally feel the blunt head of Hayden's cock at my hole. He teases me with it, pushing in only a fraction of an inch before pulling out again. I try to shove myself back on him, but his hands on my hips are too strong. He keeps me exactly where he wants me—going out of my fucking mind.

"Put it in me, babe, please, just put it in me," I beg. I don't know how much longer I can take his teasing.

Then, without warning, his hands tighten on my hips and he's pulling me backward while his hips shoot forward. He impales himself inside me in one blinding thrust that drives all the air from my lungs. My mouth hangs open as I struggle to catch my breath, but Hayden doesn't give me time to adjust.

He starts fucking me like he means it. Like he wants to wedge his cock so deep inside my body he'll never be able to extract himself again. The sound of skin slapping against skin mixes with sloshes of water as it ripples out in waves around us. Pleasure screams through me, setting me on fire from the inside out.

I reach between my legs and squeeze my dick as hard as I possibly can. I have to if I want to keep from coming too soon. With the connection between me and Hayden burning so bright and knowing thousands of people will see him destroying my ass, I'm barreling toward my orgasm way too fast.

Hayden's hands slide from my hips to my front and in one swift movement, I'm hauled upright, water flying everywhere from the change in position. Now I'm exposed to the camera in full sunlight, Hayden still buried in my ass.

He knocks my hand away from my dick and replaces it with his own. I drop my head back on his shoulder as he starts jacking me off, his hips still driving into me from behind.

"Oh, fuck!" I scream. The dual assault is too much. I turn my face to press it into Hayden's neck as a sob escapes me. I need to come. Right now. I need to come so fucking bad.

Reaching my hand up, I wrap it around the back of Hayden's head, turning it so we can kiss. It's an awkward angle, but I don't care. I need to kiss him, to share breath with him, to let him know in every way I can that I love him.

I'm a split second away from coming when he drops my dick and pulls out of my ass. His arms stay around me, holding my limp, dead weight so I don't sink under water.

My dick is spasming as it struggles to come, but can't. My ass clenches, looking for a cock to suck back inside, but there's nothing there.

"Nooo…" I whine, squirming in Hayden's arms as the orgasm slips out of my reach.

Hayden chuckles, low and evil, the sound rumbling right in my ear and vibrating from my back through the rest of my body. "Don't worry, babe. We're just moving to the lounge chair."

HAYDEN

Santino is adorable and clingy as we towel off and slather each other with baby oil. His hands are everywhere—my chest, my back, my legs, my arms—and honestly, I'm not any better. This might be the most fun I've ever had on a shoot before. Like genuine, laugh out loud, don't want it to end, kind of fun. And it's all because of Santino.

The lounge chair's cushions are covered by fresh towels and the adjustable back is set to about sixty degrees. I lie down, legs hanging over either side of the chair. Santino's in front of me, facing away, straddling my lap and the chair at the same time. He reaches behind to grab my cock and guides it into his ass.

We both let out sighs of relief as I slide back into his body. I love being in here. I love the way I fit inside him. I love the way it makes me feel so at home.

Santino leans back, legs hooked over the outsides of my knees, letting me take his weight. I drag my hands up his inner thighs. The skin of his taint is so velvety soft and I follow the seam running down the middle to that tight ring of muscle stretched around my cock. Tracing the rim of his hole, feeling how my cock disappears into his body, it has us both shuddering in pleasure.

"Fucking hell," Santino groans as he grinds down on me.

His hands find mine and together we explore where we're connected. He clenches tight around my dick and I can feel how the muscle contracts under my fingers. It's strangely intimate, touching that area, learning the difference between his skin and mine, knowing exactly how we fit together.

I turn my face into Santino's neck and breathe in his spicy cinnamon scent. It winds through me and fills me up. It chases away the darkness and turns down the volume on the voice. It makes me whole.

Santino lifts his head from my shoulder and glances down his body. "Oh, fuck."

Sebastian's positioned at the foot of the chair, camera pointed right between our legs. He's probably getting a close-up shot of us touching ourselves.

Santino drops his head back again, turning his face toward me so our cheeks are pressed together. He starts writhing on top of me, his ass grinding into my lap, his hole trying to suck me in deeper. "Oh my god, oh my god."

Lying on his stomach, his cock is so engorged the head is a deep shade of purple. I can almost see the veins pulsing as blood rushes through them. Pre-cum leaks from the slit, a steady stream dripping down the side of his hip.

Santino pushes himself up to get more leverage, then

starts fucking himself on my dick. He lifts one foot up onto the edge of the lounge chair and braces himself with one hand on an armrest. Then he bounces up and down, lifting up halfway and dropping himself into my lap.

My hands roam over his body. His thighs, his waist, his back with the deep valley of his spine. I take his free arm and loop it around the back of my neck, then run my hands across his stomach, up to his chest. I catch his nipples between my fingers and pinch.

"Oh fuck! Yes! Oh god!" Every muscle in Santino's body is contracted and taut, standing out in sharp relief. The sunshine lights up his skin and sweat gathers along his back, his chest, his temples.

He's so caught up in the moment, so lost to what he's feeling. There's no self-consciousness, no hesitation. Just the simple chase for what he wants, what feels good. I'm amazed how comfortable he is in his own skin, how easily he accepts himself for who he is. He's confident, but not arrogant. Self-assured, but not obnoxious. It's hard to believe he's real. It's hard to believe he could ever want to be with me.

Santino collapses against me, exhausted from his exertion. His body is heavy and hot, glistening with baby oil and sweat. I want to stay like this, buried inside him while he lies on top of me.

But Sebastian gives me the signal to change positions, so I carefully help Santino up.

He lies on the flat part of the lounge chair and lifts his knees toward his shoulders. I scoot in, facing him, legs straddling the chair. With my hands on his thighs, I pull him down a few inches.

My dick slides in easily now. His hole is nice and loose

from all our fucking. Santino grabs the backs of his knees and grins like he's offering himself up to me. I grin back and snap my hips forward.

"Fuuuckkkk. Yes!" A look of utter euphoria graces his face as he whimpers and whines and sobs each time I bottom out. "Oh my god, yes! Jesus Christ!"

It's almost more fun watching Santino's reactions than it is actually fucking him. Especially since there's no doubt every single one is genuine. He's not acting. He's not putting on a show. I know him well enough to know he's always that expressive, always that vocal when he's feeling good.

"Yes, right there. Oh fuck, right there. You're going to make me come. Oh god, I'm going to come!"

I don't even have time to reach for his dick to give him a hand. Cum shoots out of his cock, landing on his stomach, his chest, his chin. I help finish him off with a few light strokes as the last of his cum dribbles out.

God, he looks so hot like this. All fucked out and covered in sweat and cum. I did this to him. I brought him all this pleasure. I sent him soaring.

Santino blinks slowly at me, panting, and reaches for me. "Come on, babe, come for me."

It's as if my body was waiting for his permission. Pressure gathers in my balls so fast it leaves my head spinning and catapults me into the heavens. I'm barely able to pull out of his ass before I'm coming, adding my cum to Santino's all over his body.

My ears ring. My heart races. Waves of pleasure rock through me again and again.

Santino takes my arm and pulls me down on him. I'm

cradled between his legs, our softening cocks snuggled next to each other.

He kisses me. Slow and lazy. I kiss him back, so thankful he walked into my life.

———

I tuck the towel in around my waist and grab a second one to dry my hair while I pad out into the bedroom from the en suite. Santino's already dressed in white shorts and a bright yellow tank top. He stops in the middle of packing his bag, eyes roaming over me.

"If I didn't just have one of the best orgasms of my life out by the pool…" He trails off.

I loop the towel around my neck and hold it by the two ends. "You would what?" Obviously, I know what, but the playful, mischievous side of me that's been missing for months has finally decided to make an appearance. I want to stay like this for as long as possible. I want to grab hold of this feeling and never let go.

Santino's eyes narrow in consideration, but then he shakes his head and zips up his bag. "Nope. I can't. If I stay in here a second longer, we'll both need another shower." He swings his bag over his shoulder and heads toward the bedroom door.

He pauses in the doorway to give me another once-over before sighing dramatically. "I'll meet you out there."

I jump into action, not wanting to be apart from Santino for longer than I need to be. It only takes me a few minutes to dress and clean up the room, but when I find Santino in the kitchen chatting with Sebastian and Christian, I pull him to me like I haven't seen him in ages.

Hugging him from behind, I wind my arms around his middle. He tilts his head to the side so it doesn't bang against my chin and rests his hands on top of mine.

Sebastian regards us with an assessing look, a hint of a smile playing at his lips. "My parents are coming into the city today, otherwise I'd suggest we all go grab lunch or something."

"That's cool." Santino peeks over his shoulder at me. "Anything you want to do, babe?"

There is. But right before I'm about to suggest it, the voice sneaks in.

He doesn't want to go to the library. God, could you get any more boring?

"Um…" I blink, startled at how suddenly the voice rears its ugly head. It's been so quiet the past few hours and the darkness has been so distant I almost forgot they were there.

Santino picks up on it immediately. He cocks an eyebrow in question. "Babe?"

"Um…" My brain scrambles, not sure what to do. I know I should just tell him my original idea and if he doesn't like it, we'll do something else. But the darkness has taken control over my tongue and it won't let me say it out loud.

Santino will think it's a stupid idea. He's not into reading the way I am. What would we even do there? He follows me around while I wander the stacks? It's not like I've even been reading these days. I probably have a ton of late fees from all the books I haven't returned.

But then, Santino's been picking up the books lying around the apartment. Sometimes he reads to me. Sometimes he flips through the pages and asks me what the book is about. I don't *have* to borrow any new books, right? I can just show him my favorite spot in the library. I can tell him why I like the place so much. And I haven't been there in so long… I miss it.

Santino waits patiently as I silently battle with myself. He doesn't prompt me or make his own suggestion. He lets me figure it out on my own.

Out of the corner of my eye, I notice Sebastian and Christian sharing a knowing look. Then Sebastian crosses the kitchen and fits himself into Christian's side. With his head on Christian's shoulder, they both watch us with amused smiles on their faces.

No one rushes me. No one looks annoyed or restless. They're all just giving me the time and space I need. Gratitude fills me, lodging in my throat as I try to swallow around it. My friends care about me. They really do care about me.

I've spent so long trying not to be a burden to them, trying to protect them from myself. But they never asked me to do that. They never asked me to leave them alone. Just the opposite, in fact. I knew they were worried about me. They tried to ask me what was wrong so they could help me. And I didn't let them. I didn't let them be the friends they've always wanted to be.

The reminder gives me the courage to untie my tongue.

"Um, how about the library?"

Santino's eyes light up like I've offered to take him to Cancun. "You want to go to the library?"

I wince at how nerdy and pathetic that sounds. "Yeah? We don't have to if you don't want to. I mean, I'm okay doing something else instead."

Santino stops me with a kiss. "The library sounds hella cool."

I don't think he actually thinks that, but there's something shining in his eyes that stops me short. It looks like love. I'm almost too afraid to believe it... but what if it's true? What if Santino loves me?

CHAPTER
THIRTY-SIX

SANTINO

We stop by a chicken and rice stand on our way to the library because I haven't really eaten anything in the past couple days—the joys of being a bottom, heh.

In the park next to the library, we find a bench and scarf down our lunch. The chicken is tender and the rice has more flavor than I thought rice could have. The white sauce is creamy and smooth and the hot sauce gives just the right amount of kick.

"Holy shit, this is good," I say around mouthfuls of food.

Hayden's chuckle is halting and short. "I thought you'd like it," he says, kind of subdued.

I bump him lightly with my shoulder. "I mean, your food is better, but this is a close second."

He smiles but there's a hint of strain in it. I'm pretty sure it's the depression, which doesn't surprise me. It always hits right when Hayden's having a good time and he was having a hella good time during our shoot.

I'd never seen him like that before—at least not in person. Like, genuinely happy and truly enjoying himself. Not distracted by whatever's going on in his head. I've only seen that version of Hayden in the videos I found online.

When I first met him, I wondered whether that version was only a persona he put on for the camera. But now I know that's the real Hayden. He's still inside there some-where—I just have to help him get back to who he really is.

It'll take time, I'm sure. I can't expect him to miracu-lously get better overnight because he's seeing a therapist now. But I'm in no hurry. I can wait. It's not like I'm going anywhere.

The library doesn't look like any library I've seen before. The place is *huge*. It honestly looks more like a museum or a monument of some kind. The front of the building is this ginormous, imposing wall of smooth stone that curves inward like it's purposefully trying to intimi-date you. The main entrance has these massive black doors that reach almost to the top of the building. Golden figures of animals and famous people I don't recognize decorate the doors and also the two towering columns on either side.

Walking into the building feels like I'm walking into a temple of some sort, like a mammoth shrine to books. The inside is just as impressive. The lobby is like, three stories tall, with that hushed echoey vibe you only get with really important buildings.

Hayden actually looks kind of nervous as we head inside. I'm not sure why. Does he think I won't like it? Or is he afraid he'll feel differently about the place than he used to?

I mean, he doesn't have to worry about me. The library is obviously important to Hayden, so it's important to me too. I just hope he can still find the same joy in books and reading that he once did.

In the middle of the lobby, Hayden stops and lifts his head to look around as if this is his first time here. It's kind of hard to read his expression. There's some wonder in it and some nostalgia too. Like he's trying to match up what he sees now with what he remembers.

After a moment, he takes a deep breath and as he lets it out, some of the tension he's carrying melts away.

He turns toward me, a little sheepish. "Can I show you my favorite place?"

He has a favorite place in the library—god, he's adorable. "Hell yeah, you can."

Hayden takes my hand and leads me down hallways and up stairs. We turn left, then right, then left again and go through so many doors, I have absolutely no idea where we are.

Then suddenly we're in this super quiet area with almost no one around. Huge windows look out over the park with small padded benches in front. Hayden sits down on one, peeking up at me through his blond lashes with a hesitant smile.

"This is it?" I ask, sitting down next to him.

"Yeah." His voice goes up at the end like it's a question.

I look around at the long bookshelves in front of us, filled with books. Then turn sideways on the bench so I can glance out the window. I can totally see Hayden curled up here for a few hours, getting lost in a book.

"I like it," I declare, leaning back against the wall and settling in.

"You do?" Hayden sounds surprised and kind of amazed, like he was expecting me to hate it.

I nudge him with my foot. "Yeah, of course, I do. It's really nice."

He takes another look around, a small smile gracing his lips. "Yeah, it is, isn't it?"

We gaze into each other's eyes. His are a bright green, shining with the light of the sun through the window. There's a hint of uncertainty in them, like he's teetering between a bunch of conflicting emotions and he doesn't know which one to feel.

I take his hands and thread our fingers together so our palms touch.

He takes a deep breath and lets it out, his grip tightening. "I love you."

I blink, stunned by his unexpected declaration. He does? I mean, I know he does. At least, I was pretty sure he did. Except I thought I'd end up saying it first. I thought he might need more time to come around to the idea. But nope, he beat me to it.

When I don't respond right away, Hayden rushes ahead.

"You don't have to love me back," he says, dropping his chin to his chest. "I totally get it if you don't. I know I'm hard to love. And I'm so messed up. Why would you love me? Sorry. Forget it. Forget I said anything."

"Whoa, babe." I put one hand under his chin and lift his head to meet my gaze. I make sure he's looking right into my eyes before I speak. "I love you too."

He looks as stunned as I felt. "Really? You do?"

"Yeah." A laugh bubbles up and bursts free. "Fuck yeah, I love you."

I watch as moisture gathers in his eyes. He slaps a hand over his mouth as he gasps, trying to contain a sob.

"Babe, I love you so much." I cup his cheeks and lean in so he fills my entire field of view. "I love all of you. All the nerdy, silly, sad, and broken parts. I love everything."

He sniffles as tears escape down his cheeks. "But… why?"

"Why?" I laugh out loud. "Do I need a reason? I love you because… you're you. And you were made for me. We were made for each other."

He shakes his head, dropping his chin as his shoulders shake with a quiet sob. I pull him into a hug and he clings to me.

"I'm sorry. I don't know why I'm crying. I'm not upset, I promise."

I laugh again—or maybe I haven't stopped laughing— and press a kiss to his temple. "You're allowed to cry as much as you want, babe. I know you're not upset."

"But I don't want to cry anymore. I'm so sick of crying."

I rock him side to side, rubbing my hand up and down his back. "I know, babe. It'll get better, I promise."

He doesn't cry for long this time and when he pulls away from me, he doesn't look as miserable as he usually does after a cry session. Actually, he's kind of cute, with that like, half-joyful, half-sorrowful expression people get when they shed happy tears.

I wipe the wetness from his cheeks, then plant a fat kiss on his lips. He melts into me, his lips moving against mine.

"I love you," I murmur against his mouth. I want to

make sure he knows it without a single shred of doubt. I want him to know it in the deepest part of his soul. "I love you. I love you. I love you."

"I love you," he repeats back at me and my heart fills with so much joy I'm floating on clouds. "You're so good to me. Even when you didn't know me, when you had no reason to be. When things were the hardest and the darkness was at its worst, you were the only one there for me. I was so lost, but you found me. I was dying, but you saved me."

The more Hayden speaks, the more tears spring to my own eyes. He makes me sound like some hero, but I'm not. I'm just a guy who cares. I saw him hurting and I couldn't not help. I knew I could do something, so I did. Isn't that what everyone should do?

"I was lost too," I say, swiping at my eyes before the tears can fall. "I didn't know what I was doing with my life when I came here. I took a chance and hoped for the best. And then here you were. Beautiful and perfect."

Hayden scrunches up his face at that last word.

"Okay," I chuckle. "Maybe not perfect, but you're perfect for me."

He looks a little skeptical, but that's okay, I plan on spending a lifetime proving it to him.

Hayden shows me around the library some more, where the novels are, where the biographies are. We stroll through the bookshelves hand in hand, whispering quietly to each other. I can see why he likes this place. It's peaceful and serene.

We stop by an ice cream shop on the way home and Hayden orders a honey pistachio scoop in a cup while I get a butterscotch scoop in a cone. We sit on a bench in the park while we eat, watching the pedestrians walk past with their dogs and strollers and the picnickers lying out on the lush, green lawn.

Slowly, we make our way home, enjoying the warmth of the summer sun and the light breeze keeping the humidity at bay. I've never been happier in my life.

There's a liveliness in Hayden's eyes I'm not sure I've seen before. It's like he's soaking in the energy around him and letting it refuel his batteries. Like he's here with me in the world rather than battling the demons inside his head.

We're both pretty tired by the time we get home, but that good kind of tired when you know you've made the most of the day. We collapse onto the couch together, cuddling up close.

"What do you want for dinner?" Hayden asks.

I prop my chin on his chest and trace invisible patterns on his shoulder with my finger. "You're always asking me that. What do *you* want for dinner?"

Hayden thinks for a moment. "I think I want ramen."

"Ramen?" I ask. "Like going out for Japanese ramen?"

He shakes his head. "No, just the instant packaged stuff. I haven't had that in ages."

I laugh, dropping my forehead to his chest.

"What's so funny?"

I give him a quick peck on the corner of his mouth. "Babe, I can't cook for shit, but that is one thing I know how to make."

CHAPTER
THIRTY-SEVEN

HAYDEN

Santino's version of ramen is just pouring hot water over a bowl of dry noodles, mixing in the seasoning, and letting it sit for a few minutes. I'm going to show him how to *really* make ramen.

"Is it really ramen if there are so many steps involved?" Santino asks as he washes the bok choy in the sink.

"Of course, it is. It's basically the same thing. We're only adding a few extra ingredients."

Santino eyes the eggs, green onions, and slices of cheese on the counter. "There's not even any meat." He pouts.

I laugh, marveling at how foreign it sounds to my ears. It's been a long time since I've laughed like this. Like everything is right with the world. "You won't miss it, I promise."

Pulling out two pots, I fill them both with water and set them on the stove.

"Is this good?" Santino shows me the bowl of washed bok choy.

"Perfect." I grab my chef's knife from the magnetic strip on the wall. "Do you know how to chop green onions?"

Santino eyes the knife warily. "My dad taught me how to carve a turkey?"

I tilt my head. "Not quite the same thing. Come here." I wave him over to the cutting board set out on the counter. "Give me your hand."

When he holds it up, I help him wrap it around the knife's handle. "A lot of people hold a knife like they're shaking hands with it. But actually, your palm should be on top of the knife handle, like this." I let go and Santino turns the knife back and forth, getting used to its weight. I grab the green onions and set them on the chopping board.

"When you're holding the veggies or meat or whatever you're cutting, you want to curl your fingers so your knuckles stick out." I reach around him to position his other hand on the green onions. "Then lean the flat part of the blade against your knuckles. That way you won't chop your fingers off."

With my arms around Santino and my hands on top of his, we chop the green onions together. It's a little awkward, but about halfway through, he picks up the feel for it. I lift my hands off and settle them on his hips as he keeps going.

"That's it. Perfect."

"This is dope." He sounds so excited.

"It's just chopping vegetables, babe," I plant a kiss by his ear.

He looks over his shoulder at me and steals another kiss from my lips.

I show him how to soft-boil an egg, then dunk it in ice water so it stops cooking. And what order all the ingredients should go into the ramen. He stares slack-jawed when I lay slices of cheese on top of the boiling pot of noodles and soup.

"You can put cheese in ramen?"

"Yup. At least with Korean-style ramen. It might not be as good with other kinds." Pulling out two bowls, I divvy up the noodles, then drop one peeled egg into each.

We carry it over to the dining table and Santino lets out an indecent groan when he takes his first bite.

"Oh my god, this is so good," he says around a mouthful of noodles.

I take a bite too and I have to agree. This might be the best bowl of noodles I've ever had—because I made it with Santino.

We've just finished eating when Santino's phone starts buzzing. He pulls it out of his pocket and the sated, content expression he's wearing melts into dread. "It's my mom."

Anxiety grips me. He hasn't spoken to his mom since that day they argued. "Do you want to answer it?"

His gaze flicks up to mine. "I should, right?"

My heart starts racing as wild thoughts flood my mind. She's going to convince him to go home. She'll make him see I'm not worth his time. "Do, um, do you want some privacy? I can go…" I start pushing my chair back, but Santino grabs my hand.

"No! Stay. Please." His grip is tight and his eyes are a little wild with panic.

It's weird seeing him like this. It's weird being the one holding his hand rather than him holding mine. He's always been the strong one between us, but now I have to be strong for him.

Santino answers the call and immediately puts it on speaker. "Hello?"

"Tino? Hold on a sec."

He glances up at me and whispers. "That's my sister Luisa."

"Mom, you have to speak to him!" Someone shouts in the background. His mom's answer is too muffled to make out. "We talked about this, Mom."

Santino stares at the phone like some kind of monster might jump out of it. I don't like it. Still holding his hand, I stand and tug him to his feet. We go to the couch and I curl myself around him as we wait for someone to start talking on the other end of the phone.

"Sorry about that, Tino. Here's Mom."

There's a fumbling sound as the phone is handed off, but no one else comes on the line.

Santino and I exchange a look. "Hello?" he asks.

"Mom!" Luisa, I think, hisses in the background.

"Yes?" Santino's mom finally speaks, sounding as if Santino was the one who called her and not the other way around.

"Uh, hi, Mom."

"Hello."

"Um… how are you doing?"

I give him a squeeze and nuzzle the crook of his neck.

"I'm fine."

"That's great." A beat passes and when his mom

doesn't say anything, Santino continues. "I'm doing good too. Thanks for asking." He rolls his eyes.

"Oh my god, Mom, you agreed to talk to him." Louisa's loud enough that we can hear her clearly.

A sharp huff of air blows across the microphone. "Your sisters said I need to talk to you," she finally says.

"About what?" Santino's expression grows more and more dour by the second.

"About you leaving me."

"He's not leaving you. You know what? Never mind. Give me the phone." More fumbling sounds before Luisa comes back. "I'm so sorry, Tino. I thought she was going to be reasonable." She puts so much emphasis on that word that she's probably saying it as much to Santino's mom as she was to him.

"That's okay," Santino says, but the disappointment in his voice is more than obvious.

"No, Tino, it's not okay. She's taking this way too personally when it's not actually about her." Louisa sighs and the sound of voices in the background fades. "Don't stress, though, Paola and I are working on her. She'll come around. Eventually. So tell me about New York. Do you have a place to stay? What are you doing there? Do you like it?"

"Yeah, I really like it. I'm working with this um, indie filmmaker and I've made a lot of new friends. They're really great."

"Look at you, my baby brother, all grown up and being an actor."

Santino laughs nervously. "Yeah, something like that."

"When does the movie come out? Where can I watch it?"

"Um…" Santino casts a panicked look in my direction.

I shake my head furiously and mouth "not available."

"It's all small indie projects. I don't actually know where they'll be available. But I can check?" He crumples his face into a cringe and slumps against me. He wasn't joking when he said he was a bad liar.

"Cool. Let me know. What else is going on out there?"

Santino turns to look at me before he speaks again. "I, um, I've met someone."

A sharp shriek has us both flinching away from the phone. "You have?! Oh my god, hold on. Paola! Get over here! Okay, tell us *everything*."

Santino shoots me an alarmed look, a question in his eyes. Doubt swirls around inside me. Should he really tell them about us? What if he changes his mind about me later? What if he doesn't want to be with me after all? Wouldn't it be better if they never knew? But if he's brave enough to talk to his mom, then I need to be brave too.

I nod.

"His name is Hayden," Santino says, gazing into my eyes, a smile gracing his lips. "And… he's amazing. He taught me how to cook today."

Another woman gasps. "And you didn't burn down the house?" she teases.

"Ha, ha, Paola. No, I didn't burn down the building." Santino rolls his eyes, even as he smiles wider.

My earlier anxiety begins to ease as Santino talks with his sisters. And though the voice is still whispering at the back of my mind, I focus on the warm weight of Santino's body against mine. The way he talks slightly differently with his sisters than with anyone else. The easy banter they all have back and forth. His sisters sound really nice. And more importantly, they sound supportive.

"So when are you bringing him here to meet us?" Paola asks.

"Oh, uh… I don't know. We haven't thought that far yet," Santino answers.

"When are you clearing your stuff out of your apartment in San Francisco?" Louisa asks.

"I don't know. I haven't thought that far yet," Santino repeats himself.

I can almost hear his sisters shaking their heads on the other end of the phone.

Louisa sighs. "I can go grab your things the next time I'm up there. Just call your landlord and tell him I'm coming."

"Really?" Santino double-checks, looking both hopeful and skeptical.

"Yes, really," Louisa sounds put out, but also fond at the same time. "I have a work meeting next week, so I can swing by on Thursday."

"Sweet! Thanks, Louisa!"

"Yeah, yeah, just make sure you bring your boyfriend home sooner rather than later, okay?"

"Yes! I will. Promise!" They hang up and Santino turns in my arms. He sort of launches himself at me, but because of the awkward angle, I fall sideways and we land in a tangle of limbs.

"That went okay?" I ask, wanting to make sure that Santino isn't too upset about his mom.

Santino nods and sighs. "I was hoping my mom would be over it by now, but…" He trails off. I can see just how much it bothers him that his mom isn't on board. It only lasts for a second, though, before he smiles again. "My sisters are pretty cool, right?"

They are, and even though I still have some doubt niggling at the back of my mind, I find myself smiling. "I'd like to meet them," I say and I mean it with my whole heart. "I hope they like me."

"They're going to love you as much as I do." He plants a kiss on my lips. "Well, maybe not as much as I do. But close. My dad will too. He's super chill. And my mom?" He shrugs. "We'll deal with her when the time comes."

Just like we'll deal with everything else. Together. One day at a time.

SANTINO

In the end, Bellamy managed to convince Noel *not* to hold their wedding at that hideous mansion we went to on the first day of shooting. Instead, they charter a massive yacht. The thing is like a fucking cruise ship, with a pool on board and everything. It's so big, I've already gotten lost on it a few times.

We boarded the ship yesterday afternoon and spent the evening lounging in the sun on one of the half dozen outdoor decks. Dinner was served in a formal dining room and then we had a movie night in the salon.

Hayden and I were assigned to a VIP guest room that is by far the nicest bedroom I've ever set foot in. Like, I'm kind of afraid to touch anything in case I break it.

The wedding this morning is on the bow of the yacht. It's a wide, open area with the Atlantic Ocean surrounding us on all sides and the sun shining down on us from above.

Rhys, Angel, Christian, and Hayden are already out

there with the yacht's captain, who will officiate, while Bellamy, Noel, Sebastian, and I are waiting in a couple state rooms. The cameras have all been set up, and since we're all supposed to be in the wedding, Sebastian hired a couple of his filmmaker friends to be the camera crew.

I'm actually kind of nervous. I've never been in a wedding before, never mind a wedding on a fancy yacht where we might get hit by a wave and tossed into the ocean.

But I'm also kind of nervous that Hayden's out there and I'm in here. I know it's not my wedding. I'm not the one getting married, but he'll still be standing there watching me walk down the aisle, so to speak.

"You guys ready?" Sebastian asks, poking his head into the room where Bellamy and I are waiting.

Bellamy takes a deep breath, rubs his hands together, then lets his breath out in one fast exhale. "Uh, yeah, I think so?"

I clap a hand on his shoulder. "You totally got this, bro."

He gives me a slightly wild look and for a second, I wonder if he's going to jump off the side of the boat. But then he blinks and he's back to the cool, calm Bellamy I know.

"Yeah, yeah, you're right. It's fine. It's just Noel. I know Noel. He's an asshole."

Oookay. That's a weird way to reassure himself, but then I've never really understood their dynamic, so what the hell do I know?

"Alright, the order is Santino, then me, then Bellamy, then Noel," Sebastian reminds us. "Santino, you're with me now. Bellamy, you wait for my friend Connor with the camera to come get you, okay?"

Bellamy nods, then turns to me. "Hey man, thanks so much for everything." He pulls me into a tight hug that I return.

"Dude, I should be thanking you. You've basically changed my life."

We step back from each other and Bellamy gives me one of his signature smiles that catapulted him to the top of the industry. "You deserve it, man."

With one last check in the mirror, I follow Sebastian out to the lounge at the front of the yacht. The sliding glass doors have been pulled open so it feels like one giant indoor-outdoor area. We wait in the shadows for the Connor guy to cue the music, then roll cameras, then call out action.

Sebastian gives me the signal to go.

I can't really feel my feet as I walk. Actually, I'm not sure I can feel any part of my body except for the frantic beating of my heart.

My eyes are drawn immediately to Hayden, dressed in a perfectly form-fitting earthy green suit that shows off the broadness of his shoulders and the narrowness of his waist. His blond curls blow in the wind, looking golden under the bright summer sun.

He had his hands clasped in front of him as he waited with the rest of the guys. But then he turned and saw me. His hands fell to his sides, his lips parted with a silent gasp, and I swear to god, he almost took a step toward me before remembering he needed to stay where he was.

I take my time walking past the lounging area on the bow, my eyes locked on Hayden the entire time. It feels like there's no one else in the world but the two of us, drawn together by forces way beyond our control.

I didn't know it was possible to love someone as much as I love Hayden. Like the entire fucking planet revolves around him. Like I would die if I didn't have him in my life. I didn't know I'd want to spend every waking moment with this one other person, fall asleep next to him at night, then wake up the next morning and want to do it all again.

With Hayden, I do. Every single day for the rest of my life.

I stop before I actually reach Hayden and my heart lurches at not being able to go to him. But I've been assigned to the opposite leg of the V-shape we're arranged in.

I don't really remember the other guys walking out to the bow or any of the words the captain says to officiate the wedding. All of my attention is focused on Hayden, how much I love him, how much I want to drag him back to our state room and slowly peel off every piece of clothing he's wearing. I only snap out of my Hayden-trance when Bellamy nudges me on the arm.

"Rings," he hisses at me.

Oh, shit. I dig into my pocket and pull out the box for him.

Bellamy and Noel exchange rings, kiss with a lot of tongue for the cameras, then we all erupt into applause. And all the while, my eyes never leave Hayden's.

Later, after breaking for a light lunch and setting up the lounge for the evening reception, Hayden and I are in our state room, getting changed.

He comes out of the bathroom in a pair of beige linen pants and a white linen button-down shirt, open at the collar. His hair and skin are still a bit damp from the shower and the moisture is making the linen kind of see-through.

My breath catches in my chest as I watch him pad around the room.

He's been going to his weekly therapy appointments, although he still comes out looking wrecked most of the time. Dr. Tina suggested a really low dose of medication to ease him into it and he just started taking it a couple days ago. It's too early to tell if it's working, but he seems optimistic about it.

Which is the important bit—that he's hopeful about how things are going. He's working really hard and doing all the things he's supposed to, and like, yeah, there are no guarantees or anything, but he's not giving up. That's all I can ask for.

Hayden catches me staring at him from where I'm lounging on the bed. He pauses as he's fastening a blingy gold watch on his wrist and meets my gaze through the mirror.

"Hey," I say, trying to lower my voice into something seductive, but instead I end up sounding like a teenager going through puberty.

He snorts and breaks out into a brilliant smile. A calming peace settles inside me. Hayden's going to be okay.

He turns and sets a knee on the foot of the bed. Warmth fills me as he crawls up the bed and lies down next to me. I turn toward him and hook my leg over his.

"Hey," I whisper again.

"Hey."

"I love you."

"I love you too."

We lay there, just soaking in each other's presence until it's time to go back out to the lounge.

The sun is at its golden hour, bathing everything in a warm glow. Fairy lights are strung up around the lounge and giant burgundy flowers are scattered on every surface. Next to the bar is a table filled with enough food to feed everyone on board for three days. And next to that is a massive cake. They went with champagne and crème de cassis—good choice. Upbeat music filters in through hidden speakers.

"When are you guys leaving for California?" Rhys asks, perched on the edge of a couch in the lounge, champagne glass in hand. He's wearing a peach-colored flowy floor-length dress with his long hair curled into beachy waves.

"Next week," I answer from the opposite couch. Hayden's beside me, discussing the catered food with Angel, who's sitting beside Rhys.

"That should be fun! Right?" I appreciate Rhys's attempt at being encouraging and concerned at the same time.

"Yeah." I'm excited to see my family again. I've missed them more than I'm willing to admit. It'll be nice to actually say a proper goodbye to them this time rather than just running away without telling them. But things with my mom are still… not great. I did finally talk to her for longer than half a minute. She's still not thrilled about the whole situation, but we're making progress.

"And how's…" He tilts his head subtly in Hayden's direction. "He feeling about the trip?"

I slide my hand onto Hayden's thigh and he covers it with his own. "Nervous. But he doesn't have to be. They're going to love him."

Rhys smiles and shoots a quick glance at him. "Oh, definitely. Everyone loves Hayden. I watched your videos, by the way."

A tickle of nerves makes my stomach twist. "Yeah?" I want to ask what he thinks. But I'm scared. What if they're bad? What if I'm terrible in them?

Rhys reaches across the low coffee table between us and grabs my hand. He's surprisingly strong for someone so petite. "Girl, they're fucking amazing. Like, seriously. It's so different from the stuff the rest of us do. It's so, like, fun! Not that the rest of us aren't fun. But you two make fucking look like you're frolicking in the meadows or something."

I'm not sure what to say to that. I mean, sex with Hayden is definitely fun. It's one of my favorite things to do. But frolicking in the meadows? Okay, I guess. "Thanks. I hope the videos do well. Sebastian thinks they will."

Rhys nods eagerly. "Oh, they totally will. Be prepared. You're going to be the next superstar."

I don't know about that, but I'll take his vote of confidence.

Rhys drains the rest of his drink and sets it down on the table. He takes the half-eaten plate Angel's holding and sets it down too. "Come on, I feel like dancing." Grabbing Angel's hand, he jumps to his feet and leads the way toward the open area that's been designated the dance floor.

I settle back on the couch, cuddled next to Hayden. "Rhys asked how you're feeling about meeting my family next week."

He leans into me a little harder. "I just don't want to… you know… while we're there."

Have a depressive episode, he means. "You haven't had one in a bit."

He shrugs. "Yeah, but it could happen again."

I cup his cheek and turn his face toward me to plant a kiss on the corner of his mouth. "Then we'll deal with it. Just like we've done this whole time."

He looks at me with so much love, it feels like I'm being physically swept off my feet. I forget to breathe. The world around us fades away. And I have to pinch myself to make sure this isn't a dream.

The music changes to something slower and softer. "Want to dance?" Hayden asks.

I cast a look out toward the dance floor. "I don't really know how."

"Neither do I," he says, standing up and holding out his hand. "But Rhys says all you have to do is sway side to side."

I think I can do that. We take up a spot next to Rhys and Angel on the dance floor. Hayden's arms wind around my waist, his hands settling warm and weighty on the small of my back. I slide my hands up around his neck so I can fiddle with the delicate hairs at his nape.

We gaze into each other's eyes. It's hard to believe we're here. That only a couple short months ago, we were total strangers shoved together to share an apartment. And now… he's the love of my life.

He's someone I can have fun with. But he's also someone I want to go through real-life shit with. Because neither of us will give up when it gets tough. We'll just lean in closer and get stronger together.

EPILOGUE

HAYDEN

"Denny! Tino!" Rhys waves his arm over his head as we step out of the train station in Staten Island.

My heart twinges a bit at Rhys calling Santino by his nickname. It means Rhys thinks of him as one of the guys, as part of our chosen family.

Rhys throws his arms around my neck in a big hug and I let myself sink into it for a moment. I miss Rhys and the relationship we used to have. I think I always will. But Dr. Tina says we're entering a new stage in our friendship. We might not spend as much time together as we used to, but there are other ways we can be close. So I've been making a point of reaching out to Rhys more often and telling him what's on my mind, even if we don't see each other for a couple weeks at a time.

Rhys lets me go, then pulls Santino into an equally tight hug. Santino hugs him back like they've known each other for years rather than months. The two of them have kind of teamed up against me—in the nicest way possible.

They're always giving each other updates on what's happening with me and if one of them is having a hard time getting through because I'm too deep in the darkness, then the other one will try.

Although, the darkness hasn't been as much of an issue lately. It's been three months since I started medication, and while I'm not a hundred percent back to my old self, I'm noticeably better than I was at my lowest point. Dr. Tina says I might never be Old Hayden, though. Old Hayden didn't know what it's like to have depression. Old Hayden didn't need to fight through any of that. And, I guess she has a point… but I'm not giving up.

"Come on, our house is this way." Rhys takes off down the street and Santino and I hurry to keep up. "Angel's at home. He's so excited about having you guys over. We don't usually have guests because, you know, we live so far away. So he only ever gets to cook for his family. I swear, he's been in the kitchen for like, two days straight."

I don't know if Angel's actually been in the kitchen that long, but I do know he's been planning this meal for at least a week. I have a dozen messages on my phone from him to prove it.

"I told him you guys are cool and you'll eat anything, but he really wants to impress you, Denny. Shh, don't tell him I said that." Rhys winks at me.

"You guys should totally have a cook-off!" Santino jumps in. "Like you both make a bunch of dishes and the rest of us can be the judges."

I bump him with my shoulder. "You just want to eat all the food."

"Hell yeah, I do!"

I laugh as gratitude and love fill my heart. Never in my

wildest dreams would I have thought I'd find someone like Santino. Someone who makes me smile and laugh, who wants to listen to me talk about all the random things I read in my books. I can play video games with him or hang out at the park with him. We talk late into the night, never running out of things to say. Or we cuddle together in silence, simply enjoying each other's presence. Most days, I still don't think I deserve him. But that just makes me want to be a better man for him.

We flew out to California and spent a week with his family. His sisters are exactly like they sound on the phone —really fun and supportive—and they welcomed me into their family without a second thought. His dad is really chill too and I spent a lot of time helping him with the barbecue in the backyard. His mom, though… she wasn't bad. She was nice to me and all that, but I definitely felt like she was keeping me at arm's length. Santino, on the other hand, she barely let him leave her side. She wouldn't even come downstairs to say goodbye on the morning we left.

The house Rhys and Angel live in is a duplex. Angel's mom and sister are in the downstairs apartment while Rhys and Angel are upstairs. The second the door opens, we can smell the mouthwatering aroma of home-cooked Italian food. Santino's jaw drops and he practically drools.

"Teddy bear! We're home!" Rhys takes our jackets and hangs them up on the hooks by the door, then leads the way into the kitchen.

It's several degrees warmer in here. There are pots on every burner and the oven's on too. Angel's wearing a frilly maid-style apron I'm certain Rhys picked out for him.

He stops when we come in, a slightly alarmed look in his eyes. His cheeks are flushed, but I can't tell if it's because he's embarrassed or because of the heat. "Oh, hi, um, I'm not ready yet."

"That's cool, man. Can we help with anything?" Santino asks. His knife skills have gotten pretty good in the past few months.

"Um…" Angel's gaze darts frantically around the kitchen.

"Okay! How about let's get you guys some drinks in the living room?" Rhys spins around and ushers us out. "See what I mean?" Rhys whispers under his breath.

Now I feel bad. This was supposed to be a simple dinner with friends. I didn't mean for Angel to get all stressed trying to cook a fancy dinner. We could've gone out to eat. Rhys must see the guilt on my face because he immediately jumps on it.

"Hey! It's all good! Totally not your fault. I *told* him to take it easy. This is totally on him." Rhys goes over to a stocked mini-bar on a cart. "Denny, can you make us some Aperol spritz? I'll go make sure Angel's okay."

"Sure." I scan the cart, which has everything I need. "And let us know if we can help."

Santino pulls out his phone as I start making the drinks. He shakes his head as his thumb swipes and swipes again. "This is wild. I got another hundred followers in the time it took us to get out here."

Our first video went live a week after the documentary released and Santino's brand-new social media accounts went from a couple hundred followers to thousands almost overnight. Fans love him, but then, I knew they would. What's not to love?

We just filmed our third video yesterday and I almost didn't need to take any of those pills. My dick problem has gotten better as my depression has. Sometimes I can get hard totally on my own, but it doesn't always last as long as I want. Baby steps, though. Every day is better than the day before and that's all I can ask for.

I measure out prosecco for four glasses. "You need to turn off your notifications."

"Yeah, no kidding." He slides his phone back into his pocket then gives me a hug from behind. "Thank you."

I glance over my shoulder at him. "For what?"

"Nothing. Everything. Just thank you for being you."

My brain starts compiling reasons why he shouldn't thank me. It makes a list of all the ways I'm a failure and haven't lived up to expectations. But I cut off those thoughts, reminding myself that yes, I've failed before, but I've also succeeded.

I set down the bottle of prosecco and turn in his arms. "In that case, I should thank you too. I wouldn't be alive if it wasn't for you."

Santino runs his fingers over my face like he's remembering the shape of my features. "Then I'm really, really glad I found you when I did."

BONUS SCENE

There's thirty-three minutes before the library closes and I know for a fact Hayden's lost track of the time. That's a thing he does now apparently—get so engrossed in a book he forgets the rest of the world exists. I would be annoyed if it wasn't so damn adorable.

I still find the library huge and intimidating, but I've

been to his secret hiding spot enough times that I know the route like the back of my hand. I try not to run while checking the time on my phone. Thirty-two minutes.

I have a surprise for Hayden. Well, it's not really a surprise. The group chat's been blowing up for the past hour, so he'd know about the news if he bothered to check his phone. But I can't trust Hayden to do that when he's at the library. It's okay, though, because I want to see the look on his face when I break the news to him.

It's *really* good news.

To read the rest of the bonus scene, sign up for Linden Bell's Very Important Reader newsletter here: bit.ly/santi nobonus.

SEBASTIAN

Up and coming camboy, Sebastian, discovers what it's like performing with legendary porn star, Christian, in the first The Camboy Network book, *Sebastian*, bit.ly/sebastianbm.

THANK YOU

If you've enjoyed *Santino*, please consider recommending it to your friends. Leave a review on social media, your own blog, Amazon, Goodreads, or Bookbub so other MM romance lovers can get to know Santino and Hayden too.

If you would like to stay up to date on future Linden Bell books, join the Very Important Reader mailing list and also receive the exclusive bonus scene! bit.ly/santinobonus

You can also follow me on:
Instagram - instagram.com/authorlindenbell
Facebook - facebook.com/authorlindenbell
Amazon - amazon.com/author/lindenbell
Goodreads - goodreads.com/authorlindenbell
Bookbub - bookbub.com/authors/linden-bell

ABOUT LINDEN BELL

Linden Bell writes romances that heat you up and make you smile. Her books are low angst, feel good reads with no third act breakup!

instagram.com/authorlindenbell

facebook.com/authorlindenbell

amazon.com/author/lindenbell

goodreads.com/authorlindenbell

bookbub.com/authors/linden-bell

ALSO BY LINDEN BELL

Mars Fitness Series

Where the jocks of Mars Fitness meet the nerds of their dreams.

The Camboy Network Series

When sex on camera turns into love behind the scenes.